WOODY AND JUNE
VERSUS THE APOCALYPSE

WOODY AND JUNE VERSUS THE APOCALYPSE

VOLUME 1: EPISODES 1-7

ROBERT J. MCCARTER

LITTLE HUMMINGBIRD PUBLISHING

To my amazing wife Aleia... Woody and June exist because of your delight in these stories and your unending support.

Woody and June versus the Apocalypse

Volume 1: Episodes 1-7

Copyright © 2019 by Robert J. McCarter

Cover photography © Steven Cukrov - Dreamstime.com

"Zombies Ahead" image by ducu59us

Version 1.0, October 2019

ISBN: 978-1-941153-25-3

Find out more about this book at: WoodyAndJune.com

Visit Robert's website at: www.RobertJMcCarter.com

Published by:

Little Hummingbird Publishing

P.O. Box 23518

Flagstaff, AZ 86002

www.LittleHummingbird.com

Little Hummingbird Publishing is a division of Arapas, Inc. Find more about Arapas at: www.Arapas.com.

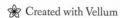 Created with Vellum

INTRODUCTION TO VOLUME 1

What you have here are the first seven episodes of *Woody and June versus the Apocalypse* in one handy, novel-length volume. These seven stories are each sold separately, so if you've been reading one episode at a time, there is nothing new here besides the Afterword and Acknowledgements.

These seven stories together truly do comprise a novel and take us through the first stages of Woody and June's adventures together.

To stay abreast of all things Woody and June, head over to WoodyAndJune.com and sign up for the fan club and don't miss out on a thing! You'll get behind-the-scene secrets, some cool digital *Zombie Arizona* postcards and know about all things Woody and June first.

PART ONE

WOODY AND JUNE VERSUS THE WANNABE WARLORD

MEETING A GIRL AT THE END OF THE WORLD

MAYBE YOU'RE SMARTER than I am. Maybe you get up in the morning with a clear direction for your day. Knowing what you want to do, having a clear list of things to get done, and checking them off one at a time. Like this:

1) Kill a few zombies for exercise; the apocalypse doesn't mean you can stop doing cardio.

2) Outwit a psychotic, petty, wannabe warlord freeing your little group from his or her (the apocalypse is equal opportunity) cruel grasp.

3) Find enough food, water, and medicine to get through the day.

4) Lead your hearty band to shelter where you can sleep and not worry about zombies or psychotic, petty, wannabe warlords.

Yeah, you probably are smarter than I am.

I guess my day has a list of sorts, but with only two things on it:

1) Survive, and...

2) Laugh, 'cause what is surviving without at least a

slice of joy. Oh yeah, and one addendum to item two: Don't laugh like a psychotic, petty, wannabe warlord because then you would just suck. Mwahahas are strictly off limits. Also cackling, and schadenfreude is frowned upon. We're looking for real laughter here.

I say all of this as preface to my tale so maybe you'll get where I'm coming from. And, you know what? I do know that you are smarter than me, because you actually have the time and leisure to sit down and read my story. Well, I hope someone reads this, I really do. So, if you are reading this, that makes you way smarter than me—or existing in the post-post-apocalyptic world where zombies have been eradicated, and well, that makes your ancestors smarter than me.

A character in a story, me in this case, my name is Woody, has to have a problem. My problem is staying alive. Every day that's my problem. It can get a bit monotonous. At the opening of this story it seems just like another day full of checking off my short list of survival and laughter. I awake to a cold morning, my shoulder and hip aching, the sun just peeking up over Interstate 40 above a ridge of pine trees.

"Shit," I say, because that is the proper way to greet a post-apocalyptic morning. Especially when you wake up on top of a semitrailer, your body sore like you've just been through a dryer cycle, your mouth drier than the Sahara, and your stomach as desolate as... enough damn metaphors, you get the idea. All of that is true, but the "shit" is mostly because I can hear the Zs weakly banging on the trailer I took refuge on. They know my fresh brains and delicious entrails are up here just waiting for them to eat.

Ironically, they, the zombies, have the same problem I do. Survival. Although they never laugh—ever—which is one of the reasons why it's second on my list (of two things, so don't be thinking yourself all cool, number two). You see, a zombie needs to eat, too, or they will dry up like a mummy and eventually blow away. Problem is, it takes about four years (a wild guess at this point) for a Z to starve to death, and it takes me about thirty days. That makes trying to wait them out fairly unworkable. Besides, the Zs continue to feast on the living, making the end date of their reign of terror further and further out.

I push myself up into a sitting position, yawn, roll my shoulders trying to loosen them up, put my baseball cap on, and look around. I'm in the loading area of a dog food factory on the east side of Flagstaff, Arizona, camped out on the top of one of twenty semitrailers parked there.

I'm a Phoenician, but let me tell you that the dry, hot, flat desert is no place to be during a zombie apocalypse. This is experience talking. Not unless the idea of living in a world dominated by the undead is just too much for you and you'd just as soon get it over with. Then, well, the Valley of the Sun is just a fine place, but I digress. Again.

Back to the cold morning in May on top of that semi-trailer, the Zs milling below me. I get myself standing and stretch my aching body some more, pulling my army surplus jacket tight—who says you can't look like a badass after the world ends?

Once I loosen up a bit, I check two things, and I can be rather obsessive about this. The first is my Arizona Diamondbacks baseball cap. It's red with the logo of a rattlesnake curled into a "D" in black. This is kind of my touchstone to my past and my humanity. I love baseball, I was an all-star in high school, played in the minors briefly, but tore my rotator cuff and never got back to it. And now... well, if humanity survives, it will be a while before baseball gets much attention.

The other thing is the packs of seeds zipped in the inside pocket of my jacket. This is food and the future, hope really. I've got carrots and beans and lettuce. It's not much, not enough, more of a symbol. You gotta have something to keep you going out here.

I move slowly, wanting to stay quiet so I don't attract more of them, and get a count of how many I'm up against.

"Shit," I whisper, because some things just need utterance, even when you don't have anyone to talk to. There are twenty of the beasts, all hungry for my deliciousness. It seems I attracted all the Zs in the area last night when I took refuge up here. Noisily and ungracefully, I might add. Do you have any idea how hard it is to get on the top of one of these things? It's not like there's a ladder or anything. I lucked out and there was a big pickup that ran into it, so that kinda saved my life—because it was getting dark and the Zs spotted me as soon as I got here.

I'm on the south side of the building, the walls are made of cement in a corrugated pattern about thirty feet tall. Two towers rise up above it and behind those, Mount Elden, which is my destination. I'm up on an isolated trailer in the parking lot, nothing close by except for that pickup.

I finally made it up to Flagstaff yesterday evening. I-17 joins I-40 up here and the bulk of the town sits around that. When the infection hit, I tried the whole survival-as-a-group in the city where there is lots of food to scrounge for, but it got ugly. When number one on my list, survival, looked doubtful, I found a truck and as much food and water as I could and headed out.

I didn't have that truck very long and that is a story for another day, but suffice it to say that in this new world, if you have something worth taking, someone will take it. Now, I have a general policy of not having anything worth taking and to have nothing to do with anyone else. Groups just get messy and fast.

If I'm telling the truth, and I'm trying my best to do that, Phoenix got more than ugly, it got weird... I got weird... but I'm not ready to write about that yet.

I spent a lot of time in the North Country as a kid, my dad was born here and we visited a lot, so I know my way around. After the disaster of getting out of Phoenix, I left the highway and got here on foot, with nothing worth taking. There are Zs out there in the forest, but not that many. There are some people too, so I kept moving, slowly but surely, to the north. Out of the desert. Farther away from any population centers. Which brings us to Mount Elden. It's steep and rugged, rising over two thousand feet up above Flagstaff. On top is the Mount Elden Lookout Tower with a set of stairs no Z could ever manage.

Yeah, I know. It's something worth having so someone is going to want to take it, but I have some fond memories of my old man and me hiking up to it when there was an actual ranger there and he let us in to take a look at the magnificent view. The San Francisco peaks to the northwest, the painted desert east and south, the ponderosa pine forest all around.

Maybe I won't stay. Maybe I'll climb up and shed a tear for our lost world and my dead father. Maybe no one will have thought of going there and I'll get to stay for a while. There are lots of isolated areas up here, I'll find one to wait it out. And, actually, the lookout tower is not the best candidate because there is no water up there—and this being Arizona, not much water anywhere.

But I gotta try.

"Hey, dummy!" a voice calls.

My heart skips a beat and suddenly I'm awake. I'm

confused, but I'm sure it's not my own voice. I mean, I've been alone for way too long, not talking at all, but I do still recognize the sound of my own voice.

And this is definitely a female voice and it's not often that my own sounds that way.

CHAPTER TWO

I LOOK AROUND, trying to find the voice that is not mine, which I should have been doing instead of such introspective navel gazing. The call came from the roof of the dog food plant. It's a girl, short black hair, dirty face, blue jacket. Not much else I can tell from this distance.

"Good morning," I yell back. "I must tell you that I plan to be lodging a complaint with management. The room service around here really sucks."

Well, that just wakes the Zs up and they start moaning and groaning, a few of them trying to climb up the truck that crashed into the trailer, but quickly failing and falling back down. Zs are dumb and slow, which is the only reason there are any living left.

"You're funny," she says, with no humor whatsoever in her voice. I revise my estimate up from girl to young woman and remind myself of my strict go-it-alone policy.

"Thank you very much," I say, taking off my hat and bowing. "I'll be here all week."

"Yeah, you will. Want some help?"

I look down, and I am surrounded by zombies, especially around the truck, which is the only safe way down. There are a few more of them shambling their way towards me, our conversation having alerted them to the possibility of breakfast.

"No thank you," I yell back.

"Suit yourself, then. I'll grab some popcorn and watch the show." She pauses briefly and even from this far away I can see that she is smiling. "And by 'popcorn,' I mean dog food. There's actually some left if you manage to survive."

Oh crap, now I officially like her and my stomach growls. Yeah, I know, gross. But it was the reason I made a stop here, the possibility of well-preserved calories that others might not think of. Any calories in an apocalypse, as the saying goes.

"I'll do my best to make it a good show, then."

But I don't, not right away. Showing off for the first female that's spoken a kind word to you in months is a sure way to fail at survival. I eat, which amounts to about a hundred calories of stale crackers and roasted peanuts. I drink the four ounces of water I have left and give it a few minutes. The one concession I make to being watched by a woman is not peeing on the Zs. Oh, and I do use a little bit of that remaining water to brush my teeth. I tell myself that oral hygiene is even more important now with no dentists (and it is), but who am I kidding?

I then dig in my pack, pull out some rope and a pink two-pound hand weight and tie it to the end of the rope. This is going to take a while, but it will be safe.

It goes like this. Find an area with fewer Zs, swing the rope with the weight on it right above their heads. When the alignment is good, let out a couple of inches of rope and bash them in the head. Boom. Down they go. Except it takes a lot of attempts and sometimes a couple of hits per Z. It is slow and tiring, but it's safe.

"You're not dumb," she yells after the first one goes down. "That's kinda refreshing."

"How's the popcorn?" I yell back.

"Delicious!"

I smile and chuckle. Not a belly laugh or anything, but I'll take it.

It takes two hours, but I clear the Zs. She claps. I bow with my hat in hand and then put the hat right back on, containing my overlong, sandy brown hair. I need a haircut, for sure. My beard has gotten rather long in the last few months too.

I put everything away, put my pack on, make sure I've got my knife on my belt—long and thin, perfect for shoving through the eye socket of a hungry Z—, grab my bat, and climb down.

I'm tired and thirsty and dehydrated. To which I say, welcome to the apocalypse. Nothing new.

"Which way in?" I call up. "I'm dying for some popcorn."

She walks above the last loading bay and points down. I eye it. There's still a trailer in it and it will be kind of tight squeezing in. I don't like tight places. It's easy to get trapped in tight places.

I shrug. Nothing to be done about it. "My name's Woody, by the way."

"June," she calls back. After a pause, she adds, "Let me guess, the folks just loved *Toy Story*?"

"Yes, they did!"

I've got a smile on my face anticipating a full stomach—even if it's dog food—as I walk toward the loading dock. I'm keeping an eye on June, because... well... I should. Trust is hard these days, but I watch her mostly because of biology. It doesn't stop for the apocalypse. I've been lonely and as I get closer it becomes clear that she's fairly cute and in her twenties like me. And she's got a sense of humor. This makes her a post-apocalyptic babe.

As I get closer, I hear some banging from inside one of the trailers. I stop and stare.

"They're trapped in there," she says. "No worries."

But I *am* worried. What else don't I know about June, about this situation?

"Ummm..." I begin. "I don't mean to be rude or anything, but is there, like, a normal way in? You know, a door, preferably with some glass?"

She shrugs. "Yeah. West side of the building, just go around that way. No idea if any Zs are left over there, but knock yourself out." She starts walking along the roof towards the west.

I stay in the open away from the service road, which parallels I-40, and away from the building. I swing around where I spent the night, plugging my nose against the rotting-flesh-zombie smell of the breakfast crowd I just took out.

As I get past the parking area, the building juts out and the way narrows. I slow down and listen. The wind has picked up and I don't hear anything. I jog along until things open up again and come to a treed area, mostly pines and a few fir and deciduous trees. From her perch above me, June is pointing towards a lower building and I head over.

Being on foot these days is nerve wracking. I prefer heights, the kinds the Zs can't get to. See why that lookout tower is so appealing?

Once in the trees, I slow down and make my way towards the front door, a sidewalk leading up to it.

This is looking to be a good day, but like is often true for the post-apocalyptic world, things can go to crap in an instant. The wind is whipping which is why I don't hear the zombies until they are almost on me. A group of five shambling my way. And they look hungry—but then again, Zs always look hungry—and I'm the only food around.

CHAPTER THREE

I DON'T NEED to do extensive descriptions of these beasts, do I? They move slow with a lurching gait, maybe 1.5 mph at their fastest, like when they think it's dinnertime. They are dirty, stink like rotting meat with a fungal overtone, have glassy eyes, and most have some kind of wound. Guts dangling out, a compound bone fracture sticking out their sleeve, or ribs jutting out their side, that kind of thing. And they hiss and snarl, and moan. Their teeth snap together in anticipation of eating you. Classic zombie stuff. And while I have an ample supply of theories, at this point I don't know much about the science of real zombies, but I'll give you a hint: It's not quite like the TV shows and comics, but just close enough to be freaky.

Well, I see the five and turn around only to see a group of eight heading through the narrow area I just passed through.

Shit.

They must have heard us when I was too busy flirting— hmmm, do I even know what that is anymore? Maybe I was just talking to a member of the opposite sex and at the same time noticing that they were indeed a member of the opposite sex. So, I was too busy maybe-flirting to follow proper survival protocol.

I look to I-40, but there is a fence with three strands of barbed wire on the top, and my way through it was about a quarter of a mile to the east.

I'm trapped.

I tighten my grip on the baseball bat and start thinking about odds. The five are definitely the better bet. I put my odds at 50/50 on getting through.

And then there's a whistle and June yells, "Hey dummy, over here."

I've been on my own for months—on purpose—with no one to rely on, and there wasn't one thought in my brain that this young woman I mighta flirted with would try to help me.

She's at the corner of the building and has thrown a rope over the edge with strategically placed knots—probably how she gets to the roof in a guaranteed zombie-free way.

Both sets of Zs are closing in and shuffling faster. They think they've got me. From the larger group, there's two close to the rope, so I rush to the one that is closest, whack his head with the bat, which makes a gross wet sound like I just bashed a watermelon. As I wind up for the second, he's on me.

You've smelled morning breath, probably some really bad morning breath, I know you have. The breath of a zombie is a hundred times worse than that. Seriously. I've almost died from their halitosis and I'm about to again. The Z grabs me and his exhale makes my eyes water and I have to force myself not to wretch. I'm holding him off with one hand while going for my knife with the other. Zs aren't superhuman strong or anything, but they're not weak either.

He's snarling and his jaw is snapping and two more are almost on me by the time I get my knife and plant it in his left eye. He goes down in a heap. I back up a step, almost to the rope, but two she-Zs are on me then. I go for the bigger one with the knife, but realize too late that the other one is closer. In a most cliched, B-movie way, things slow down. Her mouth opens and moves towards my extended elbow. Here it is, the bite, the infection, the eventual death when...

The second one's head explodes, covering my face with the grossest, stinkiest, most disgusting goo of an undead rotting former human. I don't look, I'm not that dumb, not with more Zs almost on me, but I know June shot her.

I finish off the larger one and scramble up the rope.

CHAPTER FOUR

I FLOP on the roof of the building, my breath coming in ragged gasps from the forty-foot climb—yeah, I might have said the building was thirty feet tall earlier, but I upped my estimate after climbing. These things are relative, you know. Well... at least one's subjective experience of them is, and in this case, mine, and it felt like at least forty feet.

I pull a rag from my pocket and begin wiping the splatter off my face. This is godawful stuff I've got on me. It's stinky, slimy, and tepid. Since zombies run cool, it's noticeably cooler than human norm and that just freaks me out. I rub it off and spit and gag and am anything but graceful, ignoring June for the moment.

It's the zombie goo, you see. I suspect that ingesting too much can be detrimental to my health—especially their brains. Either the bacteria in it will make me too sick to take care of myself and I'll die of dehydration and become a zombie, or it will supercharge the Z-infection we all have, and I'll die and become a zombie.

Life these days is all about avoiding that "die and become a zombie" part.

I actually got lucky. My eyes blinked shut at the right moment and I got very little in my mouth. But I spit and gag and carry on just to be sure.

Don't get me wrong, I am grateful to be alive, but now I'm going to be tasting zombie for the rest of the day. And the taste... If I were trying to make it sound a lot better than it is, I'd say it tastes like moldy, rotting meat. Suffice it to say it tastes a lot worse than that.

"Thanks," I say when I'm done with my ungraceful cleaning. I turn to June and freeze.

She's got a hunting rifle slung over her shoulder—what she must have offed the Z with—and a handgun, a 9mm I think, pointed at me. She's ten feet back and I have no chance if she wants to shoot me.

In the adrenalized moment, I don't stop to consider that if she wanted me dead she could have just left me to the Zs... or shot me instead of the Z. I'm thinking I'm out of the frying pan and into the fire. I'm thinking that I should have fled in the opposite direction as soon as I saw her. Solo survival is hard, the Zs are relentless, but they're not devious like the humans.

"Happy to help," she says with a small smile. "Now divest yourself of all your weapons."

A thin part of my mind, one I just want to kick in the teeth, realizes that she's not just cute, she's CUTE! Round face, olive skin, delicate nose, compelling ocean-blue eyes. She's petite, dressed in jeans and an oversized grey sweater. I'm not sure of her age, anywhere from twenty to thirty. My heart, my stupid heart, starts beating faster.

My bat got abandoned down below, so I slowly pull my knife out of its holster and drop it on the roof. I take my pack off and step away, my hands up. I don't say anything. I don't know enough about what's going on to try to talk my way out of it.

"No guns?" she asks.

I shake my head. Guns are useful, for sure, but they're the kind of thing other people with guns want to take from you, so I don't use them. Oh, and I really hate guns, a past trauma, pre-apocalypse.

"Nothing strapped to your ankles?"

I pull my pant legs up, there's nothing.

She lets out a sigh, the gun lowering a bit, her shoulders slumping.

"Thank you for saving my life, June," I say and really mean it now that I'm not dealing with zombie goo all over my face and in my mouth.

"Sure, Woody."

We stand there in awkward silence and the one thought that keeps roaming through my head is, "God, she's cute." And I do mean "cute" because there is something about her beauty and petiteness that portrays innocence. She's on her own and alive well into the zombie apocalypse, so she's got to be more tough and smart than cute. And believe me, I know this, but I've starved myself of companionship for so long that she's like an oasis in the desert.

"Look..." I begin after the awkwardness has had babies, raised them, and sent them to college. "Trust was never easy, and now..." I shake my head. "There really is no way I can convince you to trust me. Words just don't count. You saved my life, so I kinda trust you."

She nods, her face passive. Our kinda-sorta flirting is out the window now that we are in the same space. That only worked when we were thirty yards away from each other.

"So, you make the rules here. I can go, right now, all I ask is we find me a clear way down."

She nods again, no data there, just a signal to continue.

"Or, if you are being super generous, maybe you can share some of your 'popcorn' with me and let me spend the night up here. I can't imagine there are any Zs on the roof."

She shakes her head, the gun still pointed at me, although it has lowered some more.

"I wouldn't mind, you know, a conversation with someone besides myself," I add.

She cracks a smile.

"Don't get me wrong, I'm a wonderful conversationalist, it's just that I always know what I'm going to say."

She smiles wider, but then it disappears transforming her face into a grim mask. "Woody, if you... I swear, I'll..." The gun is pointed right at my chest now.

"I get it. I swear I do. Tell you what, I won't move unless you tell me to move."

She nods, her face relaxes again.

I hold up my hand, like a first grader trying to get the teacher's attention.

"What?" she asks, clearly a bit exacerbated, her fore-head crinkling up, which is totally... cute.

"I gotta take a leak. Can I go pee on some Zs?"

She laughs, a real laugh, and nods towards the edge of the building.

CHAPTER FIVE

DOG FOOD IS... well, it's a bit dry and very bland. On the plus side, it clears the taste of zombie goo but leaves you with dog food breath.

We're in the middle of the large roof. This section has regular skylights, farther to the north and east the roof is covered in solar cells—now that's valuable, but also bait for the psychotic, petty, wannabe warlords in the vicinity. To the north of us there is a small tower and a higher section of the building. At the northwest corner is the tall tower, rising about one hundred feet in the air. It's the tallest building on this side of town and kind of a landmark.

June has some kind of shelter either up here or in the building, but she hasn't shown it to me. She's sitting about ten feet away, her legs crossed and the pistol in her lap. She gave me a mostly empty bag of dog kibble—senior formula, because it's easiest on your guts—and a bottle of water. Both she pulled out of her pack. And I gotta admire that. She's probably been up here for a while but carries her pack at all times just in case. And in the post-apocalyptic zombie world, just in case happens all the time.

"You been here long?" I ask, trying to make conversation around the dry crunching.

She purses her lips. Okay, then, that topic is out of bounds.

I nod to the tower. "Everybody around here knows about this place."

Her eyes narrow, she's thinking carefully about everything I say.

"I'm not going to be your only visitor," I say, making myself clear. "Not having anything anyone wants has served me pretty well lately."

"What kind of life is that?" she asks.

I take a sip of water and swallow. June said to eat this stuff slowly and I am understanding now, it's hard to get down. "It's a life, at least. The Zs have lowered the bar on 'quality of life' quite a bit."

She nods. "So where are you going?"

I point past the tower to Mount Elden rising behind it. "There's a lookout tower up there. I mean, yeah, lots of people know about it, but mostly locals. Someone might be there, but if not, that's a place I could really sleep."

"That sounds like something valuable," she says.

I nod. "Yeah, if a bunch of gun-toters want it, I'll leave. But it's remote, survival up there is not going to be easy. But it is close to this side of town and could be a good sanctuary."

Her forehead crinkles again, cutely I might add, and then she says, "Why are you telling me all this?"

And that is a good question. I shouldn't have, it was violating so many of my rules. I shrug.

"Really," she says, her hand moving closer to her gun. "I need you to tell me."

I sigh. "You saved my life and... I've been kinda starved for human companionship." I feel my cheeks begin to flush as I ponder a different kind of human companionship with the decidedly cute June and wonder what is under those baggy clothes. I dig in the kibble bag as cover.

When I look back up, her blue eyes meet mine. "I get that."

"Wanna go?" I ask before I can even think about it, and I'm sure my cheeks are bright red by now.

She looks away and is still for a moment before getting up, her gun in hand. "Stay there," she says with a smile. "I'll be right back." She jogs off across the roof.

🧍🧍🧍 🧍🧍 🧍🧍🧍

OPTION NUMBER ONE: Run to the rope, grab my stuff, and escape. Continue on this loner path.

Option number two: See what this intriguing pixie woman is going to come back with and violate my guiding survival principals.

I pick option two, slowly munching on dog food and sipping water for ten minutes. It's the best meal I've had in two weeks.

When she gets back, she rips open a cheap candy bar, the kind I would have turned my nose up at pre-apocalypse, splits it in two, and tosses me half. She then steps back and sits down, only six feet away.

"What's this for?" I ask.

"To celebrate. We're going on an adventure."

I'm both surprised and delighted, and scared to death.

What have I gotten myself into? We chat then, not about anything pre-apocalyptic and personal, and not about anything too serious. About the weather and TV shows we used to like. Scrounging tips and the weirdest places we've slept (me, I climbed and tied myself onto many a pine tree to rest on the way here; she found dumpsters to work in a pinch). It's fun, like actually fun. A simple, easy conversation. I don't even think about how cute she is... well, not that much anyway.

When the sun starts getting low, she asks me to wait again and comes back with a camping pad and some blankets. I thank her, make a joke about how the hospitality has improved, but she's serious now.

"You stay here, understand?" she asks.

I nod. A big, flat, zombie-free roof with some padding and plenty of blankets sounds about like heaven.

"'Cause if you follow me, if I see you anywhere but here, I'll shoot you. Got it?"

I agree and she walks off. When she's gone, I realize that I have to go to the bathroom, and we didn't cover that, and I really don't want to get shot.

I wait a few hours and sneak to the corner of the building under the cover of darkness and take care of my biological necessities. I then go back to my pad and blankets and sleep like a baby knowing there are no zombies up here.

CHAPTER SIX

FROM THE PET FOOD FACTORY, the trail up Mount Elden is north about half a mile. To get there we have to get down off the building, go past the mall and a bunch of other shops, and cross State Route 89.

As we're eating breakfast—you guessed it, dog food, senior formula to keep you regular—we plan this out. She's six feet away, the gun in her lap, but she's relaxed. We are going to use the rope to get down off the north end of the building and stay in open areas until we get to the trail.

And then it occurs to me. Yesterday when I asked about a way into the building she offered me one of the loading docks. There must be Zs in the building. Was she trying to get rid of me then, but somehow took pity on me when I was about to be bitten?

"What's wrong?" she asks, my face must be showing what I'm thinking. "If the Zs are on the north end, we might have to make a bunch of noise to draw them away, but it will work."

I nod and lick my lips, all the good "she saved my life" vibrations draining out of me.

"What!?" she asks, staring at me.

Trust between two humans has always been a trick. But now... it's a major feat. It doesn't take much to mess it up. I nod back to where she was when we met and tell her what just ran through my mind.

She swallows hard and nods.

"I get that you weren't going to give away any secrets at that point," I say, "but..."

"Most of the Zs are gone, just a few roamers left in the building," she says. "I would have warned you. I swear. You not going for it showed you had your head on and I needed to know that too."

There are thin, high clouds today and the weather is cooler. I draw my army surplus jacket tight. "I get it," I say. "I even respect it. It's just..."

She stares at me, those blue eyes probing, like she's trying to see into my weird brain, and it wouldn't help if she could, believe me. She then nods, picks up her gun, and stuffs it into her pack. She points to my pile of stuff about twenty yards away at the end of the building. "Feel free," she says.

It's an act of trust. I smile, it's a real smile, and thank her.

THE FIRST MILE UP towards Elden Lookout Trail is easy, relatively speaking. It's on a trail called Fat Man's Loop, which runs along the side of a deep, rocky gash in the mountain around and between huge boulders. There are short Gambel oaks, a bush that kind of looks like manzanita but with silver bark, ancient alligator junipers, and pine trees, of course.

Flagstaff and the surrounding area, if you've ever been there, is all about the ponderosa pine tree. The forest has other trees, but it is dominated by the pines, large sections of it with nothing else but a few, rare oaks. Tall, with dark brown bark, the ponderosas tend to be fairly symmetrical and are covered in bunches of dark green needles that are quite sharp. The bark is separated into sections by black crevices with the bark on the bigger trees lighter than on the smaller ones and the sections bigger and the crevices deeper. The big trees, if you put your nose near one of those crevices, smell sweet like vanilla.

These trees love the altitude, dry climate, and volcanic soil of Northern Arizona—they absolutely dominate it. It's something you might take for granted, unless you are a desert rat like me and feel yourself relax whenever you are out among them and smell their sweet scent.

Even though I've been living in the forest for many weeks as I made my slow progress north, I'm still delighted when we get out among the trees. Forests feel like safety to me.

The trail name, Fat Man's Loop, seems a bit ironic, given that it's quite steep, until you get past it. After that you are on a series of switchbacks that zigzag up one of the eastern arms of the mountain, and then it gets truly hard. All told, you climb over two thousand feet in less than three miles. Strenuous comes to mind.

It takes us a few hours to get to the trail, nothing untoward occurring, and as we start up the trail we slow down. We hardly talk, we need our ears to listen for Zs or people, and we have to go slow when the forest gets dense.

Down low, we see a few Zs in the forest, but they are at

a distance and we don't need to deal with them. Some stretches of the switchbacks have great views and we pause about halfway up and take a break.

Trust has been restored, but it is still tenuous. I go in front, we both seem to want it that way, and she always has her gun in hand.

"How much farther?" she asks, her voice barely above a whisper. A raven flies silently over us, its black wings glistening in the sunlight as it rides the currents off the mountain.

I shrug. "It's been years. Always hard to tell where the top is when you're on the mountain."

"And your plan when we get there?"

"Approach slowly. See if it's occupied. Turn around if it is."

She nods and we lapse into a companionable silence looking out over the east end of Flagstaff and the monster ponderosa pine forest beyond.

ᛉᛉᛉ ᛏᛏ ᛉᛉᛉ

BACK IN THE LATE SEVENTIES, Elden had a pretty big forest fire. As we get almost to the top and start along a ridge, the tower just visible, that damage is evident. The steep slopes are covered with downed and rotting trees, only small pines taking their place even decades later. I pause, it's an appropriately post-apocalyptic landscape.

I point to the two metal structures visible just above the peak, the lookout station and a microwave communication tower.

She smiles and nods.

I signal for her to follow and take us off the trail and

behind a boulder. "Let's rest here and see if we can hear anything," I whisper.

She nods and gets out the "popcorn" and we eat a bit and rest. We haven't seen or heard anything since the few Zs we saw out in the forest at the bottom. I'm feeling good about this plan. I lean back on the boulder and close my eyes so I can concentrate on listening, and because I'm tired. I can feel her next to me, hear her breath and her crunching on the dog food, smell her scent. Which is, to be honest, not the most pleasant scent. Sweat, dust, dog food, and... something else. Something a bit sweet and entirely human. It's distracting.

"I don't hear anything, do you?" I ask after I open my eyes.

She shakes her head. I nod to the trail and we get back to it, our pace slow and careful.

The trail ends on a small, flat-ish area at the peak of the mountain. Right in front of us is the communication tower, thick with microwave antennas which look like huge, oddly shaped drums. On the other side of the open area is a rectangular brick building painted a dark red, and right behind it, the lookout tower rises sixty feet and has a small room on the top and long switchbacking steps going up to it. To our left an old truck is parked.

The clouds have thickened and there's a healthy breeze up here evaporating the sweat from the climb.

No people. No Zs. Sanctuary. A place to feel safe.

I open my mouth to say something, but June grabs my arm and squeezes hard. A man pops up from behind the truck and points a rifle at us. Another one appears from behind the communication tower. I look back down the trail and see a third man.

Shit!

CHAPTER SEVEN

THEY'VE STRIPPED us of our weapons and our packs and walked us down the dirt road a half of a mile or so to a broader, flat area of the mountain where two dirt roads converge. There's a camp setup here with half a dozen tents and three pickup trucks. They've cut down some of the smaller trees and left trunks of some of the bigger ones. On these trunks, they've built watch platforms.

They're in the process of building a barbed wire fence and a line of sharpened sticks buried in the ground and angled out just beyond the fence for the Zs to run into. There's another half-dozen men down here working. I don't see any women.

This camp is not visible from Flagstaff, I studied the mountain and the tower on my way here quite a few times. I never saw a person. It's not visible from the trail we came up either. They are being very careful and this scares me.

On the way in, they dropped our packs at the edge of the camp but kept our weapons. There are three men with guns trained on us while a fourth paces in front of us, his hands behind his back.

June is next to me, her face hard, but I know she's scared, and I know it's my fault, and I feel terrible about it. This camp is situated here for a good reason. They are well hidden. They must have been keeping watch and laid in wait for us after they saw us coming up the lookout trail.

The pacing man, a psychotic, petty, wannabe warlord, I presume, is short and stocky with his brown-going-to-grey hair buzzed like a marine's. His face is decidedly plain, and his brown eyes are flat. He's got a pistol and a knife on his belt. He seems to be waiting for something.

A boy, maybe thirteen, comes running back from the way we came and says to Mr. Short and Stocky, "No signs of anyone else."

He nods, stops pacing, and looks at us. "So, you are alone."

"Yes," I answer, even though it wasn't really a question.

"And what are you doing up here?"

"Just trying to survive," I say. "Sorry to bug you guys. We're happy to move on."

He smiles at me, the kind of condescending look one might give a clueless child. I want to hit him.

He turns to the three men with the guns. "The girl can stay. Shoot him." He walks away towards the largest tent.

And here it is. The moment I've been trying to avoid since I escaped from Phoenix and the psychotic, petty, wannabe warlord that I ended up with down there. I have something they want. June. Not that she's mine, not at all, but she's with me and they want her. They want her for...

"Wait!" I shout. "I know things. I can be useful to you."

He snorts and continues walking.

June's got a hold of my arm again and is squeezing it

hard enough to hurt. I know why they want to keep her and not me, and so does she. This world has never been very kind to women, but the apocalypse set things back a ways. And in a weird way, she just saved my life, again. If I had come up here alone they would have killed me once they made sure I wasn't part of a larger group. I can't abandon her to them.

"Gunpowder!" I shout "I know how to make gunpowder. Dynamite, if I have the right ingredients."

He stops, his shoulders relaxing as he turns around. "Dynamite?"

"You're going to need more firepower."

He raises an eyebrow and nods for me to continue.

"You probably know this, but there's a big group that has cordoned off part of the university... NAU. They've got a complete chem lab, books, and people who know what they're doing. So yeah, dynamite. You're going to need it. It's not easy, it'll take some serious scrounging and some time. But, short term, I have some ideas on where we can find some. But I need—"

He's back in front of us and the look on his face stops me short. I was about to ask for something and he knew it.

"...but I was thinking, maybe you need gunpowder first," I continue, covering up my ask. "Ammo won't last forever, and that's easy."

He shakes his head. "Bring me dynamite. You have twenty-four hours."

Things have changed. He wants something and he is willing to trade for it. So far, he's offered time, but maybe he is willing to offer more.

"I need seventy-two hours and your promise that she remains unharmed."

He smiles at June, it's a leering, lecherous look that

makes me want to strangle him. "No harm will come to her," he says.

June spits on him and he just smiles wider. "I like spirit in a woman," he says. He must be twice her age and now I want to beat him senseless.

"No one touches her and we both go free," I say.

"Twenty-four hours," he says, looking at his watch. I glance at mine; it's almost 4:00 p.m.

He nods to one of his men, a big guy, at least two hundred fifty pounds. He comes over and grabs June, and she promptly punches him in the face, bloodying his nose. He pulls back his arm to hit her and I jump on him.

A shot rings out and we all freeze.

Mr. Short and Stocky is angry, his cheeks flushed red. "Twenty-four hours. You have my word, no one will touch the scrawny little girl." He looks like he just ate something sour and now I want to kick him in the balls. "But, she must cooperate."

I look at June, her nostrils flaring and her blue eyes dark with rage, but she nods. I don't say anything, just hold her gaze for a few breaths, hoping she can see how sorry I am that I got her into this and how hard I'm going to work to get her out of it. My much-vaunted, go-it-alone survival rules are in a shamble. It's not about me anymore.

"Agreed," I say. I then turn and run up the dirt road back toward the trail. Twenty-four hours isn't very long. I pass our packs along the way and grab them without asking.

I don't have much time.

CHAPTER EIGHT

HERE'S what I've figured out about Mr. Short and Stocky, our psychotic, petty, wannabe warlord. He's not dumb, look at the way he set up his camp up and lay in wait for us. But he's not that educated, either. Making dynamite, the key ingredient being nitroglycerin, is not something done easily or quickly, and not something I have any clue how to do. The gang at NAU—that part wasn't a lie—can. Me? Nope.

His plan for us is also clear. He is risking nothing right now. If I come back with dynamite he might keep me, leverage my attachment to June to get more. Either way, neither of us is getting away.

My attachment to June... Shit. There it is. Entanglements, those things get you dead in this world. And I've known her just a day and a half.

Maybe I should forget about her and just keep running. Sure, she saved my life, and yeah, she's cute and all, but survival is rule number one. But am I that big of an ass? Has a life of survival changed me that much?

All these things run through my mind as I tear down the trail much faster, and much noisier, than I should. I'm not leaving her. I need to get some supplies and I need to get somewhere safe before dark. I need to make some dynamite, knowing how be damned.

FIGHTING ZS, surviving the close calls, getting through the day with your life is... Well, it's a mess of adrenaline, you might even say it makes you feel "alive," but it ain't living. Racing through a post-apocalyptic town, dodging Zs, breaking into an office supply store, a car dealer, and then a Home Depot in a desperate plan to save another human being... Now that's adrenalized and stressful, and not the kind of thing you want to do every day, but it *is* living.

Despite my tired brain and exhausted body, I realize this on my climb back up to Elden Lookout Tower the next day. Maybe this won't work, maybe we are both going to die —or worse—but the last three days have been the best three days in a long, long time.

As I crest the trail with a backpack in my right hand and my left hand hidden in the sleeve of my jacket, I see them.

Mr. Short and Stocky and six other beefy boys are standing on the dirt road in front of the towers waiting for me. Half of them are wearing dark-green army surplus jackets and I resolve to change my look if I survive this. If army surplus jackets are the fashion trend with the psychotic, petty, wannabe warlord set, I definitely need another look.

June is there. She looks okay. My heart is racing because I know our odds aren't good.

The psychotic, petty, wannabe warlord looks at his watch and nods. "Punctual, I like that."

I just nod and walk until I'm eight feet away. "Let her go and it's all yours," I nod to the pack in my hand.

I'm sweating, partially because of the climb and the sunny day, partially because my jacket is zipped all the way up, and partially because I'm scared to death.

He looks at me. I know he's wondering whether there is really anything in that pack. I see his brain turn as he studies me. I don't have any visible weapons and I didn't even have a gun yesterday. There are seven of them, there is no way for us to get away. He has nothing to lose.

He nods to the linebacker holding June and he lets her go. She walks slowly towards me, and when she's halfway there, I toss the pack most of the way towards them. Attached to the zipper is a small black box with a blinking red light. It was hidden from them before by the way I held the pack.

June trots the next few steps and is right beside me. I can smell her sweat and her fear, and that something a little bit sweet. That June-ness.

"You okay?" I ask, keeping my eyes on Mr. Short and Stocky who walks forward to the pack.

"Yeah. You got a plan?"

I nod and unzip my jacket with my right hand while pulling my left hand out of the sleeve. There's a quick intake of breath by one of the beefy boys when he sees me, and then a few more as they all notice. I've got on a vest with wires, red LEDs, and about thirty sticks of dynamite strapped to it. Glued to the dynamite is an array of small nails and screws. In my left hand is a hacked-up handle off a leaf blower with more red lights and my thumb firmly on a red trigger.

"Nobody make any fast moves," I say. A total cliché, I know, but I'm hoping it'll work with this group of clichéd post-apocalyptic survivors.

June swears under her breath when she sees what I've done.

"I'm hoping we all survive the day, but I am happy to take you all with me if it looks like I'm not going to."

June's staring at me, her eyes wide. "Where'd you get the—" I can see it, she's not buying it and afraid she just gave my bluff away.

"Out east on I-40," I answer. "I remembered they had a construction site there, redoing a bridge out by Padre Canyon." I shrug. "Got lucky."

Mr. Short and Stocky looks at me, his bland brown eyes drilling into mine, his face flushing red with anger. "What's in the pack?" he asks.

"Same thing that is strapped to my chest. It's also wired to this dead man's switch and full of screws and nails so it's got a pretty good lethal range. When that light stops blinking," I nod at the device attached to the pack, "it's safe to open. Something happens to me, something happens to her, or you open the pack too soon, and..." I end with a shrug. "We get away, you get your dynamite. A deal's a deal."

He's looking at me again, but there is some curiosity in his eyes now. It appears he his reappraising me. Trying to find a way to keep the dynamite and keep us. His boys, though, are looking very nervous.

I don't give him time to think. I take June's hand and take a step back. She catches my eye, looking young and scared, but there is curiosity there too. She's also wondering if I'm not who she thought I was. I'm not sure if that is a good thing when she gives my hand a small squeeze.

Mr. Short and Stocky and his boys aren't moving.

They're staring at us. They're buying this, at least for now. We back up, slowly, until we are out of sight, and then we turn and run. I don't take my hand off the dead man's switch and I don't let go of June.

CHAPTER NINE

WE'RE down the ridge and starting on the switchbacks, our breath coming fast, before June starts asking questions. "What!? How did you do all this? Is that really dynamite—"

"Wait," I say, stopping and letting my breath catch up a bit. I widen my eyes and add, "I've had four of those 5-hour energy drinks in the last day, no sleep, and am kinda shaky." I pointedly look at the dead man's switch. "I'll tell you everything when we are safe. I promise."

She nods and I know I've scared her, probably more than I need to, but I'm pretty sure they have scouts on the trail and walkie-talkies. I have no idea if we're safe yet.

We keep moving, and when we're about halfway down the switchbacks I lead us off the trail and into a canyon. I smile when I see the pack I left on the way up, that's a good sign. I nod towards it. "Water and a gun for you. If you see anyone shoot them."

She nods and we both drink before scrambling down the canyon. When it's less steep, I take us to the southeast until we hit a trail and take that to a residential neighborhood. There a beat-up Ford Focus is waiting.

"You better drive," I say, getting in the passenger's side door. After June gets in, I add, "Get us out of the neighborhood and head north on 89." I then drop the dead man's switch and slouch down into the seat, my breath coming in ragged gasps, my heart pounding in my ears. We are alive. By some miracle, we are alive. A hysterical laugh escapes me and my hands are shaking like two fall leaves in a heavy wind that are barely clinging to their tree. June doesn't say a word but drives.

It's not fast going, there are abandoned cars, but they're not hard to get around. When we get out of town, I have her turn on Townsend Winona Road.

"They can see us," she finally says. "That damn tower. I know they can see us."

"I'm counting on it. I'm expecting Mr. Short and Stocky to track us the whole way."

"Mr. Short and Stocky?" she asks.

I nod. "Yeah, you know, the psychotic, petty, wannabe warlord. Did you get his name?"

She shakes her head and snorts. "No, I just thought of him as Asshole."

I laugh, it's a bit high pitched and just a tad hysterical, but I'll take it as my laugh for the day. "I love it. My name for him was a boring physical description, and yours was a tart commentary on how he presents himself to the world."

She's not laughing, but at least there's a smile. "So, you gonna tell me everything now?"

"Can we survive the day first?" I ask, ripping my coat and then the fake suicide vest off and tossing them both in the back.

She purses her lips, tightens her grip on the steering wheel, and nods.

CHAPTER TEN

WE'RE on I-40 heading east, crossing the bridge over Padre Canyon, the sun just having set. We had to deal with Zs a few times along the way, but nothing too difficult, and I've got to tell you, June is good with a gun. Being on the move as we were, and in such a hurry, we didn't worry about noise. In fact, if we attracted more Zs in our wake, so much the better. We both know they're going to follow. Psychotic, petty, wannabe warlords just can't help themselves.

And while June is cute and that petiteness and round face can portray innocence, that's not who she is. She's tough and competent and clearly has had some training with guns.

Her eyes widen as she sees the construction equipment and trailer on the east side of the highway.

"Did you check?" she asks.

"Yeah. No dynamite, not that I had much time to search. Given how far they can see from up there I had to have a real construction site. Pull in here," I say, pointing at Twin Arrows Trading Post, a sad white building with peeling paint and two gigantic arrows out front sticking into the ground.

The trading post was abandoned long before the apocalypse and is barely standing. Nothing here, no reason for anyone to be here. I have her pull the Focus behind the building out of sight of the mountain. There is a shiny new pickup truck there. It's jet-black with four-wheel drive and a crew cab. The bed is full of supplies and the tank full of gas.

I even found some gas treatment to add to the tank. At some point, before we run out, the gas is all going to go bad. Best enjoy it while it lasts.

June just stares at me, her forehead crinkled in that decidedly cute way. "Now. Spill."

I nod. "Fake dynamite. Got paper from an OfficeMax along with string, and then some wax to make the paper look realistic and glue. Scrounged electronics from tools at Home Depot. Got sand for the 'dynamite,' nails, and everything else there too. Used a lot of glue. Drank way too much caffeine. Drove out here last night without any headlights and a scooter in the back of the truck. Drove the bike back in the dark. Survived numerous encounters with Zs. Climbed the damn mountain for the second time in two days. Bluffed my ass off, and here we are!" I end with a big smile on my face and tip my hat to her.

She looks like she's about to cry. "What's next?"

I nod to the truck. "After it's dark and before the moon comes up, we double back the long way, staying off the road we came in on, which they will be using at some point. We then head north on 89A. They're coming after us, we both know that, but we won't be here. I'm thinking the high desert, past Wupatki National Monument, down by the Little Colorado River. There's no tower, of course, not much in the way of buildings, but there were never many people out there, and there is water."

She nods and sniffs. I wrack my exhausted brain trying to figure out why she's upset, what I missed. A crying woman is for me, like many men, akin to kryptonite; it just makes us weak. It was a decent plan, pulled off in short order, and actually, unbelievably, worked. There's more danger right around the corner, but that's just life in the post-apocalyptic world.

"Hey, cheer up," I say. "We outwitted a psychotic, petty, wannabe warlord today. We're alive. We're not..." And then I pause and start to understand why she's near tears. "...and we're not alone. We've got..."

My words hang in the air as her blue eyes look deep into mine. Tears well up in her eyes, but don't quite spill, unlike me. The tears are flowing, and I don't know that I care. Today was the first day I really lived in a long time, and I'm still alive.

She sniffs, nods, takes a deep breath, leans over and... kisses me on the cheek. "Thank you, Woody," she says.

I nod. "Any time, June."

That kiss, that little peck on the cheek. I bet you're a bit disappointed, that you think she should have fallen for me right then and there. But I wasn't, not one bit. She trusts me now, and that is never a small thing. Hell, I've got the rest of our lives to convince her that I'm the man for her. Now that's something to live for, something beyond survival, although I'm going to keep laughter on the list. You just gotta laugh.

And really, who is June? She's this wonderful, decidedly cute mystery to unwind. Pixie small and wicked with a gun, punching guys over twice her weight in the nose, and a sense of humor to boot. Now that's something to live for.

Let's just hope I'm smart enough... no, that's not right. Let's hope that *we're* smart enough to stay alive so our relationship can grow.

She grabs my hand and holds it until it's dark enough for us to embark on the next leg of our adventure... together.

PART TWO

WOODY AND JUNE VERSUS THE FUNGUS-HEAD ZOMBIES

SERIOUSLY? YOU CALL THIS A FIRST DATE?

CHAPTER ELEVEN

JUNE'S too much for me. She is. And I'm freaking out a bit.

"Look, Woody, just relax." She's behind me and touches my shoulders which are hard as cement and have been since the zombie apocalypse started.

I mean, yeah, she's cute, she's funny, she sometimes laughs at my lame jokes. And she's got those ocean blue eyes, that short black hair, that petite body and pixie vibe, but...

"Take a deep breath, bend your knees, don't lock your elbows, and slowly pull the trigger."

I lower the gun, a 9mm handgun of some sort, and look at June. Her face is hard, she's focused. We're in the high desert north of Flagstaff, Arizona, at an overlook to the Little Colorado River Gorge. It's fairly flat, great visibility, and the right kind of place to make noise in this new world. We've got some cans setup on a big tan sandstone boulder for me to shoot at.

We're fifty miles away from where we've been staying,

and if the noise attracts Zs, we'll see them coming and be able to get away in time. And if the noise attracts humans... well, that can get trickier, but we won't be here much longer.

We're in the top of the parking lot of the overlook. A small tribal park on what was the Navajo Nation. Well, I don't know, still could be the Navajo Nation, but right now it's just June and me. Below us are old wooden stalls where the Navajo used to display their wares—turquoise and silver jewelry, pottery, and all kinds of touristy kitsch. Below that is the river gorge, deep, sheer, and dramatic, eroded by the Colorado's little sister through limestone and sandstone.

For the last few hours she's drilled me on the basics with an unloaded gun. It's now loaded and it's time for me to fire a gun for the second time in my life.

She's all of five foot two with her hands on her hips as she studies me and chews on her lower lip. We've known each other for four days now and in that time, she saved me from a zombie—by shooting it in the head and showering my face with zombie goo—and I saved her from a psychotic, petty, wannabe warlord with a manic, all-night prep session and an epic bluff against a bunch of armed men. But, I had, admittedly, gotten us into that mess.

There was a moment when our escape was assured that felt like... well, there was a peck on the cheek and laughter and hope. Hope for a future, a life worth living when most of the living are now the undead.

But this gun thing. She's good with guns, and by good, I mean "oh, my God, I didn't know people could really shoot like this, I thought it was just a Hollywood thing." She's good with a rifle at long distance, she's good with a pistol at close range, she's accurate, she reloads quickly, and she can take the gun apart blindfolded, clean it, all the while tap dancing to Queen's "We Will Rock You."

Okay, okay, I made that last part up.

"You have to be able to defend yourself," she says, still studying me. I get the impression that she is constantly reevaluating me. She trusts me—in so far as I don't mean her any harm and will put my life on the line for her—but other than that, I think her estimation of me has varied quite a bit.

"I don't like guns," I say.

And I guess my estimation of her has varied a bit too. It was like, "she's cute," to "my God she's cute!" to "wow, she just laughed at my joke, this is one post-apocalyptic babe... but, how long until she figures out how lame I am and moves on?"

"Why?" she asks. Lips are pursed and hip is cocked now. It's warm out here and gone is the grey oversized sweater she was wearing when we met at the dog food factory and she's got on jeans and a long-sleeve, navy-blue running shirt that hugs her petite torso. God, she's an athlete too. But after my long go-it-alone-no-matter-what phase, she's basically the most beautiful girl on planet earth to me. And she's a bit like Linda Hamilton's Sarah Connor in *Terminator* 2, although younger, and definitely cuter, and... well... it's attractive, *very* attractive, but it's rather intimidating.

"Guns kill people," I say with a shrug.

"Guns kill Zs," she counters.

"I know. It's just..." We haven't talked about our pre-apocalyptic lives. We've just avoided it. To me, those lives, those people, and that world is gone. We've all seen some bad shit, done some bad shit, and we've all lost too much. Some of it weighs on me, but talking about it doesn't seem like it's going to do any good. "I..."

"Come on, Woody, spit it out."

I bite my lip and shake my head, my eyes roaming from the gorge below us, across the gravel parking area, to the rough desert hills above us and Route 64 we came in on. While my mind is divided between cute June and "I hate guns," I'm still keeping an eye on things—I don't want to be surprised by the living, or the undead. "I would have to delve pretty deep into my past," I say, my eyes finding her round face, "pre-Z life, and..."

And I don't want to tell her what I did, not even this one, which is understandable. I mean, I was only six. My four-year-old brother and I were playing Cowboys and Indians and I knew that Dad kept the gun in a locked drawer of his desk. For once it was unlocked and I wanted something better than the pitiful plastic gun I had with the melted end—a candle experiment I had done a few months previously.

My brother had a toy bow and arrow, he hit me in the head with an arrow while I was holding the gun and I squeezed the trigger. It went off and went flying out of my hand. I didn't mean to...

June nods, her eyes finally looking away from me. She gets it. Dredging up the past can get in the way of surviving the present. Cute women, I might add, can get in the way of surviving, but are a lot more tempting than the past. A lot more.

"Besides," I add, "knives and bats work fine on the fungus-heads."

Her forehead crinkles and she's staring at me. "Fungus heads?"

I nod. "Yeah, the Zs, the dead. Their brains turn into this big ball of fungus, kind of like a head of cauliflower. Didn't you ever notice?"

She shakes her head.

I hold my hands out, palms up, and smile. "See... too much shooting, not enough bat swinging."

"You're serious?"

I nod. "Yeah. Not like the TV shows where it was some mysterious virus or something that didn't make a damn bit of sense. I think it's a parasite. There has to be something that digests what the Zs eat, give them energy to move their muscles, drives them to spread the infection. You've noticed that they move better once they've been dead a while, right? Seen that the ones that have bled out don't move so good?"

She blinks, her face blank. And then she's giving me that reappraising look again. I think I just went from "wimp who is afraid of guns" to "brainiac who has a theory on how the Zs work."

"Okay," she says with a sharp nod. "You're going to show me. Where can we find a Z around here?"

"Now?" I ask. I mean, we're in the middle of dealing with my nearly pathological resistance to guns, which I wouldn't mind avoiding a while longer, but—

"Now!" she says, marching towards the truck.

See what I mean, I think she's just too much for me.

CHAPTER TWELVE

YOU DON'T GO LOOKING for zombies, you just don't.
Nobody does. You look for a place where the Zs aren't,
where the Zs can't get to. Our little target practice was out
on the Navajo reservation and I thought of taking us back to
Cameron Trading Post, maybe ten miles away, but don't. I
head us towards the Grand Canyon.

June notices. "Wasn't there a trading post just back
there? We could try it."

I'm driving the beautiful, brand-new Toyota pickup I
recently liberated, going slow down the road through the
high desert, a long ridge of low lumpy hills to the left, the
flat desert sloping down on our right with the Little
Colorado River Gorge not far away. The land is a patch-
work of brown and salmon and red, with low grass and sage
brush.

"You didn't grow up in Arizona, did you?" I ask.

She shakes her head and I catch her frowning out of the
corner of my eye. I've strayed into pre-apocalypse territory,
but it's necessary this time.

"We're on the Navajo reservation," I say. "I just... Well, I kind of figure that somewhere out here they figured this zombie thing out. They know how to grow corn in the desert and how to live in the heat with little water. They're probably doing better than the rest of the world. And... I..."

"You what?", she asks, her forehead crinkled in that cute way.

"Well, they have centuries of white men taking things from them." I shrug my shoulders, it's mostly a feeling and hard to express. "So... I don't want to go dissecting a Native American zombie."

She nods and is, I am sure, reappraising me. Probably thinking I'm filled with white man's guilt, even though everyone is equal now. The zombies don't discriminate, they want to munch on us all no matter the color of our skin, what our sexual preference is, or how much money we used to make.

June's skin has an olive tone, so maybe Italian heritage, or maybe Hispanic. With those blue eyes, though, it's hard to tell. Me, I'm decidedly white with sandy brown hair, a sprinkling of freckles, and a beard that's gotten longer than I like. Something I notice a lot more now that June is around.

"But haven't we been staying on the reservation?" she asks.

I shake my head. "Not strictly speaking. Wupatki is a national monument. We were on the rez when we went down to the river, but not for long."

She's studying me now. And yes, I'm not completely rational or clear about this. Wupatki worked because it was so empty; going to where the Navajo live out here doesn't feel right.

"So where to?" she asks.

"The Grand Canyon. The Desert View Overlook is not

far and has a tower." I flash her a big grin and she groans. The last tower I took her to required that mad, manic bluff of the psychotic, petty, wannabe warlord. "There will have to be Zs there. Tourists. Lots of them."

She shakes her head and then checks her rifle.

CHAPTER THIRTEEN

DESERT VIEW IS my favorite overlook on the Grand
Canyon. It was never the most popular one, those are all to
the west around Grand Canyon Village. The canyon is not
as deep at Desert View, despite it being the highest elevation overlook on the South Rim, but the view is spectacular.

It sits on Navajo Point where the Colorado River is
making a sharp turn from the north to the west. You can see
to the west into the deeper portion of the canyon and to the
north into Marble Canyon, where it is not as deep but you
can see the river for a long ways. You see the work of water
on land, the slow erosion over millennia eroding away layer
after layer, color after color, of rock. To the northeast, the
desert is flat with mesas rising up, the land spotted with
vegetation here and there, but mostly the tan to brown to
red colors of the desert.

We cruise past the overlook turnoff a mile or so, we
need to scout a bit before stopping, but we only see one Z in
the distance at the crest of a hill off the road a bit. I turn us

around, drive back, and pull into the Desert View turnoff and ease down toward the parking lot. The visibility isn't great here, the desert crowded with short, twisted juniper with shaggy silvery bark.

"My first time here," June says.

"You're gonna love it."

"We're here for a Z, remember? You're gonna show me this fungus brain thing, right?"

I nod. God, she's focused. The road in is clear and we make it to the big parking lot and I pull in at the far end where no cars are. Good visibility is what you always want.

I get out, feeling the weight of the gun holstered on my hip. I don't like it. I make sure the knife is on the other side, put my pack on, grab my baseball bat (I found a replacement during my all-night, save June prep session in Flagstaff), and snug down my Diamondback baseball cap. June gets her rifle and her pack. We never assume we are coming back. You just never know.

Things are spread out here. There's a small visitor's center and some bathrooms near the parking lot. Farther in there is a store and a snack bar, and right on the rim is the watchtower with an attached gift shop.

The air is warm and still as we move through the lot. The cars are a tangled mess at the other end with doors open, a pileup where one car rammed into another, and trash on the ground. I don't like it. I look to our right and there is another road and a gas station that I had forgotten about.

I signal to June and head that way. The time for chatting is when you are safe, not when you are hunting Zs.

The gas station is built in an adobe style with sand-brown walls and faux wood beams peeking out right below the flat roof. There are, surprisingly, no vehicles here. The glass door and windows of the convenience market are broken, and behind it is a tall, square garage and there are four pumps out front. We'll be needing to see if we can get any gas later.

We circle slowly, listening, and I think it's clear, we only see a few squirrels and the ever-present ravens. Just as we are about to head back to the front of the building, I hear banging coming from the garage. It's two bays with both garage doors closed. The doors have two sections of clear plastic starting about six feet up and going to the top of the door. I signal for June to wait and she readies her rifle. I slowly walk up and hear the snarl of a zombie. It increases in volume and the banging gets louder as I approach.

The Zs can sense the living. I'm not sure how, I'm really not. We are as quiet as can be and it can't smell us through that door, still it knows we are here. Whatever this sense is, I don't think their range is good, maybe a few hundred feet, but it is unnerving.

The Z slaps its leathery hand on the clear section of the door as I get close, and despite knowing it's there, I jump, my heart pounding in my head, adrenaline dumping into my bloodstream. I hold still, listening carefully until I am convinced it's only one Z, but boy is this one ripe.

I walk back to June.

"Only one," I whisper, "and probably there since the beginning. There could be things worth scavenging inside."

She nods and smiles.

"We need to go in the front, though. I don't think we can open that door from the outside."

We circle around and enter the cleaned-out convenience store, junk everywhere. We should pick through it later, someone might have missed something, but it doesn't look like it. To the right of the counter, there is a single metal door to the back and the Z is banging on it, knowing we are here now. It is surely starving over a year into the apocalypse and will be good to illustrate my fungus/parasite theory.

"Are you sure you want to do this?" I whisper.

Her blue eyes are hard as she nods.

And by "do this" I mean "risk our lives to kill a zombie and then dissect it to see if its brain has turned into a ball of fungus because the guy you met four days ago has a theory which in all probability is fueled by too many comic books as a kid and too many zombie movies and TV shows as an adult." But I don't say all that. She's stayed alive long enough to infer all but my self-doubts and recriminations. But, hey, she's known me for four days, so she probably gets that about me too.

We clear the junk out from in front of the door—can't have any tripping hazards in case we have to run—and I find a candy bar and hand it to her. She smiles, pockets it, and continues to clear a path to the door. We don't talk about this, we just do it. It makes me like her even more, that we don't have to discuss the basics of survival in the post-apocalyptic era.

It's tight, the door is right next to a wall, but it should work. She grabs the door handle with her left hand and has her gun in her right. I stand on the other side of the door, bat ready.

The Z is there, banging on the door, a pitiful whine interjecting here and there between the snarling. It almost sounds like a sad puppy for a moment, but the stink quickly dispels that image. I wrinkle my nose at the rotting meat smell and pull my T-shirt up over my nose. This one's going to stink.

I nod and June jerks open the door, using it to shield herself. The Z lurches out and the stench overwhelms me. It smells of rotting, putrid meat overlaid with a sharp spike of mold. My eyes water and I swing my bat down onto its head, hard. It's going to make a mess, but we need to crack open its skull anyway. It goes down in a heap. I drop my bat, kneel on its chest and knife it in the eye to make sure it's not coming back.

The Z is emaciated with dried-apple skin and is skeletally thin with wisps of black hair hanging on his head. He's dressed in filthy shorts and a T-shirt with what looks like a bite wound on his leathery arm. He must have been a tourist, gotten injured, and holed up here.

This Z and his poor condition reinforces my theory that Zs will "die" eventually if they don't have any food, but I can't think about it right now. I stand up, dizzy from the funk he's putting off, turn, rip my shirt off my nose, and puke on the floor.

June is too busy gagging and coughing to laugh at me. We both run out of the building gasping for breath.

"I hadn't counted on that... that..." she says before stumbling forward a few steps and puking.

I sit on the blacktop, pull out my water bottle and wash my mouth out and then offer it to June. I smile. It's actually a good day. I'm alive. I'm not alone. I have a purpose, of sorts, beyond survival. What's a little upset stomach and puke aftertaste balanced against actually being alive?

"What now?" she asks, sitting next to me.

I shrug my shoulders. "You want to look around while we wait for the stench to clear out? This is your first time here and it'd be a shame to miss it."

She looks back towards the store, her complexion just a tad green, and nods.

"Let's go look at that *tower*," I say nodding and smiling.

She shakes her head but smiles at me. No way we're going to get into trouble with every tower we encounter, is there?

CHAPTER FOURTEEN

"OH, HELL," I mutter. From the gas station we took a service road, which quickly turned to gravel, ran along a side canyon, and we are behind the snack bar. It looks like there was a bloody last stand here some months ago.

We're in sight of the Desert View Watchtower, one of Mary Colter's masterpieces from the 1930s, a pueblo-style tower that gracefully tapers as it rises up seventy feet, made of irregular-sized, sandstone blocks with windows along the top. But the jumble of decomposing bodies is all we can look at.

It's been at least a few months and the bodies are dark, desiccated, and mummy-like where the flesh wasn't eaten by birds or bugs. White bones peek out from the gaps and holes in their sun-bleached tourist clothing. The smell isn't as a bad as the gas station Z, but it's a heavier, darker smell that creeps me out.

There's a group of ten or fifteen bodies piled up near two other bodies that are lying with their feet pointed towards each other six feet from the pile of Zs.

"Watch," June whispers, going closer.

She walks gently, her feet moving slow, coming down toe first as if she were a dancer. She takes guns off each of the two separated corpses, pulls some clips off them, and comes back to me.

She hands me one of the guns and three clips. "The pile is Zs. The other two offed each other instead of falling to them. A couple, I think."

It hits me, like a fist to the stomach. Intellectually I admire the act, although doubt I am capable of it. Emotionally... I just want to cry for them having to make that choice.

June has this distant look on her face and then she mumbles, "Now, that's love." I'm not even sure if she's talking to me. We don't say anything else but skirt the bodies and head towards the tower.

WE SKIRT the watchtower and the round, low gift shop connected to it and go to the lookout. We see more bodies, but nothing fresh and nothing moving. The gift shop is the same pueblo construction as the tower, about fifteen feet tall with larger windows.

The overlook is asphalt that has that never-cleaned look, covered with dirt and leaves, and is bordered by a metal railing. It's built on top of a huge hunk of Kaibab Limestone with Navajo Point below and the glory of the Canyon beyond.

And the view... the depth of the canyon to the west, the Colorado stretched out to the north, the canyon itself full of colors from light tan to deep umber in horizontal stripes that reveal the bones of the earth. This is the desert, so while there is vegetation, it's sparse, allowing the different geological layers of the canyon to be clearly seen. After the initial cliffs, the water has worn large structures out of the limestone and sandstone layers called mesas, buttes, and temples. And... well, if you've seen it you get it. If not, some are called temples because they look like these grand buildings or pyramids and the canyon seems like a holy place. The sun is headed towards the horizon, the yellow light deepening the already spectacular colors.

All the desiccated dead make it clear that the living aren't around, but we don't try the tower. We heard a bang on one of the large gift shop windows as we went by and saw a Z there staring at us. We looked at each other and just kept going. One Z, we can handle one Z. And any roamers would have been on us by now.

"Wow," June whispers when we reach the edge.

I take a deep breath and let it slowly out. "I know, right?" The Canyon has always given me such perspective. If you know how to read it, those rock layers show the history of the earth here going from millions to billions of years ago.

"Come on," I say, trotting back towards the path and scrambling down around the edge of the fence. Last time I was here was with the family and there was no fence hopping allowed. It's clear plenty have done it, a fading trail on the sharp ridge leads down to a ship's prow-like protrusion that juts into the canyon.

Some adrenaline is still in our systems and that, I think, leads to me making that bad decision and June shrugging and following.

In my mind, this feels like a first date, almost like there hasn't been an apocalypse and I'm just showing a girl I like something special. Taking her off the beaten trail so she can get the full experience. Showing off a bit.

Whatever it is that drives us forth, we don't notice the impending doom until it's too late.

The watchtower gift shop is full of Zs—probably another group that took refuge in there. We're far enough away and there's enough wind that we don't hear them banging on the glass until they break it and the group spills out.

"Shit!" June shouts.

I look back and there are twenty or so escaping the gift shop, but there are forty more lurching past the tower towards us. Where the hell did they come from?

The Zs are at the railing, tumbling over it, a few going over the side, but most getting up and shambling toward us. The gift shop Zs are all leathery, like the gas station Z, and must be absolutely starving. It makes them quicker than your average zombie and even more determined. The other group isn't in great shape, but a little fresher; they must have been roaming and we just missed them.

In the old world, one stupid decision and you'd wake up with a hangover, or get a traffic ticket, or maybe blow your rent money. Now? One dumb mistake and you die.

There is no escape here. The sides aren't sheer, but they are steep and sweep down hundreds of feet. We don't think about it. We run.

CHAPTER FIFTEEN

WE'RE at the end of the trail on a rock jutting out with sheer drops on all sides. I stare as the horde descends, shuffling over the tan, sandy path, winding in and out of the yellowish limestone rocks and scraggly juniper trees. When the path narrows, a few lose their footing and fall into the canyon, but plenty are getting through.

They are hungry, their groans and snarls almost plaintive, their jaws snapping and teeth cracking, the sound of it getting louder as they approach.

"You gonna use that gun now?" she asks, her breath coming fast and a small smile on her sweating face.

Flashes of my childhood living room and my father's gun flicker past. The cold weight of the gun. The ear-piercing sound of it going off. The screams of my baby brother and the blood pouring down his arm.

I nod, the past is the past. I stuff my bat between my pack and my back and pull the 9mm. "These last few days have been—" I begin, but she cuts me off with a sharp shake of her head.

"Later," she whispers, a flicker of fear passing over her blue eyes, her mouth open and lips parted. The moment lasts less than a second and then the fear is gone and she's turned towards the Zs and is firing.

You know what? She's not just cute, she's beautiful, and if we're going to die a horrible death, shouldn't I at least try to kiss her?

No! Absolutely not. Are you crazy? What kind of guy do you think I am? It has occurred to me by this point that not only do I not know if she *likes* me, I don't know if she likes men. An attempt at a kiss would not only be colossally stupid, it might afford me a quick death where she kicks me in the balls and shoves me off the cliff, my last living thoughts being what a dumbass I am before the rocks below break my body.

I don't do that. I turn. I fire.

"Try to drop them all in one spot to block the path," she shouts as she drops her rifle and pulls a pistol. My ears are ringing and I can barely hear her.

I nod and think about that couple we just found, the ones that made sure they wouldn't be zombies. Yeah, I know I was just thinking of kissing her and now I'm wondering whether we should both just end it. But there's no time. I keep firing until the clip runs out, reload and fire again. I'm doing my best, but often miss the zombies, much less their heads. June is doing good and the bodies are starting to pile up, but it's not going to be enough. Not nearly enough.

CHAPTER SIXTEEN

THEY'RE BREAKING THROUGH. Most of the dead ones fall off the trail and go tumbling down into the canyon when they're shot. The "block the path" plan is not working. There are too many. They are almost on us.

Things don't slow down in a clichéd-movie-slow-mo-mode like at the dog food plant, but my brain seems to speed up. I suck with a gun. I'm great with a bat. I drop my gun, pull the bat and step forward, right in front of June.

She stops firing, thank God, and I am just on our side of the narrowest portion of the path. They can only come at us one at a time. So I swing and I swing and I swing. I don't have to connect with their heads, I just have to knock them off.

I've got my feet planted wide as I swing, lowering my center of gravity. It's a bit awkward, not like when you're up to bat, because I need to swing both ways, even though the backswing feels weird and weak. June comes up behind me, gets down low, and shoots at them between my legs.

Bam! A blow to the shoulder knocks a chubby tourist Z

over the edge, its tattered flip-flops the last thing I see. June takes the next one down with a head shot, a small splatter of zombie yuck hitting me in the face.

Whack! A hit to the head of a former soccer mom and zombie goo goes everywhere. "Home run!" I say with as much humor as I can muster amidst the stink, the carnage, and the goo.

The next one shambles forward, too quick for my back-swing, but June takes its knee out and it stumbles and I connect solidly with its midsection and it slowly slides over, its leathery hands grabbing my boot. I ignore it, the next one is on me.

Bam! A sloppy blow to the shoulder is enough to knock a little girl Z down, but she gets back up, and as much as I hate it, I swing hard for her head and knock her over the cliff. Meanwhile, June shoots the one clinging to my boot point-blank, the top of its head flying off, soon followed by the body, bouncing down the cliff.

The moment takes me, my breath loud in my head, sweat trickling down my back and slicking my hands. It's just the bat and the Zs. Flickers of stories try to invade my head, but I push them out. The Japanese man with the expensive DSLR camera around his neck, seeing the canyon for the first time. The tired Midwest mom getting one last family vacation in before the kids start going to college. The boy Z with earphones still in his ears that would have rather played video games than walk along one of the greatest wonders of this planet. The little girl frightened of heights, but bravely going to the rim only to be trapped there when the infection took hold here.

They used to be alive with lives and stories, hopes and fears, and bills and jobs. I push their stories away, the ones I imagine. They aren't alive, they are the dead. I swing and swing and swing, inelegant grunts escaping me.

The sun is hot and my nose is full of their rotting flesh, moldy funkiness, my face and arms and clothes covered in their splatter. My ears are full of their snarling sound and snapping jaws, the sharp crack of gunfire, the sound of breath being dragged into my tight chest. My breath is coming in gasps and sweat is dripping into my eyes. Jesus, how many tourists were up here when this thing started?

The bat is like a lead weight in my hand and I'm getting dizzy, my hands so sweaty I can barely hold it. There are more, but I can't do it. Is it time to ask June to put one of those bullets in my head? Is it time to grab her hand and the two of us just jump off?

I don't want to die, but I really, truly don't want to become a Z.

But I keep swinging even though I'm getting clumsy, pushing them off more by luck than skill, off balance and lurching a bit, looking something like a zombie myself. I start babbling more, mumbling "Home run," when I hit one good or "Foul ball," when I screw up. If you saw it, you might think this was more boy trying to impress girl on a first date, but really I'm just trying to keep myself focused, keep the bat swinging.

"Ground ball," I say between gritted teeth after a weak, grazing hit that has me off balance. I stumble, the long steep slope so many Zs have gone down ready to swallow me, my breath catching, and I know this is it. But June grabs me by the pack, jerks me back, and I go down in a heap. She steps forward, pistols in both hands firing one after the other. Bang. Bang. Bang.

She is simply magnificent, Linda Hamilton's Sarah Connor ain't got a thing on her.

She does it.

The last one goes down and she collapses next to me.

"Good... good job," I gasp out.

"You too, Slugger."

"Baseball... I used to play a lot of baseball."

She smiles weakly. "It shows."

I wait, thinking she might give me something, some little tidbit about her past, kind of like "I was a spy for Israel, I'm with the Mossad." But nothing, we sit there under the sun as we recover.

But those blue eyes and olive skin. I mean, she could be Israeli. And with that shooting, she could be Mossad.

CHAPTER SEVENTEEN

WE MAKE it to the top of a tower. Finally.

Just as the sun is getting ready to set and the view can't get any better, we settle in on the top of Desert View Watchtower. We picked off a few more stragglers along the way, but nothing too difficult.

The inside of the tower is as much a masterpiece as the outside, but we rush up the stairs that twist around the tower wall. We gawk at the beautiful Hopi murals and reproduction of petroglyphs, our hands clinging to the leather wrapped handrail. We marvel at the circular open-ings between some levels that create an air of spaciousness and the rounded adobe-style treatment of all surfaces. Up we go through a final sloped ladder on the top level, through a trapdoor, and out onto a glorious zombie-free roof high above the ground below.

Despite the beauty of the inside, we rush, longing for the safety of the top of the tower, to be truly safe from the Zs. We rush for the view of the sun setting. We rush for the promise of a moment of peace and real sleep.

What I think happened is our scouting west of the overlook where we saw the one wandering Z caught the attention of that little horde, we got their zombie senses tingling, and they roused themselves and came after us. At the same time, walking past the gift shop got that group's attention. I'm thinking that the zombie fresh-flesh detector thing is more like a hundred yards. I also think these old zombies took some time to rouse themselves and didn't start banging until we were too far away to hear.

"Here you go, Slugger," she says, handing me half of the candy bar I found in the gas station. We've completed a quick meal of dog food—any calories in an apocalypse—and a little chocolate is just what I need. We had a meal like this when we met. Maybe it's becoming our thing, Woody and June chasing dog food with chocolate on top of a roof.

"Thanks, Connor," I say.

"Sarah Connor?" she asks. "Like from the *Terminator*?"

I smile, delighted that she got the reference. "Yeah, you were amazing."

She looks down, shakes her head, smiles, takes a bite of chocolate, and looks back at the sunset settling over the Grand Canyon.

There are things to do, like see what kind of supplies we can find around here, and see if my fungus-head zombie theory is correct. And we've things to talk about, like whether June likes me, or boys for that matter, but I leave most of it for later. We've got a place to sleep, really sleep, the Zs can't get up here. We can relax, at least for a few hours.

"Can I explain something?" I ask after dessert is over.

She nods but frowns.

It takes me a while to get it out, but I tell her about my little brother and the shooting accident.

"Did he..." she says, a look of horror on her face.

"Oh... no," I say, feeling bad for leaving that part out. "Joshua survived. The bullet barely missed an artery and nicked his bone and his arm was never great after that. No baseball for him, but he survived."

She nods and takes my hand and squeezes it. "It was just an accident. You were only a kid."

I nod, but the guilt still lies on me heavy.

I can see that she wants to ask me about Josh, if I know where he is, but she doesn't and I don't volunteer. I am still reluctant to go too deep into the past if it's not needed. Too much has been lost and sometimes the only way to deal with a deep loss is to ignore it—well, for as long as you can.

"But, you know, it's time to get good with a gun," she says sweetly. "Right?"

"Yeah, I guess it is."

I watch her for a bit as she watches the sun set. She's too much for me, that's for sure, and not just because of the guns. She's a complicated and strong woman that is still a mystery to me. And that's okay.

"You see there," I say, pointing to the north, "that deep gorge that is entering the canyon."

She nods and I'm not looking at her, but I see it out of the corner of my eye. I take a deep breath of her scent, sweaty and sweet.

"That's the Little Colorado River Gorge," I say. "Where it enters the Grand. We saw another piece of it where you were teaching me to shoot."

She nods again, her eyes drinking in the beauty of the tableau.

"The gorge is around three thousand feet deep there. The area is sacred to the Hopi. They believe that their ancestors emerged from a place near there called the *Sipapuni*."

In some ways I'm hoping this helps her understand my reluctance to mess with Native American zombies. I'm also trying to impress my decidedly cute companion. But, mostly, I'm just trying to help her enjoy what she's seeing.

It's more than just rock and water and the effects of time. It's vast and majestic, the land so beautiful it's not surprising there are those that consider it sacred.

I happen to be one of those people.

We're silent for a while and she grabs my hand and holds it, and the setting sun deepens the rich colors.

We sit there holding hands in one of the most beautiful places on earth watching the play of light and shadow. Who knows what tomorrow will bring, but for tonight I've got beauty in front of me, beauty sitting beside me, food in my belly, and a safe place to sleep.

Even before the Zs came, it really didn't get any better than this.

I watch June as she watches the sun set, eager to see what tomorrow will bring and what new facet she will reveal.

PART THREE

WOODY AND JUNE VERSUS THE GRAND CANYON

IF THE ZS DON'T GET YOU, THE CANYON WILL

CHAPTER EIGHTEEN

I SLEPT through biology in high school and didn't even like the game Operation as a kid, but here I am dissecting a zombie. All for a girl. All to try to prove my fungus/parasite theory of the zombie apocalypse. Because the girl asked me to and that girl is June.

And June is decidedly cute, a petite pixie woman that is an absolute badass with guns, and even laughs at some of my lame jokes, helping me on both of my two goals for each post-apocalyptic day: survive and laugh.

This is day five of Woody and June versus the Apocalypse and we've already saved each other's lives a couple of times. We met in Flagstaff, Arizona, at a dog food factory looking for calories, and our adventures have led us to the Grand Canyon and the Desert View Overlook on Navajo Point.

It's been a remarkable five days, transforming my story from "Woody, just Woody, versus the Apocalypse, barely surviving and avoiding all the living because that's when things get weird" to "Woody and June versus the Apocalypse," quite frankly a much happier and much more interesting story... and a much snappier title.

But we're not out enjoying the view. We're in the gas station convenience store where we found and dispatched a Z, the corpse laid out on the counter while I cut and June holds a flashlight.

The smell is bad. Not "puke after ten seconds of exposure" bad, like it was after we let him out of the garage, but this godawful rotting, moldy meat bouquet with a high note of fermenting puss that had been concentrating in here for a year. With damp bandanas over our noses, we'll survive it long enough.

The body has been pecked at a bit, we had to shoo ravens out when we got here, but it's basically the same semi-desiccated leathery Z we dispatched yesterday.

"There," I say nodding at the cut I'm holding open. "A little water." We were lucky that there was some pressure in the pipes and we got some water out of the garage's utility sink. Not fit to drink, but fine for this.

June pours water over the cut I've made down his forearm. The skin is leathery, this dude had gotten bitten and locked himself in the garage and became a Z when he died. The zombie had been starving, although I figure it takes them at least a few years to die. Well, they're undead and all, so "die" may not be the right word, but whatever animates them needs nutrition—explains why Zs are such a hungry lot—and without it long enough I believe they will re-die... no, die again... I don't know what the terms are, but let's just say an unfed zombie has an expiration date.

"See," I say, pointing at the white cord running below the skin, embedded in the muscle. Except for the smaller tendrils spreading out, it looks like it might be a thin tendon, but it's fibrous and has a different texture than the rest of his flesh. I poke at it with my knife and it's more delicate, severing easily. "Believe me?"

She nods, her blue eyes dead serious and points the flashlight back at the brain. I wacked him with a baseball bat, so it's a bit of a mess, but we've stripped away the bone and skin, scraped off the normal looking grey matter, and rinsed it off. What we exposed looks kinda like a head of cauliflower.

I said "all for a girl" before, but that's not right. June's gone from a cute girl (twenty-something like me) to a beautiful woman. She's petite with short black hair, olive skin, blue eyes, and gives off a dancer/pixie vibe, which lends itself to the "girl" moniker. But, holy shit, give her some guns and a gaggle of approaching Zs and she's a badder badass than Sigourney Weaver's Ripley in *Aliens*.

And besides, "all for a girl" works for me when it's *this* girl.

She sighs and nods her head. "That sure as hell looks like fungus."

"Yeah, right? I bet if we opened up his guts we'd find something fungus-like in there to process what it eats. This can't be some wacky virus or super rabies like in the comics. There has to be something animating the body, driving it to spread the infection."

"But how... how did this happen?"

I shrug. "I've got a couple theories, but..." I nod outside the store at the fading light. We spent the night on top of Desert View Lookout tower and spent the day scrounging before getting back to this fungus/parasite theory of mine.

We did good, finding bottled water, batteries, canned goods, and even some power bars. Frankly, we did a little bit too good. We ran into some roamers yesterday, nearly bit it out on the end of Navajo Point, but I have a hard time imagining they've kept people away this long. I want to be back on top of the tower well before dark.

I stretch when we get out into the light, pull down the wet bandana and take a deep breath of the cool spring air. Desert View Lookout is up over seven thousand feet in elevation, so the May highs are around fifty. We're surrounded by short junipers and can't see much from here. We head toward the truck to drop off some of our scrounged goods; both of our packs are too heavy.

Five days ago, when I met June, I was a confirmed go-it-alone survivor. Now, I can't imagine this existence without her. Unfortunately, there is one question tearing its way through my brain, but I just can't figure out how to ask her about it. There was once a peck on my cheek after a daring rescue and we've held hands, but I honestly don't know if she likes guys, so I don't know if there is a chance for anything more than this.

Although, this friendship is not bad. Did I mention she's beautiful and I've seen her charge Zs while firing two guns, one in each hand, to save us? It's just—

"Holy shit..." she gasps, pointing towards the parking lot and the road into the overlook.

It's a horde of zombies, one to put yesterday's to shame. There are hundreds of them in shorts and T-shirts, flip-flops half attached to their feet as they drag them along, cameras around some of their necks, not to mention the tattered fanny packs some have dangling from their waists.

Their faces are a horror, too. I see one with an eye dangling out and bouncing against his cheek, another with nerd glasses askew over a leathery, desiccated face barely held up because half his nose is missing. Some don't have jaws, others look almost normal except for a missing chunk of hair or a sliver of wood jutting out of their necks.

This is not forty or fifty zombies. This is four or five hundred zombies. The sound of them is this weird white noise combining their moans, growls, and scraping feet. And here I was again lost in the land of lovely June and not paying attention to the basics of survival.

I now know why this area wasn't picked clean. This little Z-patrol must have turned everyone else away. We just got "lucky" and slipped through without running into them.

We're almost to the truck, but that's not going to do any good, we'll never get through them.

"What do we do?" June asks.

I put my pack on, take a deep breath, and start jogging back towards the gas station and away from the herd. "I've got a plan."

"Really? You have a plan?" she asks as she quickly catches up to me.

"Umm... I don't think now is the time to shake my confidence."

She nods, glances back, and says, "Sorry." A few seconds later when we are past the gas station and on a gravel service road, my breath is starting to come fast, but she's still breathing easy. "Maybe if you told me your plan," she says, "I could help out."

I shake my head and smile even though I'm running from an unbeatable, unavoidable horde of tourist zombies. You know how bad, how inconsiderate, how annoying tourists can be? Well, now imagine if they are zombies too... and there are hundreds of them... and what they want is to eat you.

"I hope it's not the tower," she adds, referring to the beautiful pueblo-style sandstone tower behind us. "I hope this isn't some roundabout way to get there, because we'll just get stuck."

"Seriously?"

"Just sayin'."

I wish I could stop and look at her, study that beautiful round face of hers. The playfulness is new and I do like it, but I don't know what it means, and, you know, it's survival time.

"We're going down," I say.

"What?"

"Into the canyon."

"They'll just follow," she says.

"Yeah, but they'll spread out, lose their way."

She gives me a sharp nod.

"Only one problem," I say.

"What?" The playfulness is now gone.

"The trailhead is to the west and the Zs are in the way."

She curses colorfully.

"But, I've been studying the maps. There's a drainage a mile or so this way that I think we can get down without killing ourselves."

"Great! That's just great. Let's just hike into the canyon with no trail, an old crappy map, and hundreds of Zs on our tail." Yeah, that playfulness is gone. I hope it comes back soon, provided, of course, that we survive. Because she's right. A map isn't reality and that gentle drainage I think I see could be anything, but there is nothing else to do so we keep moving.

CHAPTER NINETEEN

AFTER THE SERVICE road turns in the wrong direction, we keep jogging to the east through the juniper forest. The ground has sandy soil varying from tan to the color of clay with plenty of rocks to trip on and sage and other bushes to avoid.

The rim of the Grand Canyon has a microclimate with the junipers thriving here when they generally prefer a lower elevation. Some of these junipers are old with twisting limbs and tufts of silvery bark hanging down like fur. We have to do plenty of zigging and zagging to get through them.

I'm sweating hard and my mouth has that stale "shouldn't you be in better shape than this?" taste. June is breathing heavy now but seems to be fine with her over-stuffed pack. We've got some distance on the Zs, so we slow to a fast walk.

The annoying tourist zombies are back there, we catch glimpses of them, and we know they won't give up. That living flesh radar of theirs will keep them on our trail even if we get out of sight.

When we hit the rim of a side canyon, June's mouth falls open and it's my turn to curse. It's a series of tawny limestone cliffs cascading down to the drainage that we would never survive without a lot of rope and some serious skills.

I close my eyes, take a deep breath, and try to calm myself. We don't have much time and I need to fight back the adrenaline and the fatigue and think. I looked at the maps. There is a drainage here, we see glimpses of it below.

"There," June says, and I open my eyes. She is pointing farther to the southeast. "That might work."

Yes. I remember now that she's figured it out. The end of this side canyon will be less steep. We don't run, but walk as fast as we can, knowing the Zs will gain a little on us by this change in direction. We stop and examine a few spots that are too steep to enter and lose more time.

Just as we can see the Zs again, we find one spot that is steep as hell, but not a cliff and has trees and bushes clinging to it.

"Well?" I ask June, looking back at the Zs. I'm starting to think I've gotten us into another big mess.

"Anything else up top here we could head for?"

I shake my head. "There really isn't, just forest and desert for a lot farther than we'd want to walk with an army of zombie tourists chasing us."

She takes another look down, her brow furrowed and her eyes wide. It is intimidating. "But isn't that desert down there?"

The sound of Z-herd's snarls and growls are getting louder, too loud for comfort. I don't look at them, but keep my eyes locked with June's. "Yeah, it's a desert, but there is water and there can't be many Zs down there. Way too hard to get to. We can probably lose these."

She shrugs and gives me a small smile. There really is nothing else to do. We go down.

CHAPTER TWENTY

THE TREED PORTION of the slope, mostly scrubby juniper, isn't bad. It's slow going and by the time we get fifty feet down, the Zs are starting to stumble over the edge, most of them falling, getting up, stumbling more, and then falling again.

We don't talk. We keep moving. I stay ahead of June in some lame-ass attempt at gallantry—you know, catch her if she falls—even though she's clearly the more athletic of the two of us. The trees last a thousand feet or so and then we're into the rocky, dusty drainage that is just as steep but there is nothing to hold on to.

The cawing of the ravens sounds as if they are heckling us, telling us we should just give it up, that even if we escape the zombies, the canyon will do us in. It's their home, their territory, they're not used to seeing us besides on the rim and on the trails.

We've gotten ahead of the Zs a bit, but there is no doubt that they are coming. The drainage also narrows the possible routes, so we will all be on the same path soon. We

conduct a controlled slide down the steepest part, surviving
with nothing more than a few scrapes and bruises, and get
to an area that is less steep.

Think of a steep, tawny-colored dry creek bed. It's all
dirt, rocks, and slow going. The Zs are behind and gaining
on us as they tumble down the steep section, get up and
lurch forward. I swear to God, I expect one of them to pick
up their fancy digital camera and take a picture of us or ask
us where the best place to eat is. I'm sure some are breaking
their legs or smashing their heads, reducing their numbers,
but probably only slightly.

As the grade gets easier we move faster and it's starting
to look good. Until we hit the cliff.

It's a sheer drop of twenty feet. The Zs are close, less
than a minute behind us. During the monsoons, this must
be a lovely waterfall. Today it could be the end of us.

June just stares at the open air in front of us and I
wonder if she's thinking of the couple we found when we
got to Desert View. The ones that shot each other in the
head instead of falling to a group of zombies. I wonder, for
just a moment, if I shouldn't just take her hand and jump.
End this together.

No. Not today.

I grab her hand and start running back towards the
zombies, but veer to the right and start climbing out of the
main drainage channel. I pull June up to me and give her
the best smile I can, our eyes meeting for only a moment,
and push her up ahead of me. "Climb. This will slow
them down." She nods and scrambles up. I grab onto a
bush that pokes its bark into my hand and pull myself up
after her.

The Zs are right below me, their hands reaching for my
boots, their snapping jaws and snarls loud in my ear, their

rotten smell filling my nose. I scramble up out of their reach, find a good bush to hold on to, and pause.

They were tourists. Mothers and fathers with their kids. Couples on a romantic vacation. People from all over the world come to see one of nature's great wonders. They were human once, just a little over a year ago, and now they're clawing, snapping embodiments of hunger.

They're trying to follow us, but it's too steep. They scramble up a few feet and slide back down, the next few standing on the backs of the fallen Zs and making it farther up.

Each one of these monsters has a story, a history. Somebody loved them and they loved somebody. My brain just kind of slips out of gear and the sadness of it all just washes over me.

The pile is getting bigger, the Zs are getting closer, soon one will grab my foot. Soon I'll—

"Woody!" June shouts from up above. "There's a way down over here." I look up at her standing on a narrow ridge looking so... God, how to describe it? Below me is the grasping desperate remains of undead humanity, above me is a competent, strong, and yes, beautiful woman. She's sweaty and dirty, but still glorious. "Come on! What are you doing?"

I shake off my malaise and scramble up after her.

IT'S another barely controlled slide down the other side of that ridge, but then we end up back in the main channel 150 feet below the cliff. The Zs and their damn fresh-brains radar adjust and they start tumbling over the cliff and smacking down on the bottom. I smile, thinking that this is definitely going to reduce their numbers, and it does, but the first dozen or so just create a nice, soft landing spot for the rest.

"What happened over there?" June asks as we start down the drainage again, which is now wider and not too steep so we can move.

I look at those concerned blue eyes and just want to babble out everything I am feeling. How grateful I am to have a sane, capable companion. How lonely I was for so long. How terrified I am of losing her. "It's just... I don't know. It's just sad sometimes," I say.

She nods and we keep moving, going steady on for a couple of miles, the drainage getting easier to traverse and the zombies falling farther and farther behind. We stop briefly to pull out water bottles and drink, but keep moving. I am tired, I would love to rest, but we are not safe so we keep going.

Until we hit it.

The cliff.

The real cliff.

The Canyon here is shaped like this: A sheer drop-off at the rim, mostly cascading cliffs, which we avoided with that drainage, and then it mellows out into these steep scalloped slopes, that end in a much bigger cliff. Below that there are more scalloped erosions that meander on down to the Colorado River.

The drainage I took us down ends in a sheer cliff about five hundred feet tall.

We are so very screwed.

CHAPTER TWENTY-ONE

YOU CAN'T REALLY UNDERSTAND the Grand Canyon if you don't hike it. From the top, it's these colorful layers of gorgeous limestone and sandstone erosion that seem deep and wide, but the true dimensions just aren't perceivable from up there. It had been a decade since I hiked down with my family and I had just forgotten.

There's a slight breeze that is barely cooling off my sweat-covered body as I stand there looking down, fighting off vertigo and panic. We've shed a lot of elevation and left the cool of the forested rim for the hot of the desert. I drink some water and adjust my Arizona Diamondbacks baseball cap. My jacket is off and tied to my pack. I pat the pocket to make sure my set of seeds are still in there.

These many lonely months, the hat has represented the past: baseball, friends, family, mundane jobs I would die for at this point. And the seeds have represented the future: finding a safe place and growing food. But in the last few days, June has changed that perception of the future, to something not so meager and lonely. But now—

Yeah. We've got maybe ten minutes before the Zs arrive and I go navel gazing. The mind is a tricky beast.

"I'm sorry," I say quietly.

June nods and then her face hardens. "What's next, Woody?" Her voice is calm, not like before when we were first running from the zombie horde, when she was being playful. She wasn't that worried then—she is now.

I look to the west and the sun is getting low and we can see deep into the canyon with about a 240-degree view. Right here would be one of the most spectacular places to see the sun set. Throw a few clouds in the blue, spring sky along the western horizon and it would be one of the best sunsets ever.

But the zombies are coming and so is dark.

Tanner Trail, that is the only trail down to the river in the area, the only safe way down. We have to get to Tanner Trail. But that means us bushwhacking across those steep salmon-colored erosions four or five miles to the west until we run into the trail. In the dark. With Zs chasing us.

I take a deep breath, step back from that damn cliff, put my water away, and tell June the plan.

She nods, taking it in without looking freaked out even once, just that steely-eyed look of hers. "Okay. Good plan."

She looks to the west and it slopes up from here, but not too bad. There are low bushes, a few cacti, and sandy soil. "Let's get some of those power bars out that we found up there and eat while we walk," she says. "Maybe we'll get lucky and lose the herd. Take it easy on the water, because it's going to be a while." She gives me a sweet smile, touches me on the forearm, and walks briskly to the west.

God, I feel bad, but I'm not dead yet and do take a moment to admire the view—June, that is, not the canyon—before heading off after her.

CHAPTER TWENTY-TWO

WE FIND TANNER TRAIL. Four hours later. I am punch-drunk tired, beyond exhausted, and we still have the herd following us. After it got dark we had to slow down and have been keeping just a few minutes ahead of them. The only good news is that nighttime brought the temperature down into the high fifties, which is a relief.

From the top, it's nine miles on Tanner Trail to the river. We're, I don't know, two or three miles down it and have six to go. My feet are killing me, I know I've got blisters, and my blisters have blisters, but I dare not take my shoes off. We've got a little water left, but only because we haven't drunk much, meaning we are both dehydrated. We're out of bars and stop for a minute to crack open a can of beans and then share it as we walk down the trail with one flashlight on. We've been burning through the batteries we found up top.

It's bad. I'm punchy. So, what do I do? Talk. "You know..." I say. "I have a theory about the fungus and the zombies."

"Oh, yeah?" June asks around a mouthful of cold black beans.

I'm out front with the flashlight keeping us on the trail. I think the talking is also about staying awake. I don't know if the trail has been used since the apocalypse hit, so we can't go too fast, lest we lose it.

And Tanner Trail is not like Kaibab or Bright Angel Trails, it was never used that much and is considered a primitive trail. That means a trail, at the best of times, that was easy to lose, where you have to keep your eye out for rock cairns that mark the way. And, having never been on the trail, I know nothing more about it than what I saw on the map. And it's dark. And we're hungry and exhausted. And hundreds of ravenous tourist zombies are chasing us.

"It involves time travel," I say.

"Oh, boy," she says with a sigh. I can't see her, but I hear amusement in her voice. "Lay it on me, Slugger." Slugger is the nickname she gave me when I used my trusty baseball bat to fend off the mini-horde of Zs yesterday. God! was that only yesterday?

"Okay, so in the near future, global warming hits hard, the sea levels rise, and humanity is toast. Those that survive live a meager existence under domes, but some brilliant scientists figure out how to send something back in time. But the trouble is they can only send something extremely small, like the size of a grain of sand."

"Okay..."

"So, they invent the fungus to cull the planet of most of the humans so we don't kill the Earth and the future doesn't suck."

"That's quite a theory there," she says.

"Yeah, I know. Pretty good, right? Want to hear my other theory?"

"I... Ahh... Sure...?"

I take a deep breath and forge ahead. "It's aliens, nice ones. So, they invented the fungal parasite for the same reason." Remember, I'm exhausted, dehydrated, and punch-drunk here.

"Hold up. Time for you to eat."

We stop and I trade her beans for the flashlight, point her in the direction of the cairn I last spotted, and she heads out in front of me.

"Seems to me," she says, "that your time travelers and aliens are just assholes."

"What?" I ask. In my state these seem like fine theories. Ah hell... who am I kidding? Even well fed and well rested, they seemed like fine theories to me when they were bouncing around my weird brain.

"Especially the aliens. Couldn't they help us get our act together without wiping most of us out? Sounds more like an invasion to me."

The beans are cold and bland but taste great like things do when you're starving.

"An invasion..." I mutter around the beans. "That's brilliant. I wonder why we haven't seen our new overlords yet."

"I have another theory," she offers.

I smile wide in the dark. Maybe she's getting into this. "Lay it on me, Connor."

"What if it's the earth herself, Gaia, that is the source of this infection, what if—"

"Gaia?" I ask, stopping on the trail. The word is familiar, but I'm not quite placing it.

"Yeah, Gaia," she says. "Think of the planet as a single intelligent organism, trying to survive, to thrive, and it finds itself infested with humans who are spreading all over her surface, creating pollution, changing the climate, setting off nuclear bombs, and she..."

She trails off. It's dark, so I can't see her face without shining a flashlight in it, but the way she trails off made it sound like she's remembering something. Something not that pleasant.

"Wow," I say, jumping into the lull. "I'm not sure I buy that planet as a single conscious organism, but that's a great theory. Zombies as an immune system, right?"

"Yes, exactly," she says, but it's clear her mind went somewhere else. Probably to the past, to what used to be, to what is lost. I don't push it and the subject changes.

We go on like that for what seems an interminable amount of time. Walking, talking, eating a little, hardly drinking, staying just ahead of the Zs.

Besides our fatigue, we've got a couple of things working against us. First, we lose the trail several times and have to backtrack to find it. Normal given it's dark and a primitive trail and it probably hasn't been used since the infection hit. Second, Zs don't care about the trail, or running into cacti, so they ignore switchbacks and come at us by the most direct path.

A little later when things fall silent, and I really can't stand the silence right then, I say, "You know, hiking down the Grand Canyon is a lot like time travel."

After my "origin of the zombies" theories, she's probably a little leery to hear any of my other ramblings, but I'm trying to redeem myself.

"Okay," she says, and I can hear the humor in her voice. Not a laugh, but she sounds amused. "How *is* hiking down the Grand Canyon like time travel?"

"Well..." I begin, gesturing wildly, the flashlight sweeping over the rocky desert around us. "Up top, that light tan layer is Kaibab limestone, used to be an ocean here, it's about 260 million years old. That's where we slid down through that drainage."

"Okay..." She clearly has no idea where I'm going with this.

"And then the Toroweap Formation, Coconino Sandstone—that used to be a desert—and then the Hermit Shale, and the Supai Group. Then we're about 280 million years old. That's probably where we hit that damn cliff."

"Oh... I see," she says. "The deeper you go, the older the rock. Thus, the whole time travel bit."

"Right! The Supai Group which was ancient mountains and we're over 300 million years old, and then down through different layers of limestone, shale, and sandstone, going further and further back in time. The inner gorge cuts into Vishnu Schist, and that stuff is a billion and a half years old."

The entire night is this battle to stay awake, stay on the trail, stay ahead of them, and stay alive. It seems endless until the predawn light shows the Colorado River below us less than a mile away.

We're on these rolling hills of loose soil that is a light burnt umber with little vegetation and has this moonscape vibe. The river is its typical reddish-brown doing its millennia-old job of carrying the eroded land away. It's that color that gave the river its name. "Colorado" means "colored red" in Spanish.

"Yes!" I shout, my voice raw and cracking.

"Oh my God!" June exclaims.

And then she's hugging me and she's crying, or maybe I am, or maybe both of us are. For a moment, it's like we haven't been up for twenty-four hours, haven't hiked fourteen miles, aren't starving, and aren't running for our lives.

It's awkward with our packs, but I lift her off her feet and hold her tight while she gives a girlish squeal. When I put her down, we just stare at each other in the dim light.

I'm blinking too much and so is she. We've got chapped lips and are so exhausted that we can hardly stand. But it's a moment, at least I think it's a moment. If we had just been in a little better shape, I can imagine her putting her cool hand on my neck and pulling my head down to hers and kissing me... the first kiss. Forget the chapped lips and bone-dry mouths, our kiss would have transcended all those pesky real-world details. It would have been amazing, right?

The light is dim, but those blue eyes are still so easy to get lost in. Moments tick by and still we're staring at each other. I hear a noise, something besides the wind whistling through the canyon, but I ignore it. God, I do want to kiss her, even if it's not enough to transcend how messed up we are. I'm going to do it. I'm going to try. Maybe she doesn't like boys, maybe she doesn't like me, but at least she can't shove me off a cliff like she could have yesterday when my hormones had the same brilliant idea.

I'm just starting to lean in when June turns away. "Shit!" she says.

I follow her gaze and see the tourist zombie horde and reality descends upon my little romantic fantasy like an elephant sitting on a mouse.

"We've got to go!" She hustles down the path and I stand there just staring at her. Was that a moment we just had? Was it anything more than the shared relief of survival with a healthy dose of my imagination piled on?

I shrug and hustle after her. With zombies heading towards me and her away from me, it's an easy decision.

CHAPTER TWENTY-THREE

FEAR AND HOPE make us quick on our tired feet and the growing light helps. We make good time and put some distance between us and the horde.

We get down to the river, use my mini water filter to pump water into our bottles, use her life-straw filter to suck our fill of ice-cold water right out of the river, and get back on the trail.

We don't talk much, just long enough to agree it would be foolish to try to cross the river and we will keep that as a last resort.

Our plan is to get on the Tonto Trail and head downstream towards Phantom Ranch. It's a bad plan, seeing how it's over forty miles farther, hundreds of Zs are still after us, our feet our wrecked, and we are beyond exhausted. But it is a plan and right then any plan with the slimmest chance of survival is a good one.

An hour and a couple of miles later, I just can't do it. My blisters have popped and formed more blisters. Each step is jarringly painful. "Wait," I gasp to June who is up ahead.

She stops but doesn't come back, and lets me catch up with her. The water has helped, but my body is just at its limit. "Look," I point to a sandy island just peaking up out of the river. It's right below a small rapid that is roaring next to us. "We can make that."

I pull out my battered map and show her where we are, at a big S-curve in the river, the bottom half having a couple of small rapids, but the top half is calm. I then show her how far away Phantom Ranch and the bridge across the Colorado River is.

She bites her lip and nods.

"We have to try," I say. "Tell you what, I'll go first."

She shakes her head, "Together, or not at all."

I'm worried about the current, about rapids farther down, but her jaw is set and I know her well enough to not argue. Besides, I don't have enough energy to argue.

We form a plan, our voices low, from fatigue, yes, but also as if that will somehow keep the Zs away. We keep looking back, making sure they aren't on us yet, hoping we have enough time.

CHAPTER TWENTY-FOUR

HERE'S another thing that's easy to forget about the Colorado River. The water that runs through it comes out of the bottom of Lake Powell and is about 45 degrees. That's cold. Stay in longer than about twenty minutes and you are looking at hypothermia.

I didn't have time to think about it then, but I wonder what will happen to the dams without people taking care of them. Will they overflow if the spillways were set too tight or will the lake mostly drain if they were too wide? What happens to a dam that doesn't have people there anymore?

But I don't think about that, just about survival, and exhaustion, and how painful my feet are.

We work quickly and together. I have some garbage bags—light, small, and very useful in many situations—we both have duct tape, and June has rope. We strip down to T-shirts and underwear, cram our clothes into our packs, and put our packs into bags. I get a glance at my feet and they're a bloody mess, as are hers, but we don't have time for that. We blow air into a couple more garbage bags and tape them onto the packs for floatation. Despite their weight, we even pack our weapons, including June's rifle and my baseball bat. Their weight could mean the difference between our contraption floating or sinking, but you don't leave your weapons behind. You just can't.

Each pack has two air-filled garbage bags taped to them and six feet of rope tying them together. We're at the bottom of the rapids standing in a few feet of water and my feet have already gone numb and I'm shivering, the cool morning air is in the fifties and not helping.

The roar of the water hides the sound of the approaching herd of tourist zombies and we almost miss them. They're right on us.

We push off, trying to use our packs and the bags as floatation, but it's a disaster. The air-filled garbage bags counteract the weight of the packs okay, but staying on them is impossible, they just slip out right from under you. Even though we've been standing in it for a while, being immersed in that water just takes our breath away. We lose precious seconds and the Zs are walking into the water after us. I can smell their funk over the clean scent of flowing water.

"Go!" I shout to June, shoving my pack and air bags out into the water. "Take them! Swim!" The cold is creeping into me and I'm pretty sure because of the cool morning we don't have any twenty minutes before hypothermia. June is ahead of me and gets away. As I dive forward, a Z catches my foot, its hand digging into my open blisters, and even with my face in the water, I almost scream it hurts so bad.

I have nothing, no gun, no bat, no knife, and the icy cold of the river is sapping what little strength I have left.

The Z that's got my foot is a chubby tourist in a filthy ripped T-shirt from a tourist trap in Winslow that says

"Standin' on the Corner." Half his face is ripped off and hanging down in a leathery sheet. Probably damage he sustained chasing us.

I do the only thing I can. I kick with my other leg, and hard. Once, nothing. Twice, I hit his wrist solidly and pain shoots up my leg as three more Zs get within striking range of me. The third time, I kick as hard as I can, hear his wrist bones cracking, and he finally lets go just as the other Zs are reaching out to grab me. I swim like I've never swum before.

When I know I'm clear, I look and see June on the downstream end of the island waving towards me, she collapses on the sand holding the rope that ties our packs together which are bobbing in the current.

The island is about five hundred feet downstream from the rapids and two hundred feet out. The current is fast and it's not easy, but I make it and crawl up onto the land gasping and shivering, my teeth chattering so hard my whole head is vibrating.

It's not lost on me that my jaw is snapping like those hungry Zs we just escaped, just for a different reason.

Together we drag the packs past some low bushes onto dry sand. Each step hurts like hell and I can barely stand, but we make it. We survive.

June points and laughs, a brief barking sound, as the herd, one by one, marches into the water and gets swept past us.

"Adios, amigos!" she shouts, her teeth chattering. "Vaya con dios!" I'm dimly aware that her Spanish sounds perfect, no casual American butchering of the words, but I'm too spent to really think about it.

We rest for a few minutes before relocating to the upstream end of the island that is free of vegetation and wider.

I flop down onto the sand exhausted. I can't move. I can't do anything but lie there and shiver and pray for the heat of the day to come.

June stands above me—and yes, she's dressed only in black panties and a blue T-shirt, both wet, not lost on me I can assure you. Her arms are wrapped around her chest and between shivers and through chattering teeth she says, "Ffff... Fire. We need fire." Sunrise comes late to the canyon and it will be a while before it gets warm here.

She then walks off toward some driftwood we passed and I tear into my pack to find my matches. It's not going to be easy, there is some wood here, and it is dry, but most of it is too big and we'll have to shave it with a knife to make kindling.

"Second thought," June says digging into her pack. "Clothes. We should save the wood in case we are here tonight."

I nod and turn away while she strips off her wet clothes and puts on dry clothing while I do the same. We get our weapons out and go watch the herd walk into the water and try desperately to swim to us.

Some of them just sink, some float and are swept past, and some of the more functional ones get pretty close. At one point, I head back to our packs for water bottles when a shot rings out and I almost have a heart attack.

I look at June who has her rifle to her shoulder and looks back to me, a sheepish look on her pixie face. "One was getting too close. It's not as if we need to worry about the noise."

I laugh out loud. It's not an elegant laugh and it doesn't last too long, but it is a laugh. "Hell, shoot it up, Connor," I say, referring to the nickname she earned up top when she went after a group of Zs with a gun in each hand and saved us. "Connor" being a reference to Sarah Connor from the *Terminator* series.

June gives me a devious look and nails a Z in the head as it sweeps past us. But then she's done. While the moment of fun was needed, we have to conserve ammo.

As tight and short as that laughter was, it helps complete my very short daily to-do list: survive and laugh. But I guess there's a third item on there now: spend time with June. And, well, that just makes the first two better.

CHAPTER TWENTY-FIVE

LATER WHEN THE sun is up, and the herd has been swept past, we have a small meal and relax now that we are finally warm. As we share another can of cold beans, June looks over at me, a wry grin on her face. "Next time you have a bright idea about escaping an approaching horde of zombies, we're going to discuss it. Right?"

"Yes, ma'am," I say, saluting her.

"Seriously, Woody."

I wipe the grin off my face. "Yes. Absolutely."

"And before we leave this island, you're going to tell me everything you know about the Grand Canyon and our next step."

"Yeah. Sorry. I got us in a little over our heads there."

She gives me that look of hers, the penetrating one where I often think she's reevaluating me. And then she smiles. "No need to be sorry. We're partners, right?"

I look closely at her, at those lovely eyes, that delicate nose, and I can see that she means it. We *are* partners. And yeah, that hormone-driven, male part of me wants more, will always want more, but this is... Well, in the post-apocalyptic world, this a lot.

I extend my hand and say, "Partners." We shake, eat beans, and rest up from our time being chased by hundreds of zombie tourists and surviving the wilds of the Grand Canyon.

Sure, we've got to get off this island, sure we've got to find a place to try to survive this apocalypse, but June and I, we're partners, so we'll figure it out. Together.

For now, we're safe, we've got food and water, and we can rest. These days that is a rare and wonderful thing.

PART FOUR

WOODY AND JUNE VERSUS THE EX

EVERYONE'S GOT A CRAZY EX, EVEN AT THE END OF THE WORLD

CHAPTER TWENTY-SIX

I THINK June used to be an Army Ranger or something. Not that I know exactly what an Army Ranger is, and this being post-zombie-apocalypse Arizona, I can't exactly look it up on my smartphone.

She is lying on the sand, her hunting rifle propped up on her backpack, sighting a straggler from the zombie horde that chased us down into the Grand Canyon. We're on a sand island in the middle of the Colorado River under the hot spring sun. We swam over two days ago to save our sweet, fresh brains. The Zs tried to follow but got swept downstream.

I've given up on the idea of her being an Israeli secret agent with Mossad, despite her olive complexion and blue eyes. The little Spanish I've heard her speak is perfect, lacking the usual sloppy American accent. I can't speak Spanish properly—I've got that sloppy American accent— but I know when it's spoken properly.

"There, Woody," she says. "Can you see it?"

I'm sitting next to her looking through my binoculars, trying desperately to focus on the beautiful desert landscape of the Grand Canyon and not on the gorgeous pixie woman lying next to me. "Yup. I see it. One zombie tourist wandering around the— oh... he walks right into a prickly pear cactus and keeps on going, a couple of 'em clinging to his leg. The poor guy lost his flip-flops, but at least he's still got his fanny pack."

I briefly considered that she might be a spy from Spain or Mexico—no idea what their intelligence agencies are called—but discard that too. She's just too American.

"I can take him," she says, even though he's at least a hundred yards off.

So that leaves me with something like Green Beret or Army Ranger. Although the idea of ending up post-apocalypse with an international spy is rather... intriguing, the mystery of June is intriguing enough without that.

"Yeah you can," I say, "but how about we save the ammo, and keep a low profile." We're just downstream from some rapids, so we haven't been worried about conversation attracting attention, but a gunshot definitely could.

She nods and sits up, brushing the sand from her T-shirt. It's hot, so she's down to a T-shirt and undies, as am I.

See why I'm distracted?

"We polluted the Grand Canyon with Zs," she says, shaking her head.

I nod. "Yeah. Sucks. I think a lot of them washed to shore after chasing us and are just wandering now."

This is day eight of Woody and June versus the End of the World and our second day on this sand island. The trip down involved a lot of bushwalking, a lot of miles, and some very close calls. We've been resting and letting our blisters heal in this rare zombie-free zone.

"We can't stay much longer." She nods at our packs, the food we scrounged at Desert View Lookout is running thin. "What are we going to do, partner?" She looks at me with those beautiful blues of hers and I just want to melt... or kiss her. Yeah, kiss her is definitely the choice.

Our relationship has progressed nicely since we met up in Flagstaff. We've gone from wary, to saving each other's lives, to trust, to officially being partners when we made it to this island alive. I think mostly because she doesn't want to try to survive one more of my hair-brained schemes again without a discussion.

Me? I want all the June I can get. Every day, year-round, give me June, month after month. She's strong, smart, beautiful, and capable. Take any "gun-wielding female force to be reckoned with" from the movies and I'd put my money on her every time. Sarah Connor, no problem. Ellen Ripley, you bet. Dana Scully, pa-lease...

"At least they haven't found us with their fresh-brains zombie radar," I say with a grin.

She shakes her head. "But why not?"

"I've got a theory," I offer.

She rolls her eyes. I have a history with my theories, even in our short time together. My fungus/parasite theory of zombiedom has kind of checked out. My "time travelers did it to us to save the planet" theory of the origin of the infection hasn't gotten any traction.

"Please enlighten me," she says, taking a sip from her water bottle and scanning our surroundings for danger. It's a good habit to have.

There are several challenges here. I don't know if she's into me, or guys for that matter, and the apocalypse doesn't actually leave much time for romance, what with all the running from flesh-eating zombies and psychotic, petty, wannabe warlords.

My approach? Be nice. Be patient. Be charming... well, at least amusing. I can amuse, not at all sure if I can charm.

"So, fungus head zombies, check," I say. "We proved it with that poor dried up sap we dissected."

She nods.

"Super large horde had a super good sense of where we were. We couldn't lose them on the way down here despite putting some distance between us."

"Check," says.

"Singles," I say, pointing towards the one who we sighted just in time to watch him tumble into a wash, "not so good."

"Right..."

"Ergo, presto—" I say, doing a silly jazz-hands gesture.

"I don't think that is the way it goes," she says, one eyebrow arched.

"Presto...?" I wave my jazz hands again.

She shakes her head, but she's smiling, so that makes me happy.

"Ergo, the more zombies, the better their flesh detection ability. Their fungus minds must be more powerful together."

I stand up, doff my hat, and take a bow and she laughs. This puts me in a good place for my goals for a post-apocalyptic day. There's the laughter, and on our zombie-free island, survival seems assured. And I'm here with June, so that means it's a good day.

A shot rings out, the sound bouncing off the canyon walls, and June is back down on the sand scanning the terrain with the scope of her hunting rifle.

I hit the sand and start looking with my binocs.

Shit!

We're not the only living at the bottom of the Grand Canyon.

Yeah, I might have been a bit preliminary on that survival part.

CHAPTER TWENTY-SEVEN

WHAT'S next on the June and Woody hit-parade? Digging a long shallow hole in the sand under the hot Arizona sun, mounding the sand along the edge so it kinda looks like a natural bump from a distance, and lying in the hole—maybe trench is a better word—until dark.

This is June's idea, which adds another check to the "Army Ranger or some such thing" list.

The shot isn't that close, so we figured we have time. It is clear we need to leave. Our sand island is perfect for zombie protection, but we're sitting ducks for people with guns. Leaving in the middle of the day is not smart either and we don't have a plan yet, thus the digging like crazed gophers.

After all, it has been well established after our last close call on the shore of the river that all plans must be discussed. Most specifically any plan hatched out of my strange brain.

But hey, I get to lie down in the damp sand next to a beautiful woman for six hours. Not so bad, really.

"They're shooting our zombies," she says once we're settled in with our bodies and all our stuff below ground level. It won't help if folks are up high, but it will work for people close or on the trail.

"*Our* zombies? So, have we adopted them or something now?" I ask. "Are they our unruly children?"

"Shut up," she says, elbowing me in the ribs. The elbow is teasing but the tone is serious. Perhaps I should save the silliness until we survive this.

"Phantom Ranch is a long ways downstream," I say. "That would be the best place to hole up down here, but it's forty miles or so of hiking."

She sighs. "We never get a break, do we?"

I want to tell her that she's the biggest break I've had since the Zs started. Hell... maybe the biggest break ever. But I don't. This is not the time, but I resolve to find the time. This is just silly. I like her, I need to find out if she likes me.

"We got this, June," I say. "There are a lot of campsites along the Colorado that the river runners used. Maybe someone set up camp when there were no Zs down here. Now they're too busy fighting Zs to worry about us."

She nods and another shot rings out and I jump. We are in a canyon and sound will travel farther than in the open, so I really have no idea how far away they are.

"I'd say they're three miles away, give or take," she says. There goes another tick on the military trained bad-ass list.

This island is very shallow, the sand damp and blessedly cool. Our prone view of the world is pretty nice too, the blue sky above, scalloped reddish sandstone rising up. The lull of the rapids and the river. I want to take a nap, but we don't have a plan yet.

"Back the way we came?" I propose. "Up Tanner Trail,

properly, no confronting five-hundred-foot cliffs. Over to Desert View, get our truck, and be merrily on our way? It will be a very long day, but the Zs are thinned out, so it should be doable."

"Good plan," she says, and she grabs my hand and squeezes it. "I'll take first watch if you want to snooze a bit."

Have I mentioned how completely awesome this woman is?

As I close my eyes and begin to drift, it occurs to me that in the pre-Z world, I wouldn't have stood a chance with this one. She's too... *everything*. And I'm... just a guy who can think on his feet and isn't an ass.

Even if she does like guys, I'm sure it's just not enough. She's way out of my league.

CHAPTER TWENTY-EIGHT

I'M ON LAST WATCH, sitting in our trench scanning our surroundings as the Colorado rushes past. It's in the low sixties and I am not looking forward to a dip in the forty-five-degree river.

The eastern horizon is just starting to lighten and it's time for me to wake June, but I hesitate. This moment here seems rare, almost holy.

The stars are bright above and the Canyon is indistinct shadows above us. I hear the roar of the rapids just upstream and the rush of the breeze against sandstone. June is breathing deep and steady and I take a deep breath of the cool, fresh air.

This moment is peace. It's almost like the apocalypse didn't happen and June and I are on a river trip camped out under the stars, happy and relaxed.

Like, maybe we've been together for a while and have just hit that point when you can start being yourself around your partner. You know, where you can both admit that you're human and not perfect.

Not quite to that been married forever and leave the bathroom door open and farting—as long as they're not real stinkers—is not a big deal, but a comfortable familiarity.

And June, despite my romantic ramblings, is not perfect. I still know almost nothing about her, and that is in part about keeping the past at arm's length—we've all lost so much—but there is more there. She's very guarded. She is good at survival, but is she good at anything beyond that? Are any of us at this point?

Before we met, I was a loner and was going through this life with nothing left to lose, nothing of value anyone would want to take from me.

June has changed all of that, but she's still such a mystery.

"June," I whisper. "Time for our nice cold bath."

She wakes with a start, her breath coming fast, her gun in hand before she even sits up. Her eyes are wide as she looks around, and then her gun is trained on me.

"It's okay, June," I say, my hands in front of me and my heart pounding. "It's just me, Woody. We need to get going."

She nods and is back to herself quickly. "Sorry," she says, rubbing at her eyes.

Maybe it's just the apocalypse that did this to her, the strain of daily survival. That's what I tell myself, anyway.

We split a can of cold green beans for breakfast and pack up.

Getting off the island is a reverse of what we did to get on it. Bag up our packs in garbage bags, blow up a couple of bags for flotation, and duct tape to each pack. Tie a rope between the two. I even stow my red Diamondback baseball cap in the pack, I don't want to lose that, even though I feel naked without it and my sandy brown hair is long enough to be falling into my eyes and quite annoying.

Down to skivvies again, we haul our stuff to the upstream end of the island and look. The guns are sealed in with the packs as well as my baseball bat, so we need to make sure there are no Zs here. This time, though, we both have knives belted to our waists.

It's light enough now that the sandstone along the river is like a grey moonscape and the layers of the canyon's cliffs are distant ghosts. We see no movement, we hear nothing beyond the roar of the river.

"It's gonna be cold," I say, already chilled from the air.

She smiles. "If it's the only indignity today, this'll be one for the record books."

"June, I..." I start, tugging on my beard nervously, needing to say things, but being too damn scared. Happy to take on a zombie, but scared to tell a woman how I feel.

"What? What is it?" She's looking around, her eyes wide, worried about danger again.

"No. There's nothing wrong." I touch her cool shoulder. "I... I just wanted to say, I'm really glad we met." And that's as close as I can get to saying what should be said.

"Me too," she says with a smile. "Ready?"

I nod and we walk into the freezing cold water. I curse. She laughs at me.

We're at the top of a big S in the river with a wide sandbar on the inside of that S-curve. We swim hard, dragging our gear, which floats nicely, and make it with ease. It's quiet on the other side, and we unwrap our packs, dress, and get going.

I get my hat back on and my jacket, checking the inside pocket, which I do a dozen times a day, and make sure my seed packets are still there. When every day is on the edge of survival, it seems like a silly dream—having a place to grow some food and maybe being a tiny bit normal. But since I escaped the mess in Phoenix and especially before I met June, this is the dream that kept me going.

We don't talk, we get our weapons out—June her gun, me my baseball bat, and set off. The Tonto Trail is up some rolling sandstone slick rock and soon we are heading northeast to Tanner Trail and our way out.

Not one Z sighting—this is looking like a good plan.

Not far down the trail, we're coming off the sandstone, down a steep section that is a bit of a scramble. We're getting close to the river again and that rapid that's just above the island.

"You'll be dropping your weapons now," a man says from behind a boulder, just off the trail. It's still not full light and I don't get a good look at him, but he has a bit of a southern twang to his voice.

We both freeze. June has her gun in her hand and I've got my bat. She's staring at him, doing the odds in her head, I am sure, and I think she would have tried, but—

"We gotcha covered," a woman says from the other side of the trail down a little, crouched behind another boulder. She's got a southern accent too.

June gives me a nod and drops her gun, slowly pulls her rifle from her shoulder and lowers it to the ground. I drop my bat and pull my pistol and put it on the ground.

"I guess we can't catch a break," I whisper.

"Now the knives," the man says, standing up and taking a step towards us, his pistol pointed at me.

"No," June says.

"I beg your pardon, young lady?" he says. He's shaggy

and maybe forty with grey invading his brown beard and his long brown hair.

"No," she repeats. I'm freaking a bit, I don't know what she's up to. "There are Zs down here. We must be able to defend ourselves."

"You hear that, Mary," he says, glancing at the woman. "She thinks she gets ta keep her knife."

"Look," I say. "We are headed up the trail. We're leaving. We mean you no harm."

"Sorry there, boy," he says. "Orders are orders. All survivors come with us." He takes another step forward and levels his gun at me. He's five yards away and I am completely helpless. "Now, drop the knives."

We do as we're told. It's now clear that we are into psychotic, petty, wannabe warlord territory, and they are much more dangerous than zombies.

June changes her demeanor when she gives up the knife. Her shoulders are rounded and she steps close to me, her hand reaching for mine. Now, I've known her long enough to know this is an act. The man talked to me first and is clearly underestimating June. She's playing in to that.

"Now cuff yourselves together," he says, tossing us a set of handcuffs. The woman, Mary, is close, her gun trained on us. She's tall and gangly and probably around forty like the man, with long black hair pulled back.

I try to catch June's eye, but she grabs the handcuffs and puts them on us, but loosely. She then holds my hand and squeezes it.

This is not good. Even if we could get away we would have no weapons and no supplies and would be handcuffed together.

They turn us around and we start heading downstream, away from Tanner Trail and our way out. They stay about ten feet behind us. They're not dumb. Most folks who have survived this long are not.

June doesn't speak, her jaw locked and her eyes taking in everything. I follow suit, looking for Zs, looking for opportunities, trying to figure out how to stay alive.

CHAPTER TWENTY-NINE

"YOU KNOW," I say as we walk down the trail, our captors behind us, "we'll just slow you down if you're going back to Phantom Ranch. That is where you're from, isn't it? Just let us have our packs and you'll never see us again."

I can't see them, but I hear their boots scraping on the trail. The morning is warming, and I spot a few condors cruising in the updrafts high above.

"Watta y'all know about them zombies down here?" he asks.

"It's a zombie plague," I offer. "They are everywhere." There is no way I'm telling them that June and I did this.

He snorts. "We ain't seen but one or two until they started floating down the river a couple a days ago."

I shrug. "Forty miles is a long hike."

He chuckles. "Hear that, Mary? The boy thinks we're gonna hike all the way to The Ranch."

"Must be as dumb as he looks, Sal," she says.

We don't get anything else out of them except the confirmation that they are at Phantom Ranch.

They hike us about a mile and take us off the trail and down a drainage to the river. There's a grey river raft, about sixteen feet long, pulled up on the sand and tied off to a spindly tamarisk tree. There is an outboard motor on the back and the raft is just below a sizeable rapid, the air moist from the churning water.

I'm puzzled. Sure, we could float all the way down to Phantom Ranch from here—about ten miles on the river through some epic rapids—but we'd never get back up. How did they get that raft here?

Mary gives her gun to Sal and gets us into the raft and ties our handcuffs to the bowline. We could undo the knots, but it wouldn't be quick.

They push us off and down we go.

I can't say that I don't enjoy it some. In the old world, it was very difficult to get a private permit onto the Grand, and you had to know what you were doing. Or you could spend big bucks and buy your way down.

Yeah, we're handcuffed, and Mary has a gun on us while Sal rows us out into the current of the muddy river, but we're rafting down the Colorado.

We float for a while, the canyon walls becoming more sheer as the canyon deepens, cooler air floating off the cold water as the heat of the day starts to settle in.

Our captors don't talk much, and neither do June and I. What is there to say?

I hear the roar of a rapid coming, when Sal takes us into a sandy shore. They get us out, tie the boat off, and we're scrambling up a drainage back to the Tonto Trail.

And then I get it. They've got rafts staged along the river for the calm sections. They can float down and motor up. They hike around the rapids.

A half an hour later, my theory is confirmed when we

come to a similar raft tied off below another rapid. After Mary ties us in, I whisper to June, "They're smart and well organized."

She nods. "That's what I'm worried about."

I settle in and do what I can to enjoy the journey, marveling at the deepening, dark grey inner gorge, the 1.5-billion-year-old Vishnu Schist. We've completed our journey down into the canyon and back through time—so to speak.

They hike us up and around the rapids, sometimes taking us far away from the river where we see the tan, brown, and salmon layers of rock all around us and the pointed temples of rock towering over us. Blue sky above, ravens cawing at us, signs of rabbit and coyote on the trail.

We spot Zs, mostly from the raft, but don't have any close encounters. Every time I see one, I feel a little pang of guilt. We did this. They kind of are *our* zombies.

June keeps her act up, holding my hand, leaning against me. I can't say I mind it at all, but it is definitely not June. I'm sure she can be affectionate, but I absolutely cannot see her as needy.

"Ain't these love birds cute," Sal says when we push off for the third time.

"Just like a couple o' precious doves," Mary says. "Ain't got a clue what Talia gonna do with these two. Probably a waste draggin' 'em all the way down."

June sucks in a breath, her brow furrowing in what looks like fear, and then shakes her head. A moment later, she squeezes my hand three times and I squeeze back. I get it. A strategy. If we appear to be useless maybe this Talia will let us go.

Soon it's early afternoon and we're back on our feet having spent several hours scrambling up one dry creek bed, walking on the relative flats above the inner gorge, and then scrambling down another.

I'm tired and my wrist is chafed from the hiking and the handcuffs. We've each only got one hand to climb with. We've taken to holding hands the whole time, despite them being sweaty, to reduce the chaffing, and keep the "love birds" thing going.

We aren't on the Toho Trail, but our way is marked by rock cairns. It's clear that they move up and down the river fairly freely. Hunting, maybe. Looking for the living in their territory, undoubtedly.

These scrambles are on both sides of the river, probably wherever they could find the drainages that got them around the rapids. They've gotten very difficult as the inner gorge has gotten deeper. At this point, they have a few crude ladders made out of logs and sun-bleached timber setup up and we are uncuffed just long enough to go up or down them.

Right after a ladder down a thirty-foot cliff, the creek bed starts to open and I hear the roar of a rapid. We saw it on the upstream end, and it was a doozy with huge standing waves and big holes ready to suck in your raft. It's taken us a couple of hours just to get around it.

At this point, I don't hate our captors yet. They act all superior, but they haven't been cruel. We've had plenty of water, but no food, but what's a little hunger these days?

As I get my first glimpse of the river, I hear the snarl of a zombie and then spot them. There's four of them. It's narrow here and they probably floated ashore and had no place to go.

They're a mess. Ripped clothes, dangling arms, one of them clearly has a broken leg and can't move very well. We stop and look back.

"No, no," Sal says from behind us. "Let's see what you two love birds are made of."

"Sal..." Mary says.

"Oh hush, woman, Talia ain't here and she's gonna want to know anyway. We need fighters not lovers."

Out of the corner of my eye, I catch an odd expression on June's face, but don't have time for it. "How about our knives?" I ask. The Zs have spotted us and are snarling and shambling toward us, all grey-eyed fungus-powered hunger, eager for a good meal and to spread their infection.

He chuckles, it's a cruel sound, and I officially hate him.

"Rocks," June says and we step forward, each of us finding one that fits well in our fists.

Two have good legs and move ahead, and we scramble over a couple of rocks into a fairly narrow sandy section just wide enough for the two of us.

"There's something I should say," I begin as the Zs get closer. They look less like tourists now, having been torn up by the river and the rapids. Their clothing just dangles, as does some of their flesh where the river or the journey down here ripped it free. It's two men coming at us, one has an eye dangling out of the socket and the other's chest is caved in.

"I... You..." I can't get it out. I just can't.

"Later, we'll talk later," she hisses, her eyes focused on the Zs.

And then they're on us.

Rocks don't work as well as a knife to the eye, especially when you're attached to someone else. I used to play baseball, so my upper body strength is still good, but I'm working with my left hand. I get the eye dangler and hit him hard in the head with the rock and he falls back. June kicks chest-caved-in and he goes down. We jump forward and let our boots do the rest of the work.

The goo from the busted opened heads is gross, but it's the sound that's the worst. The snapping of bone, the squishing of their fungus heads. And the rotting-meat-decay smell assaults me and I wish I had the time to puke.

Then the next two are on us, a woman and a teenage boy. I miss the boy's head and land a blow on his shoulder and I hear a bone snap. He collapses against me and I go down to my knees. June crouches low and kicks, taking the woman's knee out with a sickening crunch, the woman falls forward and is on June. And then...

Hell, I'm not sure what happened, exactly. The adrenaline is flowing, the stench of the Zs making my eyes water, my nice day gone, the peaceful time on our sand island a distant memory. It's fight or flight and there is nowhere to run.

I hit, I knee, I shove, I grunt. I feel June pulling my hand and our sweaty grip slips and the handcuffs cut into our wrists.

The next thing I know, I'm standing and sweating and panting, my boot coming down over and over on the zombies who are a long ways past moving at this point.

"Enough," June says. She's doubled over and panting. "Enough." She grabs my hand and squeezes.

That jolts me out of it and I catch her blue eyes and give her a tired smile.

We check each other for bites and we don't, thankfully, find any. In a fight like that... well, you never know. I turn back and stare at our captors knowing that our "useless" act is shot. "Happy?"

"Well, you're a disgustin' mess," Sal says, referring to the stinking gore covering our arms, faces, and clothes, "but that'll do. You gotta rinse off before I let you in my boat."

The river is deep and swift here, but we kneel by the

side and splash ourselves off. June catches my eye and nods downstream. She's asking if we should try to swim for it, but the sound of rapids echo through the canyon and I shake my head. The water is too cold, the rapids too fierce, and we are handcuffed together.

There's nothing we can do until we get to Phantom Ranch.

CHAPTER THIRTY

IT'S one more short boat ride, a nasty scramble back up to Tonto Trail, and then four more hours of hiking to the South Kaibab Trail and then back down to the Colorado River. The inner gorge is just too deep here for the boat trick to work, even with the ladders.

There are two suspension bridges across the Colorado— one at the Kaibab Trail, which Tonto Trail eventually runs into, and one at the Bright Angel Trail. These are the only ways across the river by foot. As we come up to the Kaibab Suspension Bridge, the trail runs through a short tunnel and we all stop, taking a moment in the relative cool.

The bridge dangles above the river with metal railings and a wooden deck. It's just wide enough for the mules that used to come down here. And that's what I'm thinking when I step into a nice, fresh plop of mule crap.

Sal laughs and I just keep going. It's not much of an indignity as these things go. This is how they bring down supplies and gas for those rafts, they must have mules. I'm really not looking forward to this. They are way too well organized.

The north side of the bridge has a series of three chainlink gates that are as tall as the railings. The first two are easy to get through, just a simple latch, and are for the Zs. The last one is locked and manned, with razor wire on the top of it and two men guarding.

"Fresh meat," Sal says, and we're waved through.

The other side of the trail is cut into the cliff, but quickly flattens out and crosses the wide sandy delta of Bright Angel Creek.

On the west side of the delta are some buildings, they were set up for the mule teams, as I recall, and I can see the Bright Angel Suspension Bridge. We head up the trail, past the old campground which appears to be used for storage, towards Phantom Ranch which is up the creek a ways in an area of Bright Angel Canyon that flares out. It's early evening and there is already a lot of shade.

Phantom Ranch is nicely treed with a large dining hall, a few dormitories, and quaint cabins made out of sandstone rocks. I recall seeing deer wandering in at night when I was down here as a kid.

We both are exhausted and defeated. During our last encounter with a psychotic, petty, wannabe warlord, I had time to prepare a bluff that I used to get them to free June. This time? I got nothing.

They escort us into the dining hall. It's an open space with wood beams on the ceiling and lots of windows out the front. Most of the tables and chairs are stacked along the walls and two tables have been pushed together in the center. They're covered in papers and there are two men facing us and one woman facing away.

The hall is hot and smells of food, grilled onions and meat, reminding me just how hungry I am.

My eyes are drawn to the woman. She's tall, long sandy-blond hair contained in a ponytail with the sides of her head shaved. She's lean but muscular with a faded brown tank top on and lots of ink.

"Fresh meat, Boss," Sal says. The men only briefly looking at us and then back down at the papers.

June stiffens and sucks in a breath by my side and lets go of my hand. The woman, Talia it must be, straightens.

"Just a couple o' love birds," he continues. "But I must say they are scrappy. Found 'em up towards Tanner Trail hidin' from them zombies in that sandbar in the middle of the river. Say they don't know about 'em, but you wouldn't swim the river if you weren't being chased by a bunch."

Talia turns and her brown eyes go right to June and her jaw falls open. I glance at June and she is blinking and biting her lip.

"Oh, my dear, sweet Jesus..." Talia says as she steps forward. "June Medina. I... I thought you died. I thought you..." Talia blinks, her hand coming to her slack face and her eyes water up. She looks at the handcuffs and our badly scraped wrists. "Sal, you get her out of those cuffs this second, or I swear..."

Sal moves quickly and uncuffs June, but leaves my cuff untouched. "Sorry, ma'am. Protocol, you know," he says, the gruff man suddenly cowering.

At this point, it was like I wasn't there. June and Talia are staring at each other and you could just about power a blender with the electricity passing between them.

"If I found you've treated them badly..." Talia says, not even looking at Sal. Her voice is fairly deep and she speaks loudly.

"It's been a fine day," I say, eyeing Sal. "Just a nice float down the river and an easy hike." But I don't think they even hear me.

Talia takes another step forward and her hands are shaking. June's face is hard, but she's blinking rapidly. I'm desperately trying to figure this out. They know each other. They were together after the Zs. And—-

Talia shouts, "Jesus be praised and Gaia too!" and rushes up and grabs June, picks her up, and kisses her hard.

Ah... they were "together" after the Zs, as in a couple, as in... OK. Well, there's one mystery solved. I now know that June likes girls and I'm not even in the running.

CHAPTER THIRTY-ONE

AT FIRST, it's a relief. I can give up my romantic fantasies and get back to focusing on survival. While I don't know if Talia is a psychotic, petty, wannabe warlord or not, I'm reasonably confident that because of their connection, we're safe.

But then I notice that it's mostly Talia doing the kissing and June is stiff, her eyes wide.

Talia puts her down. And June wipes her mouth and then smiles awkwardly.

"Jesus! I mean, I swear. Jesus!" Talia says. "How'd you get from Albuquerque over here? What the hell happened at that market? How'd you escape?"

Everyone is staring now. The two men at the table, and Sal and Mary, but Talia seems oblivious.

June swallows. "Tal, this is my good friend Woody." She steps over, giving me a shy smile but briefly widens her eyes. She takes my hand, squeezes it, and adds, "We're... well, we're together now."

And yeah, my heart jumps into my throat, and I suck in some spit and start coughing hard. "Water..." I gasp.

"Jesus, Sal," Talia says. "I swear I'm gonna have to kick your ass again. Get the man some water and get them some food. Go!"

My eyes are watering and I look up to see Talia giving me an appraising look like she's sizing up a side of beef. "Sorry about that kiss..." Talia says, sounding shy but looking defiant. "It's just... well... Our June here is special."

I nodded, my voice a croak. "I couldn't agree more. I'd be lost without her."

Sal brings us water and some stew and takes the handcuff off my wrist. I gulp the water, which helps the coughing, and then we sit down and eat, while Talia goes on about Jesus and Gaia, pacing about the dining hall like it's the oval office, going on and on about the "miracle" of having June back.

We both eat, although I see June keeping a wary eye on Talia. She doesn't say much and I don't say anything. I don't ask about the chewy meat in the stew, I'm so happy to eat.

After our meal, we get the tour and it's impressive. With us, they've got fifty-five people here and it's well protected. On the south is the Colorado River. To the north where the canyon narrows in an area called "The Box" they've put up a barbed wire fence and have guards posted 24/7. They have another fence just north of Phantom Ranch which is much wider and harder to protect. Down by the river, near the mule stables and the Bright Angel Bridge, they're gardening and even have two mules.

I learn a bit of pre-apocalypse history during the tour. June and Talia met while serving in Afghanistan. Not Army Rangers, but Army, so I was close on that. They were visiting Talia's parents in Albuquerque when the Zs happened.

"The Ranch," as they call it, is ideal. Protected. Isolated. All the water you need. A bit hot, but that just helps keep people away.

It's nearly dark once the tour is over and Talia escorts us to a cabin. "There's water inside and a little food. Some first aid stuff for your wrists. Make yourselves at home." She pauses then and stares at June. "Jesus Christ, June-bug. I'm just so glad to have you back." She gives June a fierce hug. "May Gaia be praised!"

When we get inside, June's eyes are wide and she grabs me and hisses in my ear, her breath warm. "She's crazy. We have to get out of here."

CHAPTER THIRTY-TWO

THE CABIN HAS food and water, both for drinking and for cleaning up, and our jackets. There's even some Neosporin and bandages. It doesn't, though, have our packs or any weapons.

"God, I'm wiped out, honey," June says after she lets me go, her eyes wide again. "I could sleep for a year."

I open my fat mouth to ask her what she's talking about and she puts her hand on my lips and shakes her head and then points to her ear and then outside. They might be listening?

I think about it, and yeah, they might. Small battery-powered electronics, why not? We used that kind of thing all the time in the Phoenix group I was with.

"Me too," I say. "My blisters are back, my wrist is killing me, and I'm exhausted, but this place is amazing." I rattle on for a while about how amazing things are at "The Ranch."

June takes her boots off and tiptoes around the place looking at everything. It's just one room with a bed, a small desk, a chair, and a bathroom with a groover in it. A groover is a toilet seat on top of a big ammo can lined with a bag, the kind of toilet setup used by river runners.

I pull my boots off and lie back on the bed with a groan. A real bed. I don't even know how long it's been since I've slept in a real bed. It's soft, but that softness just feels foreign.

June bounces down next to me and is whispering in my ear again, her warm breath and her familiar scent waking me up. "She was always high strung, but a good soldier. We were on leave from active duty when it came down... she... she. She lost it. She'll never let me go. I faked my death back in Albuquerque to get away." June ends in a shrug. "Oh, sweetie," she says looking at my wrist and feet. "Let me clean those up for you."

We spend the next hour switching between banal conversation, tending to our wounds, and whispering in each other's ears. We have no supplies. We're in a well-guarded compound with only two ways out.

We'll never get across the bridge with its gates and guards, so that leaves a thirteen-mile hike north up the Kaibab Trail to the North Rim or stealing a raft and heading down the Colorado towards Lake Mead with absolutely no river running experience.

Yup. This is an ideal location... to get trapped.

CHAPTER THIRTY-THREE

THEY CALL THIS PLACE "THE RANCH." The organization is militaristic. Talia is in charge, although she has no rank. Her middle managers are called lieutenants. The whole group is referred to as "Phantom Company."

As it turns out, I can't sleep in a bed anymore and neither can June. It's just too soft. We ended up dragging the bedding down onto the floor around midnight and I am sleeping like the dead... no, that's not right, the dead roam the planet looking to consume the living now. Okay, I'm sleeping like a baby, when I am woken up by a trumpet playing reveille at 5:00 a.m.

"What the..." I mumble, rubbing at my eyes. My wrist is a scabby mess and my feet are killing me.

"Come on, sweetie," June says, sitting next to me, she's already dressed. "We need to get out there."

I blink and look at her and she has a sweet smile on her face, her short black hair is damp, so she just must have washed up. Her blue eyes... God, I'm getting used to them. And for a moment, just a moment, I forget that she's pretending that we're together just in case someone is listening. I forget that we're trapped under the leadership of an unstable personality that is obsessed with June and would probably be happy to see me out of the picture by any means.

"Good morning, beautiful," I say, my smile going from wide to nervous as all this tumbles down on me. Her eyebrows dance briefly, her forehead crinkles, and I swear I see her blush before she turns away.

"Hurry up," she says, turning her back to me. "Get dressed. We've got to get out there."

Phantom Company has a boot-camp style gathering at 5:15 a.m. Including some calisthenics, duty assignments, and a few words from Talia.

Yeah, besides being trapped, this makes this place seem a whole lot less ideal. The exercise is fine, I'm in decent shape from running away from Zs, but I don't like the assignments.

A guy that goes by Harris, a buzzed cut, middle-aged, muscly, military sort, rattles off changes in duty assignments. He was one of the men we first saw with Talia. I'm to report to Meryl, a fifty-year-old man with a greying pony-tail who runs the kitchen and farm, and June is to report to... wait for it... Talia. Her assignment is not clear. June's standing at attention and looking straight ahead, so I can't get a read on her.

I count forty-nine of us in front of the dining hall lined up in four straight lines. That leaves six people out on sentry duty. Ages vary from around fifteen to seventy. Most people have a knife on their belt, but the only guns visible are Talia and her lieutenants, and presumably the guards.

After Harris is done, Talia struts in front of "the company," her hands clasped behind her back, still dressed in that tank top despite the cool morning. The tattoo on her left arm is of a skull with a snake running through the eye.

"We've got two new members to our company," she says, stopping in front of us and smiling. "June Medina and Woody..." she gives me a questioning look.

"Beckman," I say, doing my best to smile.

"...and Woody Beckman. June served with me and we are lucky to have them. I want you all to help them acclimate to things down here on The Ranch."

She begins pacing again and takes a deep breath, her voice strengthening. "Every day down here, every task we do, we do for the survival of the human race. Each job is important. Each member of our team invaluable. Each day a victory. With the help of Jesus above and Gaia below, we will not only survive, we will thrive!"

She ends square in front of the group and raises her arms into the air and shouts, "Phantom Company!"

The call is echoed by the people around me. I'm standing there with my jaw hanging loose like some fool. She mentioned Gaia. When I offered my time travel theory about the origins of the zombie infections, June countered with a Gaia theory—that the planet had created the fungal parasite to keep us from destroying it. A shiver runs through me.

Talia pumps her arms again and everyone yells "Phantom Company." I notice June is enthusiastically yelling, and I just want to freak. The third time I join in, just so I don't stand out.

After mess, which consisted of oatmeal and dried fruit, June kisses me on the check and says, "See you later, honey," before following Talia, Harris, Sal, and another woman outside.

I sit staring at the door. Maybe this weird Jesus, Gaia

thing is the way June is. She used to be with Talia. Maybe she'll want to go back to her, maybe she'll...

I shake it off. She's terrified of Talia—June being terrified of someone is a terrible thought—and that's why she just called me honey and kissed me on the cheek.

My mind is running rampant on the June and Talia thing when a thirtyish woman walks into the building, a tired look on her round face. She's tall and pretty with shoulder-length brown hair and has a gun on her hip. She must be one of the sentries, probably coming off shift.

Her eyes meet mine as she strides through the room. She tucks her hair behind her ear and smiles as she looks me over.

It's *that* kind of smile. I smile back, unsure what to think, most of the looks I've gotten have been guarded or curious stares that last a rudely long time.

I watch her walk back into the kitchen where she's handed a tray with some food. She sits down a few tables away and smiles at me again. Is she flirting?

"Come on, Beckman. Time to get to work."

I look up, it's Meryl waving me back towards the kitchen. I shake off the thoughts of June and her ex and this new woman. Time for my first day as part of Phantom Company.

CHAPTER THIRTY-FOUR

THE DAY SPINS by with half in the hot kitchen working on tonight's dinner stew, made from some old potatoes with a lot of eyes, canned vegetables, and some dried mystery meat—I'd rather not know what. The other half of the day is out in the sun weeding and hauling water by hand from the Colorado to water the plants.

Meryl moves slow and talks slow and speaks in a monotone and doesn't get any of my jokes. I don't know how long I can do this. To be clear, the work is fine, it's the lack of laughter that will do me in. I've got my two goals for the day, survival and laughter, and need them both.

The day ends in the dining hall, cleaning up after mess, and I still haven't seen June, or Talia for that matter. This is only day ten for us, but I feel incomplete without her. I don't like it at all. I spent the whole day thinking I was forgetting to do something.

When I stumble back to our cabin, exhausted, I am delighted to see her there.

"God, you are a sight for sore eyes," I say.

She's sitting on the edge of the bed, her eyes downcast, chewing on her lip. She nods and says, "You are too, babe." Her voice is light, but her face is not. Something is wrong.

She pats on the bed next to her and I flop down with a sigh and take a deep breath. "Tough work, but they've got a great setup here," I say, just in case they are listening.

"Yeah," she says. "Talia has done well. Amazing, really."

She then grabs me, her lips brushing my ear and a chill runs down my spine and I'm suddenly awake. "You're not safe."

"Meryl is a good guy," I say, my eyes wide. "I can see why they are glad to have us. They definitely need more hands."

We go on like this, talking about how wonderful The Ranch is and whispering in each other's ears.

Talia got June alone today and made her case as to why June needs to leave me and come back to her. How together they will be the ones to "save the human race." Asked her how well she knew me, asked her if she could even trust me. Told her that I didn't seem like her type. Told her she has seen guys like me before and I couldn't be trusted.

At this point, I'm not at all sure what June's type is. All I know is that Talia was once her type and that I don't like Talia one bit.

And true believers, don't get me started on them and people with missions to save this world. I barely escaped from one in Phoenix. I understand how in these desperate times it's easy to fall prey to someone who is so confident in themselves. But it's not real. They're either full of it, or nuts, or both.

June told Talia that we are in love, that I am "the one," that she is sure about me. Talia tried to kiss her again, got aggressive, it might have gone bad if Harris hadn't walked in.

I'm up and pacing, my fatigue forgotten. I'm angry. I want my baseball bat and a good-sized group of Zs to take on. I'm having trouble keeping up the charade. I want to go out into the night right now and march down to Talia's cabin, it's one of the big ones that families stayed in. I want to...

June gets up, grabs me, and holds me tight. She's afraid and that is... I don't even know how to describe it. On one hand, this beautiful, tough-ass woman is afraid and seems to want me to comfort her. On the other hand, one of the most competent people I've met in the post-apocalyptic world is afraid and... well, that's not good.

"There was a girl in Albuquerque," she whispers in my ear, "that liked me. Not even a real flirtation, and..." She ends shaking her head and won't say more.

"We need to leave," I whisper back. "Even if it doesn't work, we have to try."

She nods.

"Still got your lighter?" While they took our packs and our weapons, they didn't search our pockets. She always has a lighter with her.

"Yes," she whispers.

"Then I have an idea."

We spend the next hour working it out.

ꓘᶘ᠀ ᠀ᶘ ᠀ᶘ᠀

THERE'S a lot I hate about this plan of ours. It puts some good people at risk, but there doesn't seem to be another way. It is, though, the first plan that we've made together, so it's bound to go great, right?

Here's the problem. We're in a well-protected, isolated area at the bottom of the Grand Canyon in an armed compound run by a woman obsessed with June. All we have is what is in our pockets and what is in the room. June has a lighter and a small pocketknife. I've got a compass, a beat-up map of the Grand Canyon trails, and a small Leatherman multi-tool.

I have a brief moment when I realize I forgot about the Leatherman when we battled the Zs, but only briefly. It's too small to be effective.

If we do escape, we could encounter zombies, we could be chased, and we will most certainly be challenged by the elements.

In the room, we have some first aid supplies: hydrogen peroxide, Neosporin, and some bandages. Plus, there's three power bars, soap, toothpaste, and toothbrushes, a small LED lantern, and two bottles of water.

That's it.

We use the scissors on the Leatherman and cut two long, wide strips from the sheet. With this we can roll things up in them, tie them at the ends and sling it all over our shoulders so we can carry a few things. The rest of the sheets we cut into smaller strips, knot them together, and fashion a bit of rope.

Using a bunch of the cotton bandaging, toilet paper, and wood shavings, we set up a fire.

It's a bit of a Rube Goldberg machine with a small fire in a trash can that will jump to the bandaging and climb up onto the chair and ignite a larger fire, which will then connect with the drapes and involve the entire cabin.

We need a delay before the whole cabin is in flames.

See why I hate the plan? I don't really want to burn

down Phantom Ranch, but we need a distraction and we need everyone to be busy.

June is the firebug and is sure that the chained fires will work.

After prep, we turn off the lights and lie down, waiting for everyone else to fall asleep. She takes my hand and squeezes it. I squeeze back. My stomach is roiling and my brain won't stop freaking out and is going over and over our plan endlessly.

At 2:00 a.m. she lights the fire, we tie our makeshift sacks on, grab the rope we made out of sheets, and sneak out.

CHAPTER THIRTY-FIVE

THERE ARE high clouds and the night is dark. It's quiet except for the babbling of Bright Angel Creek. We go low and head east to the steep slopes of this side canyon and then head north.

I follow June's lead. We go in short spurts, hiding behind trees, watching. My eyes adjust quickly and it gets easier.

We make our way a few hundred feet north until we're in sight of the first, wider fence. Our cover is good and we spot the single sentry. It's a man, not the woman I saw after breakfast.

The fence runs from the edge of the creek to the canyon wall. This fence can't really protect the entire area like the one up at The Box can.

We wait. Five minutes and I'm thinking the fire didn't take. The guard is bored, walking on the trail, kicking at the dirt. Yawning.

Ten minutes and I'm about to lose it. I look at June, but

she's focused on the guard. We have a plan B, but I don't like it.

Fifteen minutes, and it's time for plan B. June gets up to go pretend she couldn't sleep and then take the guard out, but I catch a whiff of smoke and grab her.

Soon we hear the crackling, but the camp is still quiet. The guard is whistling now, looking to the north and not seeing the flicker of flames behind us.

June grabs a rock and tosses it, making enough noise to catch his attention. He sees the fire, curses, and runs down the trail. There are shouts from behind us. Once the guard is out of sight, we run, get through the gate, and keep running.

WE ARE NORTH of the first fence, and its distractible guard and distracted camp, but south of the better fence with guards we can't distract. They have guns, we don't. There is only one other trail here, Clear Creek Trail, that starts just north of Phantom Ranch and heads to the east nine miles, ending at Clear Creek in the depths of the Grand Canyon.

Right before the trail, we drink our water bottles dry, refill them from the creek, and head up. We have no choice.

We climb up the switchbacks as quickly as we can, up and out of the river gorge. The trail then goes east and parallels the river for a while and we go down that way a few hundred yards, dropping some threads from our sheets for pursuers to find. We then backtrack, going most of the way back down and head cross-country to the north.

The backtracking is risky. We need them to waste time

on Clear Creek Trail and we're betting that the fire will keep them busy long enough for us to do this.

Clear Creek is no good. We would get trapped there.

Bushwhacking across the Grand Canyon is not what we want, but we have to get out. The North Rim is the only way. It's slow going in the dark, but we scramble slowly and carefully. We're just on top of the first steep climb up out of Bright Angel Canyon, a few hundred feet above the creek.

Not the type of hike anyone takes on willingly, much less in the dark. The flickering light from the south and the whiff of smoke makes me feel guilty until I think of Talia. She forced us into this situation. She brought this on.

It's slow, dangerous going, but we scramble along, just above the steepest part of the cliff. Around The Box, it's nearly impassable and we slow way down using our sheet-rope. One of us sits anchored and the other one carefully crawls forward. We eventually get past The Box and the north-most fence.

We make some noise—even going slow and trying not to, we make noise. Each bump, each slip, each rock skittering down is like a blow. We're just hoping that they are busy and distracted by the fire.

We find a reasonable slope, which means only scrapes and bruises, and make it down to Bright Angel Trail.

Once down, we just squat there, catching our breath and listening. We're both sweaty and exhausted and very thirsty, but we don't move. Not for ten minutes.

It's silent, so we drink a little water, exchange a quick smile in the gloomy dark, and head to the north.

We don't have much food, but the trail parallels Bright Angel Creek much of the way so we'll have water. I feel a lightness about me and am about to open my mouth to say something when I hear the unmistakable snick-click of a pistol being cocked.

CHAPTER THIRTY-SIX

"HERE'S THE THING, JUNE-BUG," Talia says as she paces in front of us. "Did you not think about walkie talkies, or did you just assume the fire would consume all of our attention?"

I hate that nickname. It implies that June is small, and she might be in stature, but not in spirit. I can't imagine what June thinks of it. And Talia left out the third option, "you're so damned desperate to get away from me that you'd try anything."

Sal and Harris have their guns pointed at us and there are a few flashlights providing some illumination. June's got my hand and is squeezing it hard.

"A daring escape, I'll give you that," Talia continues. "But the guards heard you up above and we had plenty of time to deal with the fire and get up here before you." She shakes her head, her ponytail wagging behind her. "Not good enough. I expect better from you."

She sighs in an annoyingly psychotic, petty, wannabe warlord way. "In any case, you'll be coming back with us now. You'll be made a nice example of. Both of you. Let's move."

Neither of us have spoken a word. Talia had to give her tiresome, warlord speech before anything else could happen. June is terrified and not herself. I've had zero time to prep, but there is one card I can play. A big fat bluff, but maybe it will wake June up.

"Hold on," I say, holding up my hand. "I think you can spare me a moment and let me explain why you're going to let us go." Sure, I sound like I know what I'm talking about, but my heart is pounding out an insanely fast rhythm in my head and I'm making this up as I go.

June gives my hand a desperate squeeze, as if to ask me what the hell I'm doing, or maybe to beg me to shut up. I have no idea. And sure, I could get us killed now, but, hey, that might be better than being "made a nice example of."

"Very well," she says. "Dazzle me." She injects enough sarcasm that I want to punch her.

"You've got a good thing going here," I nod back to Phantom Ranch. "If you had given us a choice, we would have happily taken our packs and been on our way, but you didn't do that."

She waves her hand at me impatiently. I'm stalling and she knows it.

"June and I are in love," I tell her and turn to June and meet her eyes. "I've been a goner since the first day we met. There is no life for me now without her."

It's fairly dark, but I can see how wide June's eyes are.

And then it clicks. I know what might work.

I turn back to the impatient Talia. "And she's told me everything. What happened in Afghanistan. How things went to shit in Albuquerque." And now I'm in complete bullshit land. I mean, I know things went down, something happened to the girl that had a crush on June. I know there are things Talia's done that she's not proud of, provided she's not a complete psychopath.

"You've got a whole new crew that respects you," I say. "It's going great. So, you can let us go now," I say with a smile. "Or we can start talking."

She's breathing heavy and steps forward and presses her pistol to my forehead. "Or, I can just kill you both now," she says.

June is squeezing my hand so hard it hurts. I slowly shake my head, careful not to dislodge or jostle the gun. "No. You can't." And yes, I'm still bullshitting my ass off and would have pissed my pants if I hadn't been fairly dehydrated. "You can kill me, sure, but I know you can't kill June. Not our special June. And she'll spill the whole way back, tell everyone there exactly what your past looks like, even before the Zs."

I can see her eyes and she is furious, her nostrils flaring, her jaw locked. And I wasn't lying when I said she had a good thing back there. The gamble I'm taking is that it's more important to her than proving something here.

The seconds tick past and I just know it's not enough. She's going to pull the trigger.

"Please," June whispers. "Tal. Please. For the good times we had. For the love we shared. Please let us go."

She cocks the gun and I swear to God I can hear her teeth grinding. I squeeze June's hand and I'm sweating like it's midday and I just ran a 1 ok. She's going to do it.

And then... Talia blinks and slowly nods her head, the gun falling to her side, her shoulders slumping.

I think we can drop the petty from my description of Talia, so now she's only a "psychotic, wannabe warlord."

She stumbles down the trail and doesn't look back.

"Give them your guns and knives," she calls back to the two men. "And anything you have to eat. Let them go. Now."

"But... Talia," Sal says.

Talia stops and even in the gloom I can see how high her shoulders are. "I swear to God, Sal, those two gave me a good reason not to kill them. Have you?"

CHAPTER THIRTY-SEVEN

AFTER THEY'RE GONE we don't move. We're just standing there holding hands, my whole body is shaking, sweat dripping down my back. I hear the water rushing down the creek and cicadas buzzing in the night. I can't believe it worked. I feel... so tired, so weak, and yet I feel invincible. We just talked Talia down. We've got weapons now. They're not going to chase us. I feel this strange high.

"I meant what I said," I whisper, that manic energy finally getting me to open my mouth.

"What?" June asks.

"I have been a goner since the first day we met. There is no life for me now without you."

I don't turn. I can't. I feel her looking at me, but I'm terrified to look at her. Bullshit an armed psychotic, wannabe warlord? Sure. Face rejection from June head-on? Nope.

She doesn't speak for the longest time and I'm half-convinced that she's going to go running back to Talia.

"It's..." she begins, swallowing hard. "You know, it's..."

I turn to her. "I know it's complicated, June. We are barely surviving, how safe is it to feel like this about someone when we have no idea what tomorrow will bring?"

She nods.

"And if being your friend and your partner out here is all I get... I'm... I'm good with that."

"Okay..." she says, biting her lip. She takes a deep breath, nods her head, and says "Okay" again, but resolutely this time. She lets go of my hand and gathers up the gear the men left us just like it's business as usual. She divvies it up and gets on the trail.

When we've been on the trail for a while and it's starting to get light, I just can't stand it anymore. "So... just to be clear, you like girls *and* guys. Right?" She must. She was with Talia, but Talia bought her being with me.

She stops and stares at me.

"I just need to know if there's a chance. Is there?"

Her blue eyes bore into me, a smile playing on her lips.

"Tell you what," she says. "I'll let you know when we reach the top and have a safe place to rest." She turns and trots up the trail.

"Seriously?" I yell after her. "I mean, seriously!?"

Her laughter bounces off the canyon walls and I happily chase her up the trail.

PART FIVE

WOODY AND JUNE VERSUS THE THIRD WHEEL

HIM AND HER AND... HER?

CHAPTER THIRTY-EIGHT

JUNE IS TOYING WITH ME. I can't say that I mind. There's nothing to take your mind off the zombie apocalypse and an escape from dangerous humans like a smart, competent, beautiful woman who you just learned likes boys as well as girls and just might be interested in you.

We've escaped Talia, her ex, who is the psychotic, wannabe warlord that runs the group of survivors down at Phantom Ranch at the bottom of the Grand Canyon. We're on our way up North Kaibab Trail heading towards the North Rim.

Down below, after we managed to escape Talia and her minions, I finally told June how I feel.

And to Talia's credit, I did downgrade her from a "psychotic, *petty*, wannabe warlord" to just a "psychotic, wannabe warlord." June was able to reach her, which is why I am still alive. My forehead still has this strange itch where Talia pressed her gun. It's like I can still feel it there as she threatened to blow my brains out. Just an echo of one of the many post-apocalyptic traumas.

And yes, this is only day eleven of Woody and June versus the Apocalypse, but there is no time to fool around with Zs roaming the land wanting to eat the living, and the living often being a lot more dangerous than the Zs.

The spring day is warm with only high, thin clouds in the blue sky and I'm sweating a lot. June has put on a good pace and I've had to work hard to keep up with her. She's petite, but ex-Army and as tough as they come. We don't have much food, but we've been paralleling Bright Angel Creek so hydration hasn't been an issue.

And I guess that is the problem. There is, literally, no time to fool around. No safety. No peace. No time for anything but survival.

June likes me. She must, right? She's still here even after all our close calls in just a few days. She walked away from Talia with me. And she promised to tell me if there is a chance for us the next time we "have a safe place to rest."

So, what do I do as the miles go by? Search the landscape trying to see if the scraggly desert canyon holds any safety, wonder if there is a secret cavern behind Ribbon Falls that could be safe, wish the few buildings at the campground we pass are far enough from Talia and her militaristic Phantom Company to seem safe. Anything at all.

I wrack my brain trying to remember what's at the top of the trail, but I was a kid last time I was at the North Rim and not really paying attention. There's a lodge and a store, that kind of stuff, but will any of it be considered safe by June?

"We better stop here," I call to June as the trail turns away from the creek and starts up the slope. We're about to leave Bright Angel Creek for the real climb up out of the canyon.

June stops and looks at me, her blue eyes tired but determined. She stands there for a moment, searching the canyon, looking for danger.

And it's what I should be doing with my time. Not fantasizing about safety and her and how everything will change if we could just find some time. I should be focused on survival too.

It's my first rule for each day. Survive. My second is laugh, because you have to have some quality in your life even if you're barely surviving. My new third rule is to spend time with June, because... well... I'm crazy about her.

I turn around and look back, worried that I've missed something.

She walks slowly towards me, her eyes continuing to search, her short black hair sweaty and plastered to her head. I should be searching too, but I find myself staring at her. How can I not. She's got this petite, pixie vibe and is absolutely beautiful.

"We're being followed," she whispers to me as she opens up her water bottle and leans down to the creek to fill it.

"What?" I hiss.

Her eyes widen, and I get the message and lower my tone. "How do you know?" I ask. I plunge my old plastic water bottle in the cold water. Our supplies are very limited. We left Phantom Ranch with almost nothing. Sheets fashioned into slings to carry things, a few granola bars, cheap plastic water bottles, and I've got my trusty Diamondbacks baseball cap, the only thing I've kept since it all went down. Talia had given each of us a gun and a bit more food, but we are not in a good situation.

"I just do," she says. "I've heard a scrape, here or there, that wasn't either of us." She shakes her head. "I just know."

I nod, all thoughts of getting to safety and finding out if

the woman of my post-apocalyptic dreams likes me gone. Now I just want to get to safety.

"Talia?" I ask.

June bites her lip. "Not her, not sneaking after us, but she might have sent someone."

I sigh. I guess it's time to add the "petty" back into Talia's title.

"We need to drink as much as we can here," I say in a normal conversational tone in case we are being overheard. "We are about to head up and won't have access to water."

June gives me a weak smile and nods, taking a deep drink.

"We got this," I whisper, but I'm not sure I believe it.

CHAPTER THIRTY-NINE

WE DIG INTO THE SWITCHBACKS, shortening our strides but keeping our pace steady. The rocks and the dirt of the trail are iron rich and all have a red hue. It's spring and it's in the mid-seventies here, but with this climb that's hot. We've got our jackets tied around our waists. It's awkward, but you never leave a jacket behind—you *will* always need it at some point.

And my dull green army surplus jacket has my packs of seeds in the inside pocket. Not a ton, just some beans and vegetables that I took when I left Phoenix. Those seeds represent the future and the ability to grow food and be self-sustained.

I know it's more symbolic than anything, but those two things, my hat that links me to my past and the seeds, which point to the future, help keep me sane.

We're just past Redwall Bridge that takes you over a narrow but steep bit of canyon. We debated bushwhacking around and waited off the trail for a while to make sure it was clear. It's a wood decked metal bridge like the one over the Colorado River, but much smaller. We ended up going across one at a time, but between the bridge not feeling safe and June's conviction that we're being followed, it's been a bit tense.

Well, that and the whole escape from Talia and living in a world terrorized by zombies. Yeah, that too.

"I have a plan," I say, pulling up next to June.

She looks amused, briefly, and I'm relieved. Given our history with my plans I'm glad to see it. "Care to explain," she says, her voice low so as to not carry.

I nod and give her the best smile I can. "There's a place called Supai Tunnel coming up. If we are being followed that's the place to find out."

"A tunnel?" she asks.

"Yeah. It's the only way up, you have to go through it."

"A good place to ambush our follower is a good place to ambush us," she says.

My smile disappears, I hadn't thought of that. "We'll be careful."

She nods, all grim determination, and my determination is to lighten things up.

Sure, someone might be following us, but I don't think their intent is to do us immediate harm or wouldn't we have been shot at by now? And yes, we are in the middle of a zombie apocalypse, but we haven't seen a Z since we hit Phantom Ranch, and if they are around here, they must be few and far between.

But what about that zombie tourist herd on the South Rim that chased us down into the canyon, you might ask. Well, the North Rim is isolated and hard to get to. I am sure there are Zs, but there can't be that many and I don't see a horde of them randomly traipsing down the trail.

"So... I've been thinking about your Gaia theory of the

origin of the Zs," I say in between breaths as we wind up the switchbacks.

She glances at me briefly and says, "Ummm hmmm."

"That was Talia's idea, right?" Talia is this weird combination of evangelistic Christian and earthy goddess lover, invoking both Jesus and Gaia pretty often.

June stops, her eyes searching mine, and then she takes a sip of water. "What are you getting at?" Even her breath is coming fast as we climb.

I shrug. Truth is this tact wasn't well thought out. I thought that discussing my time travel theory of the apocalypse versus her Gaia theory might be amusing, but I've taken us right back to her ex. "Umm... just trying to understand it," I say, attempting to recover. "Trying to understand her. You know, in case..." I nod back down the trail.

June's eyes linger on mine as if she thinks there is more there and if she looks at me long enough she'll either divine it or I'll spill—the latter is actually quite likely. She stows her water bottle in her sheet sling and nods. "Yes, her theory, but it works better than yours." She turns and marches up the trail.

"Better?" I ask. "How is a conscious planet better than our far future ancestors trying to stop us from ruining the planet, or benevolent aliens trying to stop us from destroying our race?"

She snorts and that makes me smile. "First off, your aliens and ancestors are both sadistic bastards laying this crap on us."

"And Gaia isn't?"

She shakes her head. "No. Think of the planet as a single organism and we are cells that make up that organism. Did you feel bad when you lost a few pounds after the holiday, wiping out millions of fat cells?"

The trail is wide enough so that I can walk next to her and I try to catch a glimpse of her face. There is a bit of a smile playing there. She's messing with me and that's a good sign.

"And," she continues, glancing at me, those blue eyes a bit brighter, "you have to contend with the impossibility of time travel and the huge difficulties of interstellar space travel with your theories."

"And you have to explain a conscious planet," I counter.

She shrugs. "Easily done. Explain how the individual neurons in your brain coalesce into consciousness and I'll explain how the individual, seemingly disparate, beings on this planet create a consciousness."

"But wouldn't we be aware of that? Wouldn't we know that?"

She shakes her head. "Does one neuron in your brain know of the larger whole it is a part of?"

"Well... I'm a little more complicated than a single neuron." My tone is defensive now. I've lost my intent in this conversation and am just in it.

"Then prove it, and wrap your brain around the possibility."

"Aliens are more fun," I counter.

She stops, her arms crossed awkwardly over her sheet sling pack thing. "What the hell about this is fun? Answer me that, Woody? We need water. We need food. We need shelter. How many times in the last week have we almost bought it? Where the hell is the fun?"

I'm panting hard from the exertion and from the adrenaline of our little argument. Really, our first argument. She has a point; the particulars of our survival are not very fun. But that misses the larger point. A life needs to be worth living, even a post-zombie-apocalypse life.

"Meeting you, that was fun," I say quietly. "When you taught me to shoot by the Little Colorado River Gorge, that was fun... you know, except for the gun part." At this she smiles, briefly, knowing how much I hate guns, but maybe seeing that her teaching me is what made it fun for me. "Rafting down the Grand Canyon, even though we were prisoners, that was fun."

The smile is gone and yet her eyes are wide and she's blinking too much. I think Talia and our close call added to the worry about being followed may have pushed her past her limit. She has limits, which is both comforting and scary at the same time.

"Holding hands with you," I continue, "anytime and anywhere is fun." I hold my hand out and she takes it.

And yes, I am an unabashed, unashamed romantic. Before I met June, I wasn't wanting to interact with any humans, much less an amazingly competent—and yes, beautiful—woman.

"Hiking the Grand Canyon, just you and me," I continue. "This is fun." She opens her mouth to speak, but I forge on. "I know it's serious. I know our survival is tenuous. I'm not dumb. But for me fun is doing the things I want to do, not the things I have to do. And being with you is what I want to do. It takes this existence beyond survival into a life worth living."

She's blinking again and nodding, her eyes wide.

It's a moment. The world is quiet around us, just the barest of breezes and the chirping of birds. I want to kiss her, so much. We aren't safe, exposed on these switchbacks, but it's clear that no one is near. My nose if full of her sweet and sweaty scent. I lean down and she doesn't turn her head away. I move in to close the distance and—

"Shit!" she hisses, turning her head away. "Did you hear that?"

I think back and do recall a scrape a moment ago, like a foot slipping on a rock.

I straighten up and nod. And then I hear a rock bouncing down the slope below us.

The moment has passed. It's time to figure out who is following us.

CHAPTER FORTY

I USED TO BE A WAITER. Hours on my feet taking orders, regurgitating details of the menu, hauling food, dealing with stupid requests and thousands of different diets, hoping for decent tips. It wasn't bad work, not in the least. I spent some time working construction, and being inside away from the Phoenix heat made it vastly superior, but I always felt trapped by it, by the need to make money.

I'd spend all the best hours of my day doing something I had to do, not something I wanted to do. It seemed like that job, and all similar jobs, were just leaching my life slowly away until one day I would wake up old and decrepit, no longer able to work, the world having sucked me dry.

The Zs changed all that and made each day a struggle for survival. You have to find food and shelter. You have to survive the Zs, the environment, and the psychotic, petty, wannabe warlords and their merry bands of sadists.

It makes it hard to relax, hard to breathe sometimes, but there seems to be a reason for everything.

I ponder this as we wait for our pursuer on the other side of Supai Tunnel. I think we would have agonized over going through it, worrying about an ambush, but we didn't have time. Besides, Talia was so confident about catching us down there, she wouldn't have sent someone up in front of us. And I wasn't worried about an ambush from above, this was still the territory of Phantom Company.

In the end, I just walked through to June's objections.

The tunnel is an even better spot for ambush than I had thought. It is about twenty feet long, sloping up through the red rock and curves a bit at the end. It then opens up to a flattish area that has some pit toilets, a water fountain for thirsty hikers—that no long works, of course—and long hitching posts made out of metal pipe to tie the mules to that used to drag tourists down here. The ones that didn't want to hike the two miles down—or really up, it's a 1400-foot elevation gain, so not just a walk around the block.

June is positioned on the right side of the trail and will see our pursuer first, and since she can actually shoot that gun she's holding, I offered no objections. I'm to the left and we're both crouched behind large sandstone boulders that provide decent cover.

The curve in the tunnel means we won't be able to see anyone until they are almost all the way through—it also means they won't be able to see us.

You could try to use that bend as cover and shoot your way out, so we're both squatting there with our guns out.

We're almost to seven thousand feet in elevation now, and since we've stopped moving, I'm finally cooling down.

At this point, there is no doubt about the pursuer. They are there, on the other side of the tunnel, and my heart kicks into high gear.

We can't see to through to the other side, but I heard the

footsteps and I heard them stop and can dimly hear rapid breaths. It sounds like one person and they were moving fast, trying to catch up to us, I'm sure.

I throw June a worried look with a short nod, kind of an "Oh shit, you called it" look and she returns a grim smile, her gun in hand.

I have my gun too, but still really hate the thing. If it comes down to gunfire, I will be a distraction, June will be the one that actually hits something.

Minutes drag by and it's silent except for the breeze and the cawing of some ravens, the sound bouncing around the canyon eerily. The smell of the mules that tarried here still lingers, a vague acrid scent, the ground overused by them for too long and nature has not had time to properly reclaim it. Like much of civilization, their presence lingers even as it fades. A fly buzzes me and I shoo it away, it is probably longing for the mules and its easy food source to come back.

This doesn't have the banality of being a waiter, that's for sure. It's got the adrenaline of survival. I could use the banality of a soul-sucking job right now.

Five more minutes tick past and still nothing. Whoever it is, they are being careful. Do they suspect we are waiting in ambush? They must.

June's eyes are fixed on the tunnel and I'm getting antsy, about to say something when I hear crying. A child... no, a woman crying. At first, I can barely hear it and then it gets louder, but still restrained. The kind of sobbing this zombie-filled world can bring on.

The sound echoes through the tunnel and I blink, my heart heavy. I've sobbed just like that, many a night alone, barely holding on, not knowing what's next or how I'm going to keep going, much less survive.

And then the sobbing intensifies into more of a wail

before it suddenly cuts off. "I'm coming through now," she says with a sniff, her voice echoing in the tunnel. "I'm unarmed. Please don't shoot."

June steadies herself and levels her gun, but I stand up, my gun in my hand, but at my side.

Like most males, the sound of a woman crying is a complicated and terrifying thing. And yes, this might be a tad misogynistic, but it makes me want to lend aid, to help, to make it better. If a man cried, I think my reaction wouldn't be as nearly as compassionate. I'd be more "suck it up" than "what can I do to make you stop crying?"

Yup. My discomfort with women crying is all about me. And I get all that, but it runs pretty deep.

I have a hard time imagining June crying, but this woman, whoever she is, needs help.

June stabs a look at me, but I don't sit down.

"It's okay," I yell. "Come on through. We won't shoot."

"Sit down, Woody," June hisses. "Now!"

I shake my head, but don't leave my shelter like I would have on my own. I just stand there like a dope, the perfect target for Talia's mercenary sent to get rid of the competition so that June goes running back to her.

The thought lands on me with a nearly audible thud. Well, at least my gasp is audible as I realize what has always been clear to June. Just as the woman appears in the tunnel, I duck back behind my cover, convinced that she is here to kill me. That she cried like that figuring I had the usual straight male phobia to females crying and was using me.

It's clear when it comes to survival, having women around makes it more of a challenge. My constant being distracted by June and "what might be" and my stupidity just now with this complete stranger proves it.

The woman walks through the tunnel and my heart

pounds out a syncopated rhythm in my head. Was her crying real? Is she here to kill me? Why would Talia send someone after us right after making such a show of letting us go?

And then recognition hits. I've seen her before.

CHAPTER FORTY-ONE

SHE'S around thirty with shoulder-length brown hair and a round face. She's tall and pretty with a few extra pounds, which is unusual to find these days.

Her left knee is a bloody mess as well as her right hand; she must have taken a good spill. She doesn't appear to have anything on her, no gun, no pack, no water bottle. She's dressed in khaki shorts and a grey tank top.

"I... Please don't shoot," she says, her eyes red rimmed, making it look like the crying was real.

"Who are you?" June asks, standing, moving onto the trail, her gun pointed at the woman's chest.

"Dallas. My name is Dallas... I... I escaped in the chaos back there. Please... please don't shoot."

I stand and walk up next to June, my mind a mess. In the old days, pre-June, I would have avoided the encounter, hidden, stayed on my own. My little assassin fantasy, while plausible, was crumbling in the presence of this clearly distraught person.

"You, over there," June points with her gun and the

woman walks into the open area next to the metal hitching post. "Woody, keep your gun on her, shoot her if she moves. I'm going to check the other side of the tunnel."

June moves carefully into the tunnel, I hear her footsteps echoing out, but I'm focused on Dallas. She's pretty, with brown eyes and noticeable smile lines.

"I remember you," I say. "You were one of the sentries down at Phantom Ranch. You came in for breakfast after everyone else was done."

I have this clear memory of being in the dining hall at Phantom Ranch and her looking at me intently and smiling. It was one of the few kind looks I got that day. But it was more than a smile and a look; both seemed to have a heat behind them like she was flirting with me.

She nods and bites her lip. "Talia's crazy. I hated that place, but never saw a way out until..." She nods at me, referring to the fire we started as a distraction so we could get away.

I glance at the tunnel but don't see June. I'm sure she's seeing if there is anyone else here.

"You were a sentry, why didn't you just leave one night?"

She shrugs. "We are rarely alone, and how would I survive out here all by myself?"

"How did you get past Talia, Sal, and Harris after they let us go?"

She smiles shyly. "It was dark. I hid until after they passed."

I don't know if I believe her, but I could believe it was chaotic enough last night for someone to slip out. And she has nothing, which lent credence to it being unplanned, not to mention her injuries.

"All clear over here," June calls from the tunnel.

"I'm alone..." Dallas began. "Please... I..." Her eyes well up with tears and I feel that compulsion to help again. I fight it down as best I can.

"What are we going to do?" I whisper to June when she gets back next to me.

She takes a deep breath, her eyes fixed on Dallas, her gun pointed at her chest. "We have to take her with us," June says. "We can't have her running back to Phantom Ranch and we can't have her following us."

I nod. I don't like it, but I don't see any other options.

June pulls a water bottle out of her sheet sling. It's only got about an inch of water left, but she tosses it to Dallas. "We can't have you falling over from dehydration."

"Thank you," Dallas says, and quickly drains the water.

"Get going now," June says. "Stay on the trail, don't try to run or I will shoot you."

She nods. "Thank you. Thank you both." She starts walking slowly up the trail and we follow when she's about twenty feet ahead.

"Do you think Talia sent her?" I whisper.

June snorts and raises her eyebrows, nodding her head.

"What are we going to do?" I ask.

"Get out of this damn canyon and then you're going to find us some shelter."

I nod and pull my beat-up map of the Grand Canyon out of my pocket, wishing I remembered the North Rim better than I did.

CHAPTER FORTY-TWO

THE SOUTH RIM of the Grand Canyon sits at seven thousand feet and perches over the gorgeous erosion near the river. The North Rim, on the other hand, is up above eight thousand feet and is spread among side canyons that cut deeply to the north.

The South Rim is easy to get to, full of tourists, with the overlooks close together. The environment is desert-like.

The North Rim is hard to get to, far fewer tourists, with long drives between overlooks as you thread from one side canyon to another. The environment is more forested, with the pine trees and a few spruce and fir right to the edge.

For both of these reasons, the forest and the isolation, I love the North Rim.

This difference between the rims is caused by geology, the land sloping from the north down towards the south, causing rainfall at the South Rim to flow away from the canyon, while rainfall at the North Rim flows into the canyon, producing the deep side canyons.

The three of us are standing in the parking lot of the North Kaibab Trailhead. We are fourteen miles from Phantom Ranch, it's late afternoon, and we are tired, hungry, and dehydrated.

There's an outhouse here, which we've all taken advantage of, and a sloped parking lot for about forty cars that is about a quarter filled. That's the advantage of simple things, like pit toilets, they still work even after civilization is gone. Although they would have worked better had there been some toilet paper left.

Dallas had been quiet, trudging ahead of us up the final switchbacks, it's the kind of climb that is hard enough to make most everyone quiet, but she has more reasons than that. She's got some kind of tattoo under her tank top. I see a beak and maybe feathers peeking out. We need to know more about her, but I don't think either June or I have had the energy. We just escaped Talia, lack supplies, and are in a bad spot again.

This would be much simpler without Dallas.

"What now?" Dallas asks, looking directly at me. June is looking at me too.

Who put me in charge?

"How much does Phantom Company come up here?" I ask Dallas, trying to sound confident, but it's the first thing that popped into my head.

"Plenty, with the huge herd that was on the South Rim, but I've never been out of Phantom since I arrived."

So, it's probably picked clean. A lack of food we might have to deal with, but we need to find water and shelter.

"Do you think they'll send someone after her?" I ask June.

She pointedly looks at Dallas instead of answering.

Dallas scrapes her hiking boot on the pavement, her head down. She takes a deep breath and lets out a noisy sigh. "She... Talia. She wanted to... to date me." She looks up and her eyes are haunted. "I worked in the kitchen then and turned her down, that's when I got put on sentry duty."

I'm about to ask about that when June does. "Sentry duty? Seems like a promotion?"

Dallas snorts. "Guarding gates all night, every night, never alone, bored to death, sleeping when most everyone else is awake?" She shakes her head. "No. It was punishment."

"So, do you think she'll come after you?" I ask.

She looks down at her shoes again. "She's crazy, you know. Obsessed. But it's not me she wants now."

June blinks and nods. She's still got her gun out, but the miles and this story seems to have mellowed her about Dallas. It's a story June can relate to.

And then they're both looking at me.

"Okay. A plan," I say, making it up as I go. "Let's go slow and systematic. We need transportation, so let's check these cars, and while we're at it, let's see if they have anything useful—and considering how little we have, that might just actually be possible—and then we'll head for the lodge."

June guards us with both of our guns, and Dallas and I start picking through the cars. There's about ten of them and they're a mess. They've been open to the weather with broken windows, popped trunks and hoods, dried pine needles inside, and seats chewed up by squirrels.

"How did you end up down there?" I ask as we're rooting through a minivan. I find a tire iron and grab it, any weapon in a zombie apocalypse, as the saying goes. And yes, that really is a saying if you're reading this long after the zombies are gone—I gotta have hope, you know. Anything that will stop the fungus heads from eating you is welcome. Anything that helps you survive, a blessing.

"Just an accident," she says. "I was in Holbrook holed up in an old hotel—the thing had fake teepees, for God's sake—when Talia and her group came through. I ran into them when I was scrounging and was 'recruited.'"

She shakes her head, sweeping pine needles out of the side of the van while I'm rooting around the back. I understand what she means by "recruited." Talia finds you and you're a part of the group even if you don't want to be.

I find a Bic pen, shove it into my pocket. I remove the gas cap and there isn't even a whiff of gas so we move on to an old sedan and then a Jeep Cherokee. I'm checking the cars and searching, but keeping an eye on Dallas too. She is quick and thorough, looking everywhere. She finds a pair of sunglasses in a little cubby and puts them on, but that and the pen and tire iron are the only things besides pine needles, scat, empty gas tanks, and trash we find.

While Dallas starts on another car, I eye up the trash cans up by the outhouse. They are off-white metal rectangles with sloping tops one is for trash, the other for recycling with the tricky lids to keep bears out.

"Nothing?" June asks, still keeping a good distance from Dallas and me.

I brandish my tire iron. "Not a bat, but I'll take it. I think Phantom Company drained the gas out of these long ago and scavenged them for parts." I point to the trash cans. "Might as well be thorough."

I use my superior human hand and push open the latch, the "how to" illustration still sticking tenaciously to the lid. Inside I find, you guessed it, trash and recycling—for reasons beyond me, humans didn't seem to be able to put trash in the trash can and recycling in the recycling can, although they could obey the instructions on how to open the lid. It doesn't stink—any garbage dumped in here has long rotted away. It does have this stale musty smell, though, which reminds me of the Zs.

I pull out some decent water bottles with lids, all empty, and put them in my sheet sling and go to the next dumpster. I get some empty bottles for June and Dallas and find some paper with one side blank and fold it up and put it in my pocket.

"Hey!" Dallas shouts, pulling a dirty backpack from underneath the car she was searching. It's filthy but was once pink with a big Hello Kitty on the back.

I signal her over and we stuff the little backpack full of empty water bottles.

"Let's move on," I say, signaling Dallas in the direction of the lodge. Her brown eyes lock with mine and I feel guilty for still treating her like a prisoner. She holds my gaze for a breath and then sighs, her shoulders slumping.

The parking lot slopes down to the road which then curves up and around a large tree-covered hill, kind of a switchback for cars and I know we are all sick of switchbacks. There's a nice dirt path paralleling the road, but without cars on it, the road is a lot safer. "Let's stay on the road, more open," I say, even though Dallas is already headed towards the road.

She starts walking in front of us. She's our prisoner and I hate it. I don't want to be a psychotic, petty, wannabe warlord bossing people around at gunpoint. I don't want to petty, or psychotic, even. I just want to survive.

And right now, the only thing we have in abundance is empty water bottles. We need water and food and a vehicle.

We likely haven't seen the end of Talia and need to leave the area. Now.

June's blue eyes narrow and catch mine as if to ask, "Are you okay?"

I smile, as best I can, and nod. "Let's see what we can find at the lodge."

CHAPTER FORTY-THREE

FROM THE TRAILHEAD, the road heads west, snakes up and around a big hill through a thick forest of ponderosa pines with firs mixed in and a few aspens, and then heads south towards the lodge and Bright Angel Point.

The road is post-apocalyptic, meaning it is untended and covered in debris. Dirt and pine needles cover much of it as if the forest is reaching out and trying to reclaim the road. There are large tracks of dried mud and stones where heavy rains flowed mud onto the road. There is evidence of vehicles, tire tracks through the dirt, but not that many and not that often.

As soon as we crest the hill and start heading south, a Z comes shambling forward from off the road near some buildings that I can just glimpse through the trees. The building doesn't look familiar; it's been a long time since I was here.

We just passed Admin Loop on the right, that is where the back-country office is and housing for the people that worked here. This other building is big and brown with a green roof, up ahead on the left.

"I'll get 'em," I call cheerfully, jogging ahead of Dallas with my tire iron.

Truth be told, I'm tired, hungry, exhausted, and desperate for some rest, but Dallas doesn't have a weapon and I don't want June shooting—too much noise.

The Z stinks of rotting flesh with a moldy keynote, like they all do, but he's in good shape with torn jeans and a denim jacket. His face isn't desiccated at all and he only has a gash on one cheek. He's also a bit slower and clumsier as new Zs tend to be. Strange.

It's snarling and snapping its jaw, its teeth clacking. I kick it in the chest, it goes down. I stand on its chest and it claws at my jeans. I use the sharper end of the tire iron and shove it through his eye socket and one more Z is taken care of. Only about six billion to go.

I stand up and smile at June and Dallas, sure what we need right now is a moment of humor. "How many Zs does it take to screw in a lightbulb?" I ask.

June rolls her eyes and shakes her head.

"How many...?" Dallas asks tentatively, as if she's worried there is something sinister behind my question.

"They won't do it," I say, pointing at the now still zombie. "They lack the brains!" I draw "brains" out in total B-movie style. "Braaaaiiiinnnnssss."

June groans, but Dallas laughs. It's awkward, a bit of a giggle, but at least there's some kind of laughter today.

"Don't laugh," June says to her, "you'll just encourage him."

"Why shouldn't you ever go to a zombie doctor?" I ask, sufficiently encouraged.

June's still shaking her head, but smiling now. "Why?"

"Because his diagnosis is always the same... there's something wrong with your braaaaiiiinnnnssss!!!"

June chuckles and Dallas laughs for real. These are bad jokes, not really worth the laughter, but these are desperate times. Any joke in an apocalypse. And no, that one's not a saying yet, I just made it up.

I'm pulling the denim jacket off the Z when Dallas says, "Wait... wait... I've got one."

I look up. "Let's have it."

"What do a scarecrow and a zombie have in common?" Dallas asks, a big smile on her face.

"What?" June asks. June is clearly enjoying this silliness, but she's still got her gun in her hand and is still keeping her distance from Dallas.

"Their favorite song is 'If I only had a *brain!*'"

We all laugh, but it doesn't last long. The silence and stillness of the world seem to descend heavily. There's no road noise, no voices, no people.

It's just us the three of us on North Rim of the Grand Canyon with a psychotic, petty, wannabe warlord that is obsessed with June, and we have no way of escaping.

I get the jacket off the Z and toss it to Dallas. "It's going to be cold tonight," I say. "You're going to need this." The Z has a knife on his belt and I take both the knife and the belt, again wondering what a new zombie is doing here. I search the body, but there is nothing else worth taking.

When I stand back up, June is looking at the building where the Z came from. It's a tall L-shaped building with brown walls, a green roof, and several large garage doors. Behind it are two towering water tanks.

"Okay," I say, heading down the road to the building. There is really no choice—we need water.

In front of the building are two signs. One is brown with a half-circle of colors going from green to red and a pointer. It says "Grand Canyon National Park. Fire Danger

Today." except some joker scratched out "Fire" and carved in "zombie." The needle is pointed to "Low". The second sign says "Grand Canyon. North Rim. Emergency Services". It's made of wood, with the letters carved in as well as the National Park Service logo.

With the building's size and huge bay doors, it makes me wonder how many emergencies they were having up here. No doors are open and there are no vehicles in the semi-circular driveway or near the building.

I start down the far portion of the driveway past the signs, but June doesn't follow, she's staring at Dallas who is still on the road holding the jacket I gave her, a blank look on her face.

I walk back to June. "What do we do with her?"

She shrugs.

Dallas may be telling the truth, that she escaped Phantom Ranch in the chaos, or she might have been sent by Talia to... Well, I'm not sure there. Talia wants June, so Dallas could be here to kill me so June goes running back to Talia. That doesn't make sense, June wouldn't do that and Talia knows it.

Dallas is looking scared, her brown eyes wide as she studies us studying her. She's competent, but that is pretty much to be expected at this point post apocalypse.

We could tie her hands, similar to what Sal and Mary did to June and me when they captured us down in the Grand Canyon and cuffed us together, but I don't know if I can do that. If her intent is innocent, if she really is just trying to escape, that's not right.

And if her intent is not innocent? I don't know, but leaving someone with their hands tied to fight off hungry zombies doesn't seem like the kind of thing that is ever right.

Maybe since I've experienced fighting Zs while restrained, I'm extra sensitive here.

"We have a trust issue," I say, nodding back to the building. "There could be more Zs back there, but we need the water. We need to move quickly, stay alive, and find a way out of here, and that is going to be hard if we don't trust you."

Dallas nods and shrugs. "What can I do?"

And there really is nothing. Trust comes with time. It has to be demonstrated. June and I trust each other even though we haven't been together long because we have good reason to.

I look at June and she is clearly worried. If it was anyone but Talia that was the threat, I think she would have been much more assertive. She did, after all, fake her own death by zombie to escape Talia.

"We're going to check this place out," I say. "I suggest you stay out here, watch, come get us if you see anyone or anything coming."

I grab a stick, pull out my multi-tool, flick open the knife blade, and quickly sharpen the edge and toss it over to her. "Just in case."

Dallas picks up the stick, nods, and frowns. "But don't get too close to you guys, right?" she asks.

"Exactly."

June nods, hands me my gun, and we go in.

CHAPTER FORTY-FOUR

IT SEEMS like I've done this thing a thousand times. This is life now. You approach the unknown, slowly and warily, you map out your escape routes, you stay quiet and use your ears, you breathe deep through your nose so you can smell the Zs. You feel scared and excited at the same time, your heart rate elevated, your senses sharp.

The forest is quiet, just a breeze through the pine needles, some squirrels scrambling up a tree, and the cawing of the ravens that are all over the place up here.

The building looks to be in good condition, the shorter portion of the L jutting toward the road is all large bay doors like you'd see at a fire station, the right side of the building has large vehicle doors too. I imagine fire trucks inside and for a brief moment want to go find out, go fire one up and let the siren blare, chasing away the eerie silence. But it is only a moment, water is what we need.

June and I stay about five feet apart, we don't talk about it, it just feels natural.

We slowly circle around. There's a shed to our right

past two large dumpsters and the two large water tanks in back.

This is the first pass, we aren't getting aggressive, we are just looking, listening. Are there Zs here? Are there people here?

When we're out of sight of the road and Dallas, I nod towards the water tanks. "Let's circle around those too."

The tanks are huge, maybe ninety feet in diameter and twenty-five feet tall. They're painted a fading green and were clearly the water supply for the North Rim. There used to be a chain link fence around them, but someone removed it, leaving just the metal posts sticking up. I suspect that Phantom Company gets their water here when they are up.

June nods and we widen our path and slow down even more. The forest is thick and grows close to the tanks, the hill we followed the road up dropping off not far behind, our feet crunching on twigs and dried pine needles.

When we are back behind the right-most tank, I touch June on the arm and quietly say, "Do you think Talia sent Dallas?"

June's eyes scan our surroundings before meeting mine. "Good odds."

"And what is she here to do?"

"Separate us. Drive us apart. Remove the competition."

I'm staring at her, blinking. I mean, June is amazing and competent and beautiful. I can see how she is desirable. I can see how Talia would view me as the competition, but...

"Shit!" June hisses, squeezing my arm.

It's a group of five zombies shambling towards us. These look brand new too, like the one on the road. What the hell?

"No guns," I say, no longer bothering to whisper. "We don't know what else is around here."

June nods and we start moving back the way we came, out of the forest into the lot surrounding the building.

"Let's lead them out to the road," June says, "see what Dallas can do."

I nod and hand June the knife I pulled off the other zombie and holster the gun. I still have the tire iron.

"We've got five Zs," I call to Dallas as we get in sight of her. "Can you help us out?"

She nods and runs up to us, the stick I gave her in one hand and a big rock in the other. She doesn't look scared, not really, more tense. She looks like June does. Me, my stomach is doing backflips, but it does this every time I have to face a Z. Every time.

One bite and it's a guaranteed awful ending. A broken leg and you're done. Sprain your ankle, and that's probably going to be the end too.

I'm not really a warrior. I mean, I fight, like hell, when I have to, but I would just as soon not have to. The look on the two women's faces make me think they are both warriors. I'm not saying they're not scared, that they don't worry about the same things that I do. I just feel like they have that warrior spirit that I lack.

And gender norms be damned, I'm glad to have them. The zombie apocalypse did away with all that crap. When zombies are bearing down on you, you want warriors, man or woman doesn't matter a bit.

Well, that's true with us and with Talia's group, but probably not with the psychotic, petty, wannabe warlord in Flagstaff. Those dudes seemed to be going in the opposite direction.

"You two," June says to us, "stay behind me a bit."

The Zs snarl and snap and lurch towards us, the dank rotting smell of them filling my nose. We lead them out onto the wider main road, their attention focused on June who is the closest one to them.

This causes them to not be five Zs shoulder to shoulder, but a loose line of them. I see what she's doing, thinning them out a bit; they don't all move at the same pace.

We make our way down the road in the direction of the visitor's center and lodge, staying about five yards away from them. In a few minutes, they are a single-file line with a big burly male zombie in the lead, and a flannel-shirted female right behind him. The other three have fallen a few seconds behind. Both of the lead zombies have backpacks on and show minimal damage. They're recent zombies and a bit slow for it, the fungus not having as good control over them as it soon will.

I come up even with June and see that Dallas does the same. "Now?"

June sheaths her knife and pulls her gun. "Now."

I rush the big guy and swing the tire iron hard, connecting the thicker, bent end with his head.

I am dimly aware of Dallas taking on the female Z, but don't have any attention to spare.

My blow is glancing and he stumbles, but no real damage done. I am so missing my baseball bat, I would have taken him out with one swing.

I dance back, my foot catching on a crack in the pavement and I almost go down, my attention away from the zombie and on staying upright.

When I look back up, the snapping jaw of the Z is too damn close, but suddenly he is pulled back. It's Dallas, who grabs him by his backpack and yanks him, giving me the moment I need. I rush in and shove the pointed end of the tire iron through his eye socket and he goes down.

The female Z is down and then June is there with her knife and it's three living versus three dead.

These are good odds. My butterflies are gone, my breath coming fast, my heart beating hard. The butterflies have been replaced with the adrenaline of survival. I don't think of Talia or that impending threat, I don't worry about how little we know about Dallas, I don't even think of the future I so want to have with June. It's just the fight now, just survival.

We spread out a bit, a Z heading towards each of us, mine a young man with a scruffy brown beard and a beanie askew on his head, greasy black hair sticking out.

I go in with the tire iron ready. I let him grab me and pull me towards him. I use that momentum and shove the sharp end in his eye as hard as I can... and he goes down.

I look up and June has a middle-aged female zombie she is working with. She rushes in, aims a kick at the Z's knee and then rushes out. Smart.

I look for Dallas and she's in trouble. A big male Z is on her and she seems to have lost both her weapons, which were just a rock and a hastily sharpened stick, for which I feel bad.

I rush over and grab him by the backpack and yank him off her. The Z goes down and I stomp on his chest and swing hard with the tire iron. It makes a mess, unleashing a fungal funk as his head splits open, but it does the job.

I look up and June is on top of her Z, her knife flashing down to its head.

And then Dallas is on me. Hugging me hard, pressing her not insubstantial curves against me.

"Thank you, thank you," she whispers breathlessly. "I... It..." She's shaking, and even though she has that warrior vibe, I can't say I blame her. She was under equipped and was in a bad spot.

"Yeah... Sure... Thanks for your help." I pat her on the back.

I can smell her sweat and the funk of the zombie, but I have to say it feels nice to have her pressed against me. And I feel bad that it feels nice. But I was alone for many months, and she is attractive, and it is only natural.

I had one post-apocalyptic relationship, and let's just say that it ended rather badly.

Dallas is sniffing and I can see June staring at us. The look on her face is hard to read, one eyebrow raised a bit, her lips pursed, her brow furrowed, but not in that decidedly cute way.

I try to give June a "what can I do?" look and open my arms so it's clear who is hugging who.

"I owe you my life, Woody," Dallas says. "Seriously. I'm... I'm forever in your debt."

I slowly push her away and connect with her brown eyes. She seems sincere.

"Any time, Dallas," I say. "You helped me, I helped you." I shrug and walk over towards June, making my eyes wide, to kind of say "what the hell," but she's not looking at me. She's examining the Z she took down and suddenly I'm worried. Does June think I like Dallas? And with another woman around will I ever have the conversation with June that we need to have?

But I shake all that romantic crap off. It's still survival time and we need to figure out what's going on with these new Zs and find a way out of here.

CHAPTER FORTY-FIVE

WE'VE ENCOUNTERED six zombies since we got here. Four of them have backpacks, all of them seem to be new Zs. This is a stroke of good fortune—for us, not for this poor recently alive group. It's lucky because backpacks mean supplies when we had little chance of finding any up here.

It's also a mystery. How did they get here? How did they die? Six equipped humans can handle quite a few Zs in an isolated environment like this, especially this late in the zombie game.

We're all standing there breathing deeply of the cool air, staring at the bodies, the silence again feeling sudden and somehow ominous. A place like this, there should be noise.

Both June and Dallas are looking at me. Somehow, I am the leader, because I have the most knowledge of the area, although I suspect both of them are better trained for it than I am.

June was in the Army. Dallas was... well, she was part of Talia's Phantom Company, but I wouldn't be surprised to learn that she has some military training too.

"Okay," I say, trying to get my brain moving. "Let's get anything usable off them and let's find out how they turned. These Zs are new and that is bothering me."

I can't say that I trust Dallas at this point, but it seems like it's time to give her some more autonomy and get her better equipped. June is keeping her distance from Dallas and that's just fine.

There's no more talking and we all get to work on these five Zs and I go back and drag over the one that I took care of on the way in, shooing the ravens away that were having a meal.

We pull backpacks, jackets, shirts, knives, belts, guns, canteens, and search pockets. We even find a couple of life-straw portable water filters, a bigger hand-pump water filter, and a hunting rifle that June claims. I get a pair of boots my size, and we get their socks—they'll need to be washed, but hey, socks can make all the difference when you are on the move all the time.

A group of ravens have taken up residence in the pine trees around us and are cawing up a storm. They're hungry, they want us to leave the Zs to them. In some ways this is comforting, the circle of life continues. In other ways it's just creepy, all these big birds with shiny black feathers and big beaks staring at the proceedings.

We've got a pile of the usable gear off to the side and the Zs are down to their skivvies—no one seems interested in inheriting zombie underwear (except for the socks). We all have our limits.

"How did they die?" I ask.

We stand there gazing at the pale but nearly normal-looking bodies. The heads are a mess from our fight, but the rest of them look... normal. Entirely normal. The normal scrapes and cuts and bruises you'd see on anyone living out of doors. No bites, beyond bug bites. No gunshot wounds. Nothing out of the ordinary.

"Shit," June says.

"What the..." Dallas adds in.

"This is not good," I say.

Suddenly we have a problem bigger than if we can trust Dallas or if Talia is coming after June or even if June likes me.

We have new zombies that don't have any bite marks or other obvious causes of death.

We might just have a new way that humans turn.

Shit.

CHAPTER FORTY-SIX

"ZOMBIE 101," I begin, pacing on the paved road to the North Rim lodge in front of the stripped-down zombie bodies, scraping my foot on the debris time has deposited. "We all know this, but maybe saying it will jar something loose."

June and Dallas nod.

"First, zombies are driven by a parasitic, fungal infection, source unknown." I throw June a smile, but she's not having any of it.

"Fungal?" Dallas asks.

I nod and detour, explaining how old zombies have a white mass in their skulls that looks like a big head of cauliflower and white threads of fungal fiber running throughout their bodies. I tell Dallas about the dissection June and I did on the South Rim.

"Okay," I continue, "fungus-head zombies driven by a parasitic infection that we all have. We die, we turn into a zombie. We get bit and zombie spit in the blood stream supercharges the infection and we die and then turn into a zombie. I also think that if we ingest too much zombie goo... you know, blood, splattered brains, etcetera... well, you get the picture." I stop and point at the arrayed corpses. "No bite marks, they're not covered in recent zombie splatter, something else killed them, but what?"

"Virus?" Dallas offers.

"Infection?" June says.

"Right. Something all six of them were exposed to. Either they all ingested it or it was communicable. And that means..."

"We better hope for ingestion," June says.

"Because if it was a contagion," Dallas says, biting her thumbnail, "we are all so very screwed."

I nod. "So next step, see if they have a camp around here, see if we can find something they might all have ingested. And that means, we can't eat their food or drink their water."

We had found some canned goods, dried fruit, and even a couple power bars in their packs. We are all hungry, so not eating is a big sacrifice. Not drinking, an even bigger deal.

"And we need to find water," June says. Her lips are chapped as are all of ours. It is, fortunately, not hot, but we are getting more and more dehydrated, and how these people died won't matter if we don't get water pretty soon.

I look up at the sky through the pine trees. We have about two hours before the sun goes down and it gets cold. "And we need shelter," I add.

I don't say that we need to get out of here and get away from Talia and Phantom Company. That doesn't need saying.

Without further discussion, the three of us head back past the physical plant and to the water tanks where June and I had encountered the Zs. We all have knives on our belts, but June snagged the two guns the Zs had on them, so Dallas doesn't have a firearm. Not trust yet, but more of a "bigger fish to fry right now" kind of a thing.

The camp doesn't take long to find, it is in the woods just behind the water tanks. Three tents outfitted with propane lanterns, air mattresses, and sleeping bags.

My first thought is, wow, luxury. My next thought is, that is way too much crap to be hauling around when zombies are chasing you.

June is close, her elbow brushing mine as we approach through the fir trees. She's got her gun out and I've got the tire iron in hand. Dallas is a few yards to our left with a knife in hand as if she understands the temporary truce we have here with trust.

"A van!" Dallas says, and runs right through the camp before we've had a chance to check it for the living and the dead.

It's an old white cargo van that was driven around the water tanks and hidden behind some trees. She opens the door; the light comes on and it dings a warning that the keys are in the ignition.

"It's got half a tank of gas," she calls back excitedly.

My brain freezes. This is what we need. Gear and escape from Talia. But, what happened here? I don't want to fall into the same trap these folks did—provided that it's even avoidable.

"Should we..." I begin nodding towards Dallas and the van.

June shakes her head. "Let her leave if that's what she wants, but I don't think it is." She ends up looking at me pointedly.

I hold my hands up. "Hey, that hug thing was all her."

A brief smile plays on her lips. "Don't pretend you didn't enjoy it."

I feel my cheeks flush. "I won't. But she's not who I want to be with."

And here it is. Another potential moment. June's deep blue eyes lock with mine, no danger falling on us this very moment, the sweet smell of pine and fir trees in the air, the cool breeze playing with her short black hair, and then...

Hooooonk. "Come on, guys!" Dallas yells. "Let's get the hell out of here before Phantom Company gets here."

I sigh and June chuckles.

"Hold on," I yell. "We need to figure out what happened."

Now that I'm not lost in the deep blue ocean of June's eyes, I can smell something dank just underneath the sweet vanillay pine trees and the sharper scent of the firs.

"What? Are you kidding me!?" Dallas yells.

"Better go explain it to your girlfriend," June says, but I can see the smile on her face. "And get her to stop making so much noise."

Shaking my head, I walk over to give Dallas the news.

CHAPTER FORTY-SEVEN

"SO... why didn't you just kiss her," Dallas asks, her voice low and conspiratorial when I get over to the van. The window is rolled down and she's in the driver's seat leaning towards me, a smile playing on her full lips.

"It's complicated," I say.

"It wouldn't be for me," she says, her eyes looking me up and down and my heart pounding hard. "Seriously, it wouldn't be complicated, Woody."

I sigh.

"Things are so uncertain, I'd have fun whenever I could if I could land a good guy like you."

"Dallas..."

"Come on, I'm not repulsive, although I haven't had a bath in a while." She takes a sniff at one of her armpits and wrinkles her nose rather comically.

"Look, we are going to try to figure out what happened to these six. Can you—"

"If we were a thing," she says, cutting me off, "we'd be in this van celebrating being alive right now."

My jaw is agape and I am sure I look like a fool, my heart now pounding in my ears.

"Right now," she whispers, leaning even closer, and I can smell her sweaty scent. It's not altogether bad and she's not altogether unattractive and I am healthy enough to be feeling exactly what she wants me to be feeling.

Seconds tick by in slow motion and we're just there, our faces close, her brown eyes wide, her face dead serious. My body at war with my mind.

My meeting with June was wary and comical, this Dallas is aggressive and... Well, I'm not sure exactly what she is, and part of my logical brain—the part that is barely functioning—knows this may all be part of Talia's plan to get me away from June.

"We... I..." I stammer.

Dallas laughs and shakes her head and then louder says, "Sure, Woody, I'll help search the camp." And then quieter she adds, "The offer stands, Mr. Beckman, any time you want to take me up on it... anytime, anywhere."

CHAPTER FORTY-EIGHT

IT'S like the world has changed or something as we all search the camp. I notice how tight Dallas's tank-top is and how generously endowed she is, how strong her long legs are. I mean, I noticed all that before, but now I really *notice*. I see her smile lines as cute and her brown eyes as soulful.

Stupid, I know. Biology in action, nothing more, but that doesn't negate the powerful hormones in biology's arsenal, and Dallas sure knew how to use those weapons.

I find myself isolating from the two women, facing away so I can't see either of them while I search. Seeing June makes me feel guilty and seeing Dallas makes me feel... well, I think you get the picture.

The camp has the three tents, a fire ring, some pots and pans for cooking, and a hatchet. It's perched just beyond the water tank before the hill drops steeply off, the tents situated where the trees allow but in sight of each other. I grab the hatchet and shove the handle into my belt. If I can't have a bat, a hatchet is much more appealing than a tire iron.

"Over here," June calls.

She's at the back of the water tank closest to camp where there are some large pipes and valves.

"They were collecting water here," June says when I get close, pointing to a large pipe jutting out of the bottom of the dull-green tank, with a big valve, a 90-degree turn pointing the open end down. It is slowly dripping water into a metal pot that's overflowing.

"Smart," I say.

June looks up, her eyes serious and she shakes her head, pointing to the pipe which has long bone-white tendrils of something coming out. Each drip of water slides down a tendril into the bucket. Drip. Drip. Drip.

The tendrils are maybe an inch long and look remarkably like the fungus we found running through the arm of the zombie we dissected. I squat down by June and look in the pipe—it's full of the white stuff and my nose fills with the heavy fungal funk of it, the source of the dank scent I smelled earlier.

I stand up and step back, suddenly hot, and look up at the water tanks. The fungus spores must have gotten in there and thrived in the moist, closed atmosphere.

"Shit!" I say. Not eloquent, I know, but I have no other words.

"So what's the deal over here?" Dallas asks, sauntering up, and I am thankful that the fear of fungal parasite hormones has totally swamped the horny young man hormones.

"Fungus water," I say, pointing at the large pipe, which must be some sort of emergency drain. I rub at my nose which is still full of the stench I sucked in while up close. "They drank fungus water. I guess it killed them."

Dallas is staring at the white strands, blinking. "Before...

before you told me about the fungus-heads, I would have... I would have drunk that water."

June nods solemnly and gets up, looking at me.

"Okay," I say with a sigh, trying to get my head back in the game. "Grab the sleeping bags and lanterns, let's load up the van and get the hell out of here."

"No tents?" Dallas asks, giving me a look that I am sure is meant to be sultry, but the fungus-creeps are still with me.

"In a zombie apocalypse, tents are dumb. We need to see the Zs coming."

"Right," Dallas says with a nod and then raises her middle finger and points it to the south. "We are out of here, Phantom Company and crazy Talia. Eat me!" She whoops and runs to a tent and starts pulling gear out.

I'm staring at Dallas, and beside me June sighs.

"What were you and your girlfriend talking about for so long?" June asks.

I look at her and there is no smile there this time.

"She... I..." My face is red and my blood pressure is going up, yet again.

"I need to know, Woody. Seriously."

Dallas has her arms loaded with sleeping bags and is running towards the van, chanting obscenities at Talia.

"She offered me... umm... herself," I say. I don't know how else to put it. I don't know if it was a relationship she was offering, or even what a relationship would be like with Dallas.

June's eyes look sad and she smiles weakly. "Ahh... I thought so."

"What?" I began. "How could you—"

"Oh, please, Woody. She couldn't have been telegraphing it more obviously if she had been wearing a T-shirt that said, 'Take me, Woody.'"

I shake my head, dumbfounded. I didn't really see it. And that makes me wonder what I'm missing with June.

"Everything I said to you stands," I say to June.

She smiles, her blue eyes brighter. "And that makes you a smart man."

My mouth is moving, but I don't know what to say.

"Talia," she whispers, taking my hand and squeezing it. "I don't know if this is all Dallas, all Talia, or something in between."

She lets go of my hand, walks to the nearest tent, and starts pulling gear out.

I take a stone and scratch the word "TOXIC" on the pipe to hopefully keep more people from dying. Phantom Company may still be using it and as much as I hate Talia, there are some good people down there. As I squat there, my nose stinging from the strength of the moldy-fungus smell, I realize that closed water stores like this, all over the country, probably have the same thing happening. A new wave of zombies is rising up right now.

I then write "TOXIC" in large letters on the back of both water tanks. It's not much, but it's something, at least.

After I'm done, I watch the two of them for just a few seconds, before shaking my head and joining them.

CHAPTER FORTY-NINE

THERE IS ONLY one paved road out of the North Rim of the Grand Canyon, Route 67. It runs about forty-five miles from the Canyon north to Jacob Lake across the Kaibab Plateau.

The land is gorgeous, rolling grass meadows flanked with fir/spruce forests with a sprinkling of aspen and pine trees. As dusk settles in, we drive through a burned-out section of the forest, the opportunistic aspens first up after the fire, short and thick, the scared trunks of the taller trees ghostly among them. It looks and feels post-apocalyptic, and I guess it really is. The fire was the apocalypse, the new aspen forest, although far too dense, is the beginning for the "post" apocalypse. The forest will be different, but it's returning. It's grim, but it somehow gives me hope.

By the time we get to Jacob Lake, it's dark. Our journey was slowed by several wrecks in the road we had to scout and slowly get around.

On the way, June peppered Dallas with questions such as: Does Phantom Company have vehicles and gas stores at the ready on the North Rim?—yes, but she had no idea where. How far do they range to the north?—they have been to Fredonia, but met another group in Kanab and one in Colorado City and haven't been farther. What kind of force would likely come after them?—enough to get the job done.

All of this made Jacob Lake not a great place to stop, but we needed to stop. We had eaten the power bars now that we were pretty sure the fungus water had killed them, but we had left all their water, fearing that it was contaminated.

Jacob Lake is at eight thousand feet in the middle of a ponderosa pine forest. The stop isn't much more than a gas station—and we need gas—a gift shop, restaurant, and inn, a visitor's center, and a campground.

There are enough cars here so that I'm not worried about a random van being spotted. Going down a forest service road would be more discrete, but then we would be easily trapped. Here there are multiple escape routes.

The gas station is old-fashioned with a flat-roof covering the pumps and a single-vehicle garage, the only one around for many miles.

I pull up to the edge of the roof and say, "Let's figure out how to get up there for the night. Even if they come, they won't be able to see us."

June smiles and eyes the height. We found some rope in the van so if we can get someone up there, we can all get up there. It won't make for a fast getaway, but it has been a couple of days since June and I have slept, and we need rest.

"What?" Dallas says. "That's just..." She trails off when she sees our faces.

"We like roofs," I say, smiling at June.

"Oh, get a room, you two... please!"

CHAPTER FIFTY

EVEN STANDING on top of the van, the roof is too high, but the rope is long enough to lob over the short side, get it tied to one of the poles, and from the roof of the van, June scrambles up.

"Well?" I yell up.

June appears on the edge, her hands on her hips, illuminated by the lanterns we've got going. "It'll work. We can get the rope anchored up here and then pull it up after everyone and everything is up."

It takes about an hour to haul all the gear up and stash the van in front of the inn, where it hopefully won't be noticed. I even unhook the battery, open the van door, and toss a bunch of pine needles in and dirty up the windshield so it looks like all the other vehicles. I kick around the debris in the parking lot so it's not obvious I just drove it there. I'm last to climb up, and with the van gone, I have to climb all the way up the rope. It's not as high as the dog food plant in Flagstaff, but in my diminished state, it's a challenge despite the knots we put in the rope.

After I'm up, we pull up the rope and gather around a single lantern right in the middle of the metal roof. Comfortable, it's not, but it's safe from Zs and hidden from the living.

The night is cold and the sleeping bags are welcome as we sit there. Dallas hands me an open can of green beans with a fork in it, and I gratefully get all the moisture out of it I can.

It helps, but it's not enough. I've got that spiking pain in my head that is a warning that dehydration is going to get serious soon.

June pulls her gun out and points it at Dallas. "Time to tell us everything."

I didn't know she was going to do this and my tired body dumps more adrenaline in my bloodstream. Not much, but some. Enough to, weirdly, make me feel even more tired as my heart beats hard.

Above, the Milky Way is strewn over us and I wish I could just lie down, hold June's hand, and stare at the stars for the ten seconds it would take me to fall asleep.

"I have told you the truth," Dallas says dryly, as if she doesn't believe she's in real danger. I know June a little better than she does and am quite sure she *is* in real danger.

"Not all of it," June says calmly as if she's commenting on the weather in San Diego—yes, it's going to be yet another beautiful, sunny day.

"All of it," Dallas says.

"Bullshit." June cocks the gun.

"Is this about me taking a shot with your boy toy?"

My adrenalized mind is spinning, this is not the kind of thing you want to get into the middle of, but I don't want any lives to end here tonight.

Even if Dallas is here to split June and me up, not that I

can say we are truly "together"... Okay, that's not fair. We are partners, we have been working as a team. We are "together," just not in the sense of being a couple.

"Why don't you just tell us what happened last night," I offer. "Go slow. Give us all the details."

I try to catch June's eye, but she is focused on Dallas.

Dallas takes a deep breath and sighs. "I was on sentry duty at the Kaibab Bridge, there are two sentries on each of those at all times. I was with Trent, who has the annoying habit of watching me more than the bridge, even in the dark. He's way too old for me and just stinks of desperation. Anyway, we both see the unusual flicker of light from The Ranch a little after 2:00 a.m. and I knew it was you guys and I knew it meant you were trying to escape.

"Talia talked about you," Dallas nods towards June and in fact her gaze has been fixed on June the whole time. It doesn't seem to matter at all that I'm here. "I knew that you were smart and tough and I knew that this was my chance. So, I left Trent, telling him it was a fire and he'd have to watch all on his own."

"Don't you have walkie talkies?" June asks. "Didn't you check in first before leaving? Didn't Trent?"

She smiles and shakes her head. "No, and I took the walkie with me and ditched it later. Trent isn't the brightest bulb."

June nods for her to continue.

Dallas shrugs and glances at me briefly. "I liked the look of you too, so I took a chance and followed. I saw your stand-off, freezing my ass off in the creek. After Talia, Sal, and Harris left, I waited a while and followed."

She shrugs as if that explains everything, but it really doesn't. This could be the truth, this could be a lie. Maybe that's what the shrug is about—take it or leave it, I can't prove it anyway.

June sighs and shakes her head. My eyes burn I'm so tired and my headache is even worse. It has been less than twenty-four hours since we set that fire at Phantom Ranch and a lot has happened. We are all exhausted.

The silence just hangs there, thick and nearly tangible. June and Dallas staring at each other as if it's some kind of contest.

"I wish we could believe you," I finally say, because I can't stand the tension. "But Talia could have told you all that and sent you on after us."

Dallas meets my eyes, the lantern putting her look of distaste in rough relief. "I hate that bitch," Dallas spits out. "Risking my life like this, chasing you with no weapon, no water..." She shakes her head and holds up her scraped hand. "No. I wouldn't do that for Talia." She sighs, her shoulders falling, and suddenly she looks as tired as I feel. "I left food, shelter, and security to take a chance with you two. I'm sorry you can't see it."

And then she's crying. Not like at the Supai Tunnel, this time it's a quieter, more controlled weeping, her eyes flicking between me and June. I feel that weird knee-jerk need to do something to make it stop, but I shove it down and just sit there, my mouth dry, my head hurting, and my eyes heavy.

It doesn't go on, she soon wraps her sleeping bag tight around her and lies down.

I look at June, wondering what the hell we do now. We can't let her go, even if she isn't working for Talia; she might run right back to her.

"I'll take first watch and wake you in a few hours," June

says. I open my mouth to object and she cuts me off. "Just get some sleep, Woody. We're all too tired to think."

I nod and lie down on the hard roof and stare up at the Milky Way, bright and sparkling above us. It takes me far less than ten seconds to fall asleep.

CHAPTER FIFTY-ONE

MY MOUTH IS dry and my eyes thick with sleep as consciousness slowly returns. At first it feels like a dream, just a brief bit of pre-apocalypse paranoia. I can hear people talking about me, the noise of it like buzzing flies I just want to shoo away.

I'm back in my bed in Phoenix in a two-bedroom apartment I share with two other guys. I'm enrolled in community college taking business and accounting courses, waiting tables to pay the bills, trying to claw my way out of minimum wage work.

We all had different hours in that cramped, thin-walled apartment, and I often heard people talking about me while I was sleeping. My half-asleep brain would hear my name and imagine that they were saying bad things about me, that each laugh was at my expense. I hated it, but I wasn't about to go crawling back to Mom and Dad and sleep in my old room, which had been converted into a workout room with a treadmill that no one used.

My hip and shoulder hurt and the air has a cold bite to

it and I realize that I'm not stuck in the mundane treadmill of making money, paying bills, and trying to sneak in some fun. I'm a survivor in a post-apocalypse America on a different kind of treadmill. Fight zombies, avoid the living, survive, laugh a little to make life worth living.

My eyes flutter open and I see the tops of pine trees and a grey clouded sky behind them, illuminated by the pre-dawn light. My breath puffs out in condensate in front of me.

"Put that damn gun down," I hear a female voice say. It's a bit deep and speaks the order as if it's used to being obeyed. "We don't want to alert them to our presence if they're still here."

"But, sir," a gruff male voice says, "the deer. We could use the meat."

My brain begins to engage as I slowly, regretfully, wake all the way up. Both voices are familiar.

"I swear to God, Sal, with Jesus as my witness above and Gaia below, I will beat you senseless where you stand if you keep questioning my orders."

Talia!

I sit up and suck in a breath, my not-quite-awake brain getting ready to sound the alarm when a cold hand is clamped over my mouth.

"Don't. Say. A word," June hisses in my ear.

Fully awake, I nod and she takes her hand off my mouth and I look around. Dallas is sitting there, her brown hair disheveled, her eyes wide, a sleeping bag still around her body.

June's blue eyes look filled with sleep too, and she's sitting up in a sleeping bag, the fatigue must have gotten her while she watched and she fell asleep too.

"Goddamn Dallas," Talia says from below us, the sound

of her combat boots smacking on the pavement a steady rhythm. "I gave that girl one thing to do. Distract a horny boy. How hard is that?" There's a pause, and the tapping of boots stop. "Well, Sal, how goddamn hard is that?"

June's nostrils flare and she slowly pulls the gun out of her sleeping bag and points it at Dallas in a "we might all be screwed, but you'll be first" kind of gesture.

There is a sloshing sound and the distinct scent of gas fumes.

"Wouldn't think it be hard," Sal said, "seeing how he was still in his twenties and... Shit!"

"What!?" Talia asks.

"Oh. False alarm," Sal says. "All good. Plenty of gas left and no sign of the lock being tampered with. Just some air in the line."

"Well, where the hell are they?" Talia says. "Dallas was under strict orders to not let them get any farther than Jacob Lake."

Dallas is hugging her chest with her arms, her head down, her eyes not meeting either of ours.

We don't move. We hardly breathe, until we hear Talia and Sal get in a pickup truck and drive away.

Then June cocks the gun and points it at Dallas's head.

CHAPTER FIFTY-TWO

WHAT OFFENSE CAN one human do to another that justifies murder in cold blood? Justifies as in "just," as in right, as in something you can live with. And by "live with" I mean be able to sleep at night.

Hell if I know.

Dallas has certainly danced near that line with us, but has she crossed it?

"I told you the truth," Dallas says after the truck is out of the area. "I did try to escape. I did witness your little showdown where Talia threatened to blow your boyfriend's brains out." The girls are once again having a conversation between them, and while I am the object of much of it, it doesn't really matter that I am here.

I can't say that I like the feeling all that much.

"But Talia caught me after you two left," Dallas continues. "She was so mad, but she's smart. She heard about me noticing Woody in the mess hall—everyone's a gossip down there—so she told me that if I took care of Woody then I could have my freedom."

"Took care of me?" I ask.

Dallas looks at me, but only briefly as if I am some kind of annoyance in all of this. "She was very specific that I should not kill you unless I had to, that would leave you martyred to June and she would forever wonder what might have been."

"And we can't have that, can we," I say, injecting as much sarcasm as I can into the phrase. And given the headache and dehydration and hunger, it isn't all that much. But she's not paying attention to me anyway.

"And what of the leverage we established against Talia in what you call our 'stand off'?" June asks.

The leverage was that June knew of Talia's messy past in Afghanistan and what had happened in Albuquerque with her jealousy and the band she led there post-apocalypse. (Maybe I should just start abbreviating that as post-A, it's a little long and I'm tired of writing it.) The leverage is how we got Talia to let us leave.

"Yeah. That," Dallas says with a smirk. "I asked Talia and she told me she was going to 'confess' to the entire Company as soon she got back."

I'm staring, a question on my face. I have clearly missed something.

June throws me a wry smile. "Talia was going to get ahead of it and tell her side of the story, which will be incomplete, at the least, and make her come out looking very good."

I shake my head, those psychotic, petty, wannabe warlords have a lot of tricks up their sleeves. This time, the "psychotic" part of it being at the forefront. They are definitely part of the "ends justifies the means" crowd.

"And what means will she use to find us?" June asks.

Dallas shrugs. "It would be a guess."

June gestures casually with her gun. "So, guess."

"Talia will go back before the end of today. Phantom Company means more to her than you do, and she never leaves for too long. After that, she'll send a small team after you, probably led by Harris. He's..." Her face gets this faraway look and then her lips purse in a sour expression. "He's good. He'll find you."

June nods, her face hard, not betraying any emotions. Me? I'd just as soon pee my pants, but I'm too damn dehydrated.

"And what should I do with you?" June asks.

The question surprises me, and judging by Dallas's expression, it surprises her too.

She's silent for a long time before she says, "No matter what I say, you can't trust my motives. If the situation was reversed, I'd kill you, but I wouldn't use that gun with them in the area."

June nods slowly. "Stand up. Hold your hands high. Turn your back to me."

I want to say something, but my mouth is so dry and I just can't think.

Dallas does as she is told.

June slowly walks up to her and says quietly, "You know, I like you. I wish this could be different."

"Likewise," Dallas says.

With that, June slowly releases the hammer on the gun, grabs the gun by the barrel, and hits Dallas hard on the head with the butt.

Dallas goes down in a heap.

My mouth is open, I am trying to speak, when June's blue eyes meet mine.

"Don't worry," she says. "We're not like them."

CHAPTER FIFTY-THREE

AS THE SUN crests the horizon, the thin orange glow is harsh on my tired eyes, we move quickly. I make sure Dallas is still breathing and tie her up. We leave her a can of food, her backpack, and sleeping bag.

We're not like them.

This is the thought that keeps bouncing around my head, keeps me fighting through the dehydration. The air is cool and my limbs don't quite obey me at first, but it gets better as I warm up.

We're not like them.

I sneak a few looks at June, and if I was taken with her before, well, it's an entirely different thing now. She has retained her humanity which, right at that moment, seems more important than survival, and sexier too.

On top of the can of peas, I put the sharp metal lid to the can we had last night. She can use it to cut through her rope, albeit a little slowly.

We are giving her a chance.

I slide down the rope and pull the van around. I use the

tire iron and break through the lock to the gas tanks, use the ball pump and tubing that was in the van to pump the tank full and three plastic gas cans that were in there.

June slides down the rope and lands on top of the van, cuts the rope and throws it back up top.

Dallas will have a six-foot drop getting down. Her feet will sting like hell, but it will be doable. I put her knife on top of one of the gas pumps; she'll need it if she's to survive.

June and I do all this with very little conversation. Talia is out here. We have to find another place to hide before Dallas wakes up or anyone from Phantom Company comes back around.

For the moment, our plan is simple. Head out into the forest service roads, find a cow tank, I know they are out here, and get some water. Stay ahead of Phantom Company.

We're not like them.

Suddenly I am no longer wondering whether June likes me or anything like that. It just doesn't matter. June and I are a "we." I'll happily take whatever that means.

In the van, June cracks open a can of black beans and we slowly eat it, careful to get every bit of moisture. Even that little bit of water clears my head some and I suddenly feel optimistic, like there is actually a chance for June and me.

I grin at her as I start the van up. "How many zombies does it take to woo the girl?" I ask.

She opens her mouth as if to speak and then her brow furrows, her beautiful eyes meeting mine and her face softening. "Not gonna happen, they lack the *braainnnss,*" she offers, punctuating it with a little giggle.

"Well, yeah, but that's not it," I say.

She shrugs. "Well, I don't know then. How many zombies *does* it take to woo the girl?"

"They can't do it," I say with a smile. "She's got her heart set on a baseball-obsessed guy named Woody from Phoenix, Arizona."

She's quiet for a moment and my heart leaps thinking I've misjudged the situation. She's just not into me. She's only staying because she needs me to survive—ha, as if! And then she slowly nods, her eyes connecting with mine again. "Yup, that's about the size of it."

I pull us out of Jacob Lake and head onto 89A to the east with the biggest smile in the post-apocalyptic world on my face.

Sure, we've got June's obsessed ex on our trail, God knows what Dallas will be like when she wakes up, and the entire undead population of the Desert Southwest would love to snack on us, but June and I are a "we."

And that is a lot pre- or post-apocalypse.

PART SIX

WOODY AND JUNE VERSUS PHANTOM COMPANY

DESPERATE TIMES CALL FOR FOOLISH MEASURES

CHAPTER FIFTY-FOUR

TWO BIRDS LAND on the boulder June and I are crouched behind. They are nothing special, I couldn't even tell you what kind of birds they are. They are small with mottled brown feathers, a white breast, and a long beak. The two of them light there and stare at us for a moment.

The sky above is an azure blue and disorganized cumulonimbus clouds squat on the western horizon, threatening to bring spring rain to the juniper-pinion forest.

I stare at the birds as their heads bob briefly and somehow they give me some hope. I see those birds as June and I flitting through the forest looking for safety, for sanctuary, for sustenance and rest.

They're not love birds or anything romantic like that. Just two birds deep in the forest of the Kaibab Plateau trying to survive. Like June and me.

Except those two birds aren't being hunted by a group of post zombie apocalypse survivors that live at the bottom of the Grand Canyon and call themselves "Phantom Company." They haven't been on the run for the last three days with little food and little sleep and no time to say what they need to say to each other.

"You good with the plan?" June asks, her blue eyes hard. It's been too long since we had even a semblance of peace or more than the most forced of laughs. Talia, June's ex, is the head of Phantom Company and she wants her back. At any cost at this point. And "any cost" means whether I live or die matters not one bit.

Well, that's not really true. Talia would much prefer me dead at this point.

"No, I'm not good with this plan," I say.

She sighs and nods, her hand brushing at her short black hair, her gaze flicking to her hunting rifle. "We're not like them, Woody. I will not be aiming to kill."

One of June's most attractive qualities, beyond her olive complexion, striking blue eyes, and athletic, petite, pixie frame, is that she's retained her humanity through all she has been through post-A (post-apocalypse, that is. It's a mouthful, so I'm going to shorten it from now on).

I shake my head. I don't like that part of the plan—the shooting—but have come to accept it, but it's not what bothers me the most. "June, I..."

June smiles, it's a wistful little thing. "At this point Talia or her people will kill you on sight. You know this. If it goes bad, I'm turning myself in. It's the only way."

I nod, a knot in my stomach to make the Gordian Knot look like child's play. Truth is, I have become extremely attached to June during our fifteen days of "Woody and June versus the Apocalypse." In some perverse way, they've become the best fifteen days of my life and that is without us kissing... even once.

Survival is the first rule of each day, and we have been fully engaged with that, being chased by Phantom

Company down these old forest service roads. Laughter is my second rule of the day, and I've been hard pressed to find any humor at all. My third (and very new) rule is to spend time with June. And on that count, I've spent a lot of time with her while we've been running around the forest, but it hasn't exactly been quality time.

She takes my hand, her eyes betraying a flicker of fear. She's terrified of Talia, this, the strongest, most competent woman I've ever met. Hell, the strongest, most competent human I've ever met. She faked her death, by zombie no less, in Albuquerque to escape Talia. It was just a freak accident that we all ended up at the bottom of the Grand Canyon.

"I need you to survive, Woody." She squeezes my hand and I swear for a moment she's about to cry.

"We should have made a break for it on 89A," I say. It's not the first time I've said it, and only about the ten-thousandth time I've thought it.

"She had ambushes set up in both directions," June says. "I guarantee it."

I nod and peak up over the rocks, but no vehicles are present yet. They're coming. We are sure of it, and our van is stuck, we're almost out of water, and all roads out of here are blocked by Phantom Company.

For the last three days, they've been herding us to the southeast until we lost quite a bit of elevation. The pine trees have been replaced by shorter pinion and juniper trees, the cow ponds we have been getting water from disappeared, and the roads have gotten so bad, that the van finally got epically and truly stuck.

"I need you to survive too, June," I say. Two weeks ago, I was determined to live, and die, alone in this world gone insane, but now someone else, June, is more important to me than myself. It's not the "I love you" I feel, but I'm not sure she's ready to hear it, and right before what is about to come is not the right time to say it.

The two birds fly away and June shoulders her hunting rifle and takes bead on the barely-there dirt road leading towards us.

I check the two guns and the clips laid out that are my part of this. I grab the binoculars and start scanning the forest.

It's time.

CHAPTER FIFTY-FIVE

GIVE ME ZS ANY DAY, a whole horde of them, no problem, even the annoying horde of tourist zombies that chased us into the Grand Canyon and got us into this mess. I'd gladly take them on, just keep all the psychotic, petty, wannabe warlords... please. Keep all the humans that shed their humanity so quickly when everything went to hell. Keep those that care more about power and more about being right than their fellow non-zombie human.

Keep them, please.

When the first vehicle appears, a white "U.S. Park Ranger" SUV, June takes out a tire and puts a bullet through the radiator, steam hissing up.

All their vehicles are the same. These SUVs were the park police vehicles and they must have taken them from the Emergency Services building where we found the new zombies, their camp, the deadly fungus water, and the van.

It's a strange kind of battle between us and Phantom Company, something of a dance. June doesn't want to kill anyone, and Talia knows it and is much bolder than she would be otherwise. Talia doesn't want to kill June, so the shots hitting our boulder are not as close as they might be. It's real, there is real danger, but it's not quite normal.

This three-day dance in the forest was just that, a dance. Harris, Talia's taciturn second in command, was trying to wear us out, force us into the open, trap us, so Talia could leave her precious Phantom Company and be here for the drama of our capture.

The petty, psychotic side of wannabe warlords love their dramatic victories, love to crush their opponents under their heel—literally or figuratively, they're generally fine with either.

We do some damage, June and I, but we don't take any lives. My role with those two pistols—couldn't tell you much about them, 9mm something or another, I think. I hate guns, I guess that's what happens when you accidentally shoot your little brother at the tender age of six. June has taught me to shoot, but my brain just won't retain the particulars.

Anyway, my role with the two guns is to lay down suppressing fire while June uses the hunting rifle to do the real work. The rifle, again, no clue about caliber or make, is bolt action with a scope, a long range, and she is good with it. And I mean good. She could have killed four or five of them with how bold they are being, but she settles for flesh wounds and disabling their three vehicles.

We are making good progress—and by "we" I mean June—until they pull Dallas out of one of the SUVs. Her hands are tied, she's gagged, and she has a black eye and a nasty bruise on the left side of her face.

Harris is there, Talia's muscly second in command, with a gun to her head. He's all buzz-cut, square-jawed serious.

Talia has a bullhorn—of course she does. "One more shot and Dallas dies." Talia's voice echoes over the land.

We left Dallas in a reasonable situation, as these things go, but apparently they caught her. We couldn't trust her, and I don't know if we can now.

"What do we do?" I ask June.

She licks her lips and nods her head, her eye to the scope. "What I should do is kill Talia."

My heart thumps and skips and thumps again. As much as I dislike Talia, I don't want her to die, and I really don't want June to kill her. Besides, as a strategy for survival, I'm not sure how sound it is. What will Phantom Company do if Talia goes down? "Can you?" I ask, these thoughts rumbling around my head.

She purses her lips and shakes her head. And this, right here, is what is most amazing about June. After all Talia has done, with what Talia wants to do, she still won't pull the trigger.

"Is Dallas really in danger?" I ask.

"Oh yeah," June says. "She failed. Talia knows that we let her live and is trying to use that against us."

"What now?" I ask, although I know the answer.

June sighs. "They'll be on us any moment. I think you can trust Dallas now. Remember the plan. Remember the signal. Remember that I—"

June is cut off by the click of hammers being pulled back as two men from Phantom Company reach the top of the hill.

June stands up and executes Plan B. And really, I think this was her Plan A all along. She pulls her pistol, cocks it, presses it to her head and yells, "One bullet hits him, one person touches him, and I'll pull the trigger."

Yeah. She does that.

I know it's coming and still it rips my heart out. I'm in love with June Medina in a way I didn't really even imagine possible. I hate what she is doing, but I completely understand it too. I'd do the exact same thing for her. I'd rather know she is in this world and never ever see her again if that was the only way to save her life.

"Oh, Christ, June. Come now..." Talia says as she saunters up the hill dressed in her combat boots and brown tank top. "Surely this boy is not worth *that*." Her long blond hair is pulled back into its usual ponytail, with the sides cleanly shaved, but I'm glad to see her hair a bit disheveled and dark circles under her eyes.

Harris has Dallas in tow and she looks worse than I first thought. Her left cheek is badly swollen and crusted blood is clinging to her chin.

My reaction is complicated. I want to hit whoever hit Dallas, but I'm also just a little pleased to see her in dire straits—June and I might have escaped but for her.

"Yes, he is worth this," June says, her eyes locked with Talia's.

Talia sighs. "Okay, what are the terms of your surrender? Clearly you have a plan, my June-bug, so spit it out, so we can all put this little debacle behind us."

June is most definitely not Talia's and never will be, and she's definitely not a cute little bug. It's only the petty, psychotic side of this wannabe warlord that has her going to these extremes to possess June.

June cannot be possessed.

"Food, water, water filter, and weapons for both Woody and Dallas," June says slowly. "We all sit here and watch them until they are out of sight and then I will go peacefully with you."

"No promise that I won't send anyone after them?" Talia asks.

June smiles, it's the kind of smile with an edge, meant to cut. "I would ask it if I thought I could trust your word."

Talia shakes her head. "You can trust my word, June. You don't ask it, but I will give it." Talia raises her voice. "I swear this to Christ above and Gaia below, no one is to follow Dallas-girl or Woody-boy. We will set them up for survival. But, if they are ever seen in the vicinity of Phantom Ranch or any of our territories again, they are to be shot on sight, no questions asked, no quarter given."

Everyone is silent, the six members of Phantom Company all staring at us. One of them that is holding his bleeding arm—June's doing—looks like he is hoping we end up back in their territory so he can shoot us.

The breeze kicks up and sweeps hot air from the desert and I am sweating. Dallas catches my eye and I see a flicker of hope there. She was not expecting to survive this.

"Now move, boys!" Talia shouts. "Get these two set up so I don't have to see their pathetic faces again."

Several men run back to the vehicles and I try to catch June's eye, but her gaze doesn't leave Talia, her finger right on the trigger of the gun she is holding to her head.

Dallas is untied, ungagged, and shoved forward. She stumbles and falls, but gets up and stands tall next to me, a grim look on her swollen face, her hands shaking. They throw loaded packs at our feet, give us unloaded guns and shove two clips into each pack.

I still have my Leatherman multi-tool in my pocket, and my knife and hatchet on my belt.

"Now be off," Talia says with a wave of her hand.

I take a step towards June and Talia pulls her pistol, and

for the second time since I've known her, presses it to my forehead.

"No sappy goodbyes, lover boy," she says. "Turn and go before I lose my patience."

My heart is pounding in my head, and despite my strong desire to not lose my humanity, I want to kill Talia... slowly, and with my bare hands. I want her to suffer.

"Just go, Woody. Please," June says, not turning her head.

But still I stand there. I want one more glimpse of those blue eyes, one more look at her delicate features, one more moment to marvel at her strength.

"Come on," Dallas says, her speech slightly slurred from the beating she's taken. She's got her pack on and hands me mine. "We have to go."

And still I wait, my eyes drilling into Talia's hazel eyes. I want her, for just a moment, to consider the fact that I'm not afraid of her.

And I'm not, in that moment about to lose June, I'm not. And I'm foolish enough in that adrenalized moment to think that feeling will last.

Finally, I allow Dallas to pull me away and we head east down towards the desert.

"I love you, June Medina!" I call back after we are about twenty yards away. I do it because I don't know if I'll see her again and I just have to say it. I also do it as a big middle finger to Talia.

"You better, Woody Beckman!" June calls back, the strain in her voice ripping my heart open even further.

"Oh, Christ!" Talia says. "I think I'm going to be sick."

I smile and chuckle. It's pure schadenfreude, but on a day like today, losing June and dealing with a psychotic, petty, wannabe warlord, I'll take it.

CHAPTER FIFTY-SIX

THE JUNIPERS HAVE TURNED shrub-like and there are sporadic clumps of grass and sage laid out before us as the rocky terrain slopes down. To the north, red mesas poke up just above the horizon and the pine-covered high country of Jacob Lake and the Grand Canyon are to the west.

It's been an hour, we're well out of sight of Talia and Phantom Company, and I'm so nervous I could puke.

Dallas has been, thankfully, silent so far, keeping up with the blistering pace I've set.

In my mind, I'm thinking, "This is not over, this is not over, this is *not* over." Repeating it continually like some kind of weird mantra. I rescued June from a psychotic, petty, wannabe warlord on top of Mount Elden near Flagstaff, and I can do it again.

Except Talia has attachments to June unlike that short, bald, psychopath at Elden Lookout Tower. He just wanted some dynamite to extend his little kingdom and was using June as leverage.

"Thank you," Dallas says, her breath coming fast.

I'm covered in sweat and take a swig from my water bottle, but don't slow down a bit and I don't answer her.

It's rude, and yes, my mother raised me better than that, but my mother is dead and the world is overrun by zombies and crazies like Talia.

"Seriously, I owe you and June my life."

I clear my throat and say, "You owe June your life. Twice now." Neither of us are counting when I pulled that zombie off her at the North Rim and "saved" her. That was part of her act back then. She could have handled that Z. I take that as a good sign that this is really a different Dallas.

"Yes, yes, twice. I don't know how to thank you." Her speech is still garbled from the beating she took at the hands of Phantom Company and that cracks my resolve just a bit. June and I aren't the only ones suffering because of Talia.

I stoop under the scant shade of a dwarf Juniper and look into Dallas's brown eyes. "No more bullshit, Dallas. No more come-ons. No more lies."

She nods, her eyes wide and earnest. "I'm sorry. I was just trying to survive. And... the come-ons, well, I came on stronger than I would have, but I meant it all."

I nod slowly. Somehow, I believe her. Maybe it's because I want to. Maybe it's because if I can get her to help, the odds of surviving what comes next gets a bit better.

"But no more of that," I say.

She rolls her eyes and shakes her head. "I get it. Boy, do I get it. You and June are the real deal. No bullshit there. I've got to respect that. Love in the apocalypse, now that's something even a jaded bitch like me can get behind."

I sigh, my shoulders falling, and slump to the ground, fatigue washing over me. Now that we've stopped, I don't know how I'm possibly going to summon the strength to continue.

"What happened to you?" I ask.

She shrugs. "I woke up at high noon. Got down, found the knife—that was remarkably kind, thank you—headed out and ran right into a patrol. Just bad luck."

I nod. "And your face?"

"Just sweet 'ole Talia convincing herself that I didn't know anything about where you guys went... with her fists."

"She's a peach," I say, doing my best to spit the last word out.

"That is for sure. If she didn't think I might be useful for leverage, I'd already be dead." Dallas lowers her voice, even though we are very much alone. "Listen, Woody, she thinks you're too weak to survive out here, and she thinks that your weakness rubbed off on June, and before no time, with a little help from Talia, she'll be back to her old 'shit-kicking self.'"

I stare at Dallas for several breaths. "And what do you think?"

"What do I think?" She looks out over the parched landscape, to the east the cut of the Grand Canyon is just visible. "I think Talia is stupid. I think June is going to work at this from the inside. I think that you and I are going to work this from the outside. I think that we are going to get June back or die trying!"

Dallas walks from under the tree and holds up her middle finger, pointed back the way we came. "Hear that, Talia, you sociopathic little weeny bitch! We are coming for you. Do you hear me!?"

She pokes her head back under the tree. "That's what we're doing, right?"

I don't say anything for a few beats, my face pulled down into a long frown. "Can I trust you, Dallas?"

Dallas blinks, a look of incredulity on her face that a four-year-old might wear if you insisted that she didn't like ice cream. "Shit, Woody," she says patting the gun on her hip. "If I was sent to kill you, you'd already be dead."

I do my best to smile and nod.

"I'm your best goddamn friend, Woody," she adds. "I'm June's new BFF. I want to be the best maid *and* best man at your wedding." She stands back up, both middle fingers pointed the way we came. "You hear that Talia? We are coming for you!"

When she squats back under the tree, all that energy seems to have dissipated and she looks at me, her face serious. "You've got a plan, don't you?"

I smile and nod. "And you're going to love it."

"Yeah? Why?"

"Because it's absolutely insane and we have little chance of success."

CHAPTER FIFTY-SEVEN

AS THE DAY DRAGS ON, my feet hurt more and more
and it gets hotter and hotter. But the land, my God, the
land. Redrock mesas rising up, the dry land unrolling before
us as we tromp towards the Colorado River. The vegetation
getting smaller and nearly disappearing as we go. Colors
from terra-cotta red to off-white as the composition of the
rock changes, all carved by the rare rain that falls. Land as
beautiful as it is harsh. the kind of place you would film a
gritty western where the scrappy underdogs take on an
unjust power with little more than determination.

I see it. I marvel at it. But I don't enjoy it as I might
have. And gone is Dallas's enthusiasm for getting back at
Talia, we both have to save every ounce of energy we have
to keep moving. To the east, ever to the east.

And if you are up on that hill where Talia's forces over-
whelmed us and you have a great pair of binoculars or a
telescope and can watch us, you probably think that we are
crazy. There is nothing east but the desert and then the

Grand Canyon. No trails down. No roads. Just brush, dried grass, rock, and endless heat.

And if someone is watching, and we figure there is a good chance Talia has someone doing just that, that is exactly what we want them to think.

Once it's dark, we stop, start a campfire with what brush and wood we can scrounge, get it roaring, and promptly leave. We turn to the northeast, towards 89A and a little blip in the road called Marble Canyon. It's the only bit of civilization for many, many miles.

"Do you think Talia will have someone at Marble Canyon?" I ask Dallas. The temperature has cooled slightly and we are moving slow in the darkness, not daring to pull out a flashlight. Talia's promise to have us shot on sight anywhere in her "territory" has stuck with me. Marble Canyon is a place that Phantom Company cleaned out long ago, but they may consider it part of their territory.

"If she does," Dallas says, "then it's only for spite, so she sees us both dead."

I nod in the dark. That means she probably does have someone there. And people still at Jacob Lake and west toward Fredonia, basically leaving us no way out of the desert. Talia, once again, made a show of letting us go, but had no intentions of letting us survive.

"So... there'll be someone there for sure," I say another half mile on.

"Oh, yeah. They'll be waiting for us."

Marble Canyon is near Lee's Ferry, a put-in to the Colorado River that rafters use when running the Grand. Navajo Bridge is there and goes across the river. There are two spans—the new one for cars, and the older, historic one is just for pedestrians now. It will be tough to get across the

Colorado without using one of those bridges and they won't be hard for Phantom Company to guard.

Another half mile goes by.

"So, how we gonna get across the bridge?" Dallas asks.

"I don't think we are."

"Well, I'm intrigued. What do you have in mind?"

"It's going to take a little swimming in ice cold water and a lot of hiking."

"Oh, sounds like fun," she says calmly, and I just smile. Dallas is the right kind of crazy for this particular rescue attempt.

CHAPTER FIFTY-EIGHT

POPULATED AREAS, like Phoenix, are full of Zs, full of useful supplies, and full of too many living that have taken to the apocalypse and are somewhere on the psychotic, petty, wannabe warlord spectrum.

The wilderness, like the desert we're trudging through and the high country we came from, doesn't have much of the living or the dead, but survival is brutally hard.

In some ways that's better. It's the same survival issues humans have always had. Water, food, shelter. The apocalypse doesn't even really matter that much out here.

In the three days June and I were on those back roads in the forest and this day with Dallas, not one Z has been seen. Not one.

This is something that always bugged me a bit about the pre-A zombie shows. The Zs were always there, wherever you went. But in a state like Arizona, even before the madness happened, it wasn't that hard to find a place where there were no people near you.

And this is what I want for June and me. I want a place,

literally in the middle of nowhere, with water, the ability to grow and forage food, and game to hunt. I want to be away from the living and the undead.

The moon is up, casting the desert in a silvery hue, and it's cooled down and is a fairly good temperature for hiking. My eyes have adjusted to the dim light and I can see well enough.

I glance over at Dallas and we are so deep into this hike that we haven't talked in miles. Her head is down and her shoulder-length hair has escaped her ears and fallen forward so I can't see her face.

I really don't know anything about her. In fact, I don't know that much about June, not in terms of life history. I know how she conducts herself, I know she hasn't lost her humanity. But Dallas? There's an edge there, a spark in her eyes when she's screaming and flipping off a faraway Talia, or the glint in her eye when she was propositioning me at the van on the North Rim.

We are getting close to 89A, I can see the cut of the road in the distance. We need to get to the road. It will be more dangerous, we'll be easier to spot, but I'm tired of slogging through the desert.

I open my mouth to try to engage Dallas in a conversation when I hear a weak snarl.

A Z is shambling towards us about fifty yards away.

I grab Dallas, her head snaps around, and she's got this wild look, for just a moment. The miles and fatigue must have lulled her into an almost trance. "What?" she asks irritably.

I nod towards the zombie. It's a pitiful leathery thing, tall and lanky with tufts of blond hair sticking out of her nearly bald, skeletal head.

Dallas's eyes light up. "She's all mine. Do you mind?"

"No."

"Can I use your hatchet?"

I pull it out of my belt and hand it to her and suddenly Dallas is alive again and running across the desert at top speed.

"Hi, Talia!" she shouts. "Fancy meeting you here."

If I squint, I can kind of see the resemblance. The zombie is tall with blond hair.

Dallas dances up and smacks the Z in the side of the head with the flat of the hatchet. The Z stumbles to the side, rights itself and comes back towards Dallas.

"I'm sorry, Talia, did that hurt?" Dallas says and then pokes it in the forehead. "How about that?"

I approach and watch from a safe distance as Dallas literally toys with the zombie, smacking it in the head, knocking it over, but not delivering a lethal blow.

She talks to it like it's Talia. She curses at it. Spits on it. All the while with this manic grin on her face.

The whole show is rather disturbing, especially in the eerie silver glow of the moon. I get it. Talia was cruel to Dallas and maybe this is a way for Dallas to let off some steam, but...

"How do you like that!" Dallas shouts after she smashes the Z in the nose, breaking it with a sharp crack.

I've had enough. "Catch up when you're done playing with your Talia Zombie," I say and walk away.

Dallas doesn't acknowledge me. And I can't say I know anything more about her or her history, but I can say that I know her better. Her animosity towards Talia runs very deep. It's clear I can trust her to help me get June back, it's just not clear if I can trust her to keep herself in control.

CHAPTER FIFTY-NINE

BEFORE THE NIGHT ENDS, we hit 89A with boots full of blisters and fatigue like an elephant sitting on us. We've come a lot of miles, like twenty-five or so, and we are just getting started.

Dallas's time with the Talia Zombie seemed to lighten her mood and we've chatted a bit.

She was conceived in Dallas, where her mother was from, and born in Montana. Her mother was really missing her home state when Dallas was born, thus the name. Her mother died when she was five in a traffic accident and she was raised by her father. She wasn't in the military, just the only child of a single father that liked to fish and hunt and hike and camp and did all those things with Dallas.

Once on the road, we are able to start making better time, keeping our ears open for any cars, Zs, or any other kind of danger.

I ask Dallas if she wants to stop. She's been through more in the last twenty-four hours than I have. She just snorts and keeps on walking.

Our water is getting low and we are only taking small sips at a time. Marble Canyon is another twenty miles or so and we are going to be in rough shape by the time we make it there.

When dawn starts to lighten the eastern horizon, I call a stop and we find a side canyon not far from the road and take cover.

Just as we are getting settled in, we hear a car humming along the road and we peek out to see it. It's a faded red Nissan pickup.

"Shit!" Dallas swears. "That's a Phantom Company truck. We were too slow."

I let go of the fact that Dallas once told me she'd never been to the North Rim with Phantom Company. That is the past. Things have changed.

I shrug, it's almost better knowing for sure that they are there. It will help us plan.

"Get some sleep," I say. "I'll wake you in a few hours."

Dallas is promptly snoring softly, nestled in the red dirt, her denim jacket bunched up for a pillow. I take my boots and socks off, letting my poor feet air out. I watch her for a while, wondering at what an unlikely ally she is. And I do trust her now, her animosity towards Talia is not faked, and neither are those bruises on her face.

I then turn my mind towards our next step, Marble Canyon, Lee's Ferry, and getting across the Colorado. I ponder abandoning the plan and trying to hike upstream above the Colorado River gorge to Page, but figure there's likely another psychotic, petty, wannabe warlord set up there using that bridge across the Colorado as a control point.

Actually, with the dam and the hydroelectric power,

Page would be a great place to try to rebuild civilization. Power. Water. A long growing season.

I pull out the pen and paper I scrounged from the North Rim and start writing notes and doodling, just using it as a tool to help me think.

At first the pen feels weird in my hand, it's been so long since I've actually written anything. And then it feels good, like filtering my thoughts, turning them into words and writing them down, forces some clarity from my tired mind.

We can definitely cross at Lee's Ferry, it used to be a literal ferry, but then what? We have no vehicle, very little food, and are a long ways from any kind of civilization.

We could try to find a raft at Marble Canyon, haul it miles down to Lee's Ferry and raft down the Colorado, but there are rapids there and I can swim and know how to paddle a canoe, but don't think that qualifies me to raft down the Colorado through the Grand Canyon.

We need a vehicle, and as much as I hate the thought of it, that red pickup from Phantom Company may be our only shot.

After I run through all that, I watch Dallas for a while longer, she is really out. Looking at Dallas makes me think of June. Of the crazy days since we met. I think of her blue, blue eyes and her olive skin. Her short black hair and her lithe body.

Without really thinking about it, I write "Woody and June versus the Apocalypse" on the top of a blank piece of paper. And then I start jotting notes:

Day 1: Meet in Flagstaff at dog food plant.

Day 2: Climb Mount Elden and June taken by psychotic, petty, wannabe warlord known as Mr. Short and Stocky (by me) and Asshole (by June).

Day 3: Daring escape with fake dynamite and fake

suicide vest. June kisses me on the cheek and holds my hand. Not alone anymore.

It goes on from there and suddenly I am writing as fast as I can, filling in the details, remembering the words June said or the looks on her face.

I can't help myself. I can't stop.

It just pours out of me and somehow I feel clearer, and just a little bit hopeful.

CHAPTER SIXTY

"LAY IT OUT FOR ME, BECKMAN," Dallas says, her shoulder touching mine as we peek over a sandstone boulder. We've climbed up the slope of a mesa in sight of Marble Canyon and Navajo Bridge.

"You got it, Lonestar."

Dallas doesn't like her nickname much, but she's the kind of wild spirit that you would think of when pondering Texas in the late 1800s. Annie Oakley or someone like that. Besides, if we're going to be friends, if we're going to fight this fight together, we best act like it.

It's late afternoon and we've been walking since dawn along red-rock mesas over the Arizona desert. We skirted two small developments, not much more than lodges, and made it here without incident. We're hot, out of water, nearly out of food, and our feet are a mess. Phantom Company's red pickup truck is in the middle of the bridge blocking both lanes and a man with a rifle is pacing in front of it.

From the rocky outcropping on the other side of the river, we occasionally see a reflected glint, presumably from the scope of a rifle or binoculars.

"Their weapons are much longer range than ours," I say. "The bridge is effectively blocked unless we can figure a way to surprise them."

"They gotta take a dump some time, don't they?" Dallas offers.

"Well, yeah, but we have to assume they have walkie-talkies and someone is always watching."

"And your swimming idea?"

I point to the road heading north from Marble Canyon, which is just a motel, a gas station, and a few houses. "That road runs to Lee's Ferry, about five miles away. We could swim the river there, get across, but then we are on foot and a very long ways from getting the supplies we need to rescue June, much less what we need to survive."

"But they know this, right?"

I nod. "They must. Could be there is someone at Lee's Ferry, too."

She takes a deep breath and sighs. She points back behind the buildings on 89A to some houses set right against the cliff. "And those?"

I shrug. "Never noticed them before. Houses, I guess. I would suspect Phantom Company went through everything here long ago."

We lapse into silence, each of us taking a turn with the binoculars and watching the two sentries we know about. Dallas recognizes the one on the bridge. His name is Hank, she says he's a decent guy, but will definitely follow his orders and shoot us on sight.

"There is one more thing we could try," I finally say. "As long as we get a little lucky scrounging and can deal with whoever is at Lee's Ferry and we won't die of a bullet... but will likely drown." I don't like the idea at all, but we're out of options, so the Colorado seems like the only way.

Her eyebrows dance on her forehead and she smiles widely. "I'm all ears."

CHAPTER SIXTY-ONE

LUCK IS WITH US. Well, I guess you could say that considering how dumb what we are about to do is.

After thinking about it, we completely skip Marble Canyon, the odds of us being spotted there are just too high with at least two members of Phantom Company in the area.

After dark, we skirt along the edge of the mesa we were watching from, going around Marble Canyon, and make it to the road to Lee's Ferry. It's slow going—we can't use flashlights. We parallel the road and make it to Lee's Ferry some five miles later. We stop at the campground and watch and listen for almost an hour, but no one is there.

Once we are sure we're alone, we go down to the water and use the water filter pump and fill up our bottles, being careful to drink slowly. We're pretty dehydrated and it's not good to flood the body with water. The river water is cold, coming off the bottom of Lake Powell not that far upstream.

We then go slow and search the campsites first. There's

not much there, only two RVs and one car, all of it picked clean.

As it turns out, Lee's Ferry is not guarded at all, although it takes us most of the night to determine that. There are multiple access points to the river spread out quite a bit, making it hard to guard, and that's probably the issue. Talia must not care about us continuing on by foot and probably doesn't think we'll try what we're going to try.

We move farther in and go cross-country up a hill overlooking the river that has five houses sitting on it. After watching and waiting, we move into the neighborhood and do a quick search. No Zs. No living.

We get bold, use a flashlight and search the houses. And luck is with us again, we find what we are looking for. Stuffed in the attic above a garage is an inflatable raft, big enough for four people, complete with oars, hand pump, and life jackets.

This is a small inflatable raft, ten feet long with a steel frame, oar locks, and one seat for the rower. It is not good enough to go down the Colorado, but I don't expect to find anything better than this. With the rafts moored at Phantom Ranch and the series of motorized rafts that Sal and Mary took us down to Phantom Ranch in, they have cleaned this area out of all the real rafts.

"Well?" Dallas asks, a huge grin on her face, the dim light making it look very Cheshire-like. We are in the dusty garage looking at all the gear we found.

"The truck is still probably sitting there at Desert View," I say. "If we can survive the river, we can hike out, drive to Flagstaff, avoid the psychotic, petty, wannabe warlord there, get the supplies we need, and get on with the hard part of this rescue."

Dallas is quiet for a bit, staring at me. She then snorts

and shakes her head. "I gotta say, Talia underestimated you, Beckman. She ain't gonna have a clue what hits her."

She holds her hand up palm open and I high-five her. I smile and feel just a sliver of hope. "Well, let's survive the Colorado first, shall we?"

CHAPTER SIXTY-TWO

I DIDN'T KNOW this then, but we had sixty-nine river miles to go and about twenty rapids to get through. As Dallas and I stand there in the ice-cold Colorado River, our decidedly odd raft loaded and ready to go, I'm scared. I know there are some big rapids to come, but I really have no clue. I mean, I knew the canyon had some wicked rapids. I knew that trained professionals regularly drowned. But I also knew that June had already spent two days with Talia and each day that passed with her in jeopardy was like shoving a toothpick under my fingernail.

And the Woody standing there with an awkward grin on his face had many of the same personality quirks as pre-A Woody, but really bore little resemblance to him. In fact, that Woody bore little resemblance to the pre-June Woody of sixteen days ago.

"You sure you want to do this?" I ask, fussing with the branches we cut and laid on top of the raft as camouflage.

The night is dark, the moon down with only stars illuminating, but we are worried they might have night scopes and are watching the river and we don't want to get shot as we pass under the bridge.

We've both got wetsuits on and the raft has every life jacket we could find tied to it as well as our packs and extra oars. It is a decidedly weird contraption and I have no idea if the camo is needed or if the extra flotation even makes sense.

"Stop asking stupid questions, Beckman. I am fully grown and if I don't want to do something, you sure as hell will hear it. Now can we just get on with this?"

I nod and Dallas hops in the raft and I push it out and then jump in. I row us to the center of the river and let the current take us.

The river floats us along lazily and soon the canyon rises high around us and I know we are getting close to the bridge.

We tie the oars to the raft, slip into the water, futz with the branches, and then we both grab a rope and float behind the raft. Another survival precaution, this one is Dallas's idea, in case they notice the raft in the darkness and take some pot shots.

Even with the wetsuits, the 45-ish degree water is cold, and I can feel the heat leaching out of my body.

"Here goes nothing," Dallas whispers as we approach the bridges, two dark lines high above blocking out the stars.

"Thanks, Dallas," I say, feeling a surprising amount of affection for the woman June and I pondered killing just a few days go.

"Any time. Anywhere," she says with a chuckle, echoing the words of her offer when she was trying to break June and I up on behalf of Talia.

"Likewise," I say.

We lapse into silence, hardly breathing, and...

Nothing. Soon the bridges are out of sight and we climb back into the raft shivering and toss the branches. One more piece of luck; we are sure to run out soon.

A few miles downstream we hit Badger Creek Rapids. I didn't know the name then, but that's what it is. A series of waves and troughs two to three feet high.

I'm at the oars, holding them with a white-knuckle grip, just trying to keep us in the center of the river pointing straight down. Dallas is in front, one arm thrust in the air whooping and hollering like she's riding a bucking bull in a rodeo, or knowing Dallas, more likely a mechanical bull in a bar.

The eastern horizon has started to lighten a bit and the walls of the canyon are dark grey and looming, the white-tipped waves ghostly shadows.

We make it through in about forty seconds, although it feels more like forty minutes to me.

Dallas turns around, a huge grin on her face. "More? Are there more? And bigger?"

I laugh and nod. "A lot more. A lot bigger."

She whoops and pumps her fist and I try to take a deep breath, roll my shoulders, and unwind some of the tension.

The stakes are high, but this *is* an adventure. I'm rafting down the Colorado River. No one is pointing a gun at me. There are no Zs. Dehydration is not a danger. We actually scrounged a bit of food in those houses, so we won't starve.

I let out a big sigh and smile.

And it even lasts for a while.

A few miles later, with the sun up, we strip off the wetsuits. We have bathing suits we scrounged on underneath, and for a moment, it feels like a vacation. Like we're just a couple of adventuresome friends rafting down the river. We're smiling as the first rays of the day kiss our faces, watching the colors of the Grand Canyon brighten.

Dallas takes us through Soap Creek Rapid which is a bit bigger. I'm up front, the cold water splashing me, my smile wide, and she's behind whooping it up.

And then another five miles after that we hear the roar of House Rock Rapid and no one is smiling anymore. The noise is deafening, you can just feel it coming, like a waterfall is up ahead and I can't imagine how our little raft is going to make it.

CHAPTER SIXTY-THREE

THE STANDING WAVES ARE BIG, four to five feet high. There are rocks to avoid in the middle of the river. A deep consistent trough, called a hole, looks like it can swallow our little raft whole. And there is a turn to the right where the river wants to smash you up against the rocks.

House Rock Rapid.

"We can't do it," I say.

Dallas nods. We are on the left side of the river and have a good view of the rapid.

"I mean, we can, but the boat will flip and we'll be tossed in the water."

"So what?" Dallas asks.

I point to some of the large, bone-breaking boulders in the river.

"Okay," she says calmly. "I guess this is it, Beckman. You and me making our life here until the day we die."

I glance at her and there is a smile playing on her lips, her brown eyes bright.

"I don't know, Lonestar. Stuck with you here, for years

and years." I sigh and shake my head solemnly and she punches me in the shoulder. Hard. It hurts. A lot. But I don't let on.

She points to the other side of the river, the inside part of the curve. "Since you can't stand the smell of me, I'll guess we'll have to portage."

I turn to her, a quizzical look on my face. "Portage? Where'd a country girl like you learn such big words?"

She winds up to punch my shoulder again and I hold up my hand. "Okay, okay, we'll portage. You're a well-educated, sweet-smelling Montana wilderness girl."

"Now you're talking!" she says.

ᛓᛈᚾ ᛏᚠ ᛗᛈᚾ

THE PORTAGE of House Rock Rapid goes well. We walk the boat upstream, paddle like hell across the river, and carry the boat over the sandy inside turn of the curve. There we launch again and only hit a few of the waves on the lower portion of the rapid.

And thus it goes for the rest of the day and into the evening. We are going about three river miles per hour and some rapids we run and some we get out and portage.

The adrenaline has worn off and fatigue has kicked in when we hit what is known as "The Roaring Twenties." Ten rapids between mile 20 and mile 30.

We, of course, have no idea what is going on, just that the rapids are coming fast, getting big, and getting harder to portage.

Through it all, though, I am still struck with the power of the water and the beauty of the canyon cutting deeper and deeper into the red sandstone around us.

The canyon walls, sometimes sheer, sometimes sloping

steeply, rise in colors from ochre to salmon, with creeks cutting in, and the occasional waterfall in sight.

This is true wilderness we are floating through, largely unchanged except for the dam above regulating its flow, and seen by very few people.

It's magnificent. I can see that Dallas is feeling it too in the quiet moments when we are just floating down the river, her eyes wide, staring at the ancient sandstone or up at the turkey vultures circling above us in the clear blue sky. Listening to the breeze whistling down the side canyons or breathing deeply of the warm desert air.

Even with hindsight and better knowledge of the river, I can't tell you what rapid finally did us in. Our pace had turned into a crawl, scouting each rapid, none were small, portaging where it made sense, running them when we could.

The sun had gone down in the canyon and the coming rapid was a straight shot and looks like if you just stay in the center you'll be fine.

We are not.

A hole opens up, seeming from nowhere, and swallows our little boat. The raft flips, coming up the far side of the hole, and we are thrown into the cold water.

Without our wetsuits, the frigid water hits like a punch to the gut, taking my breath away.

We have on life jackets, but I'm still sucked under the water, suddenly immersed in the violent churn of the river. Floating on it, you don't feel its strength, but down below, its power is undeniable and you are nothing. Feeling its raw power, it's no surprise that the Colorado was able to carve the Grand Canyon out of the limestone and sandstone desert.

As the water takes me, sucks me down, there is one

thought screaming its way through my mind. And no, it's not about June or worrying about dying, not yet. The thought blazing through me is, *My hat!* That beat-up red Diamondback's baseball cap is the only thing that I have from my pre-A life. As the water takes me, I feel the hat lift from my head and I thrust my arm up and, by some small miracle, snag the hat.

As I'm sucked down, I grip it tightly, like it's the life preserver. I'm under for the longest time, tumbling like some rag in a washing machine, holding my breath, my lungs burning, my eyes open, but I can't see anything but the dim, swirling water.

As the seconds tick by, other thoughts come.

I'm going to drown.

I think of June, of her beautiful blue eyes and her determined face. I think of the first time I saw her on the roof of the dog food plant, how she munched on "popcorn" (that would be dog food) while I took out the Zs that had surrounded the semitrailer I had slept on. I remember her with a gun in each hand taking out zombies on Navajo Point on the South Rim and saving both of us. I remember the feel of her hand in mine, and all our almost moments. I see her standing there in front of Talia with her pistol pointed to her forehead.

I love you, June Medina.

You better, Woody Beckman!

It's the end, I know it is, and then suddenly... I bob up out of the water sputtering and sucking in air.

I take a deep breath and scream, "Point your feet downstream." I can't see Dallas and had told her this earlier, but want to emphasize the one and only piece of advice I have for being swept down a raging river.

You want your feet to hit the rocks first, not your hands or head.

The river sweeps me down, like a pair of strong, unrelenting hands. There is no fighting the current, not directly. When the water calms, I swim towards the left shore—probably a better word for that, but it is the shore on my left side as the current flows.

I still am clutching my hat, making my swimming rather awkward.

I'm worried about Dallas when I hear a "Whoohooo! Goddamn!!" and have to smile. It is very hard to keep that woman down.

"What now, Beckman?" she shouts, not far behind me.

"Swim to the shore!" I yell.

"But what about the boat?"

The boat. Where our packs, weapons, and supplies are. The boat, the only reasonably safe way down the canyon. The goddamn boat!

"Swim for the boat!" I yell.

What else can we do?

The next rapid takes the boat through first and then us. I bounce off a boulder, getting a nasty bruise on my shoulder for my effort and my teeth start to chatter.

The river is then kind to us and calms. I put my hat on and swim like hell and catch a rope trailing off the raft and swim to shore right before the next rapid.

There's a small beach and warm sand in a large eddy and I crawl to shore panting, shivering, and collapse on the sand, glad to be alive.

Dallas is soon next to me.

"Damn, Beckman!" she says, slapping me on the back as her teeth chatter. She pulls her life jacket off and throws it farther up the beach. "You sure know how to show a girl a good time."

I stare at her, rather dumbfounded. The bikini she found when we searched the Lee's Ferry houses is a tad small for her and she is practically spilling out of it. She adjusts her top and I'm staring even harder.

"Sorry, boy-o," she says with a grin, "you turned this paradise down."

I blink and look away, grateful that something is helping me feel a little warmer. I pull the rope and get the raft firmly in the eddy.

"But tell me," she says in a serious tone. "If it was just you and me, you know, would you...?"

Dallas baffles me, I swear to God she does. But then again, June baffles me and women in general baffle me. And somehow, I doubt that I am alone in this, even with the planet's drastically reduced population.

"Seriously?" I ask. We almost died and our teeth are still chattering. Is this really the right time for this conversation?

She nods and looks away shyly.

Is this a game? Does she really care about this? I choose to believe the latter. The swelling in her face has gone down and now the bruise is edged in a nasty purple, but it's still clear that she's quite attractive.

"I'd be lucky to have you, Lonestar. You're... you're the whole package." And, yes, I'm staring at her barely restrained, generous curves in that bikini.

She nods. "Thanks for saying that."

"No, no, it's true."

She finally meets my eyes and I am shocked by what I see. She actually doesn't think of herself as beautiful, even with the way she toyed with me, even with her obvious experience using her femaleness to manipulate men.

"You're amazing, Dallas," I say, careful to keep strict eye contact. "If June wasn't in the picture, I'd be ecstatic to spend the apocalypse with you."

She smiles widely and then frowns, her brow furrowing, and her mood changing as fast as the weather on a mountaintop. "Well, too bad, Beckman. I'm nobody's second choice." She stands up and looks around and I see the large tattoo she has on her back. It's a bald eagle with wings outstretched and beak outstretched at the top of her back. Could anything else be more fitting for her?

"We camping here or what?" she asks.

I shake my head. Dallas baffles me, but I am so glad to have her along. There is a lot more river left and a lot more miles to go before we even get a shot at June.

CHAPTER SIXTY-FOUR

WE'RE up before dawn and portage our way through the rest of The Roaring Twenties and then start to make better time. We take to paddling when the river is calm so we can go faster.

We take one more spill, and while it's dangerous, it's not nearly as terrifying as the first one. We are down to our backup oars and lose those in the spill, but by paddling with our hands down a quiet stretch we find them and can resume normally.

By evening, we make it down to Tanner Trail, pull the raft up out of the water, and hide it behind some tamarisk bushes. We change out of our bathing suits into our clothes and put our packs on. We are ready to go.

The sun is setting, the yellow glow of it illuminating the tops of the canyon walls to the east. There are zombies out there—June and I led the hundreds-strong herd down here ten days ago. There is Phantom Company who makes it up this far on occasion. There are miles to go and little chance of success.

Dallas must sense my hesitation, she pats me on the back. "One more mighty obstacle between you and your love removed," she says.

I grin as best I can. We are both exhausted, but that's just the way of it these days. "Three innings down, only six more to go," I say. "But this one might go into overtime, you know?"

She smiles at me and we get back to it. We drink as much water as we can, fill all our water bottles, and we start the nine-mile hike up the trail. We've got our weapons out in case we encounter the living or the undead. We don't have a safe place to rest. We don't have time to spare, so we are doing this in the dark.

On the bright side, we are not bushwhacking our way up with five hundred tourist zombies on our tail, just hunting for the cairns that mark this primitive trail in the moonlight.

The thought makes me a bit wistful—seriously—and I miss June all that much more.

The cool of the night will help with the hike, but the dark will make it harder to see the Zs.

"Did you put your pantyhose on, like a good boy?" Dallas asks as we start up the trail.

I sigh. Back at Lee's Ferry when we were "shopping"—Dallas's term for it—in the houses, she found some knee-high pantyhose thingies and insisted that we wear them for the hike out. Said that they would go a long ways to preventing anymore blisters.

"Yes, ma'am, pantyhose in place as instructed." If they had been full, up-to-the-waist pantyhose, I would have refused, but knee high I can manage.

"That's a good boy," she says. "You'll thank me in the morning."

I have some decent socks on over them, but frankly it feels strange, the light pressure on my calf, my feet sliding more easily in the boot. The last week has been horrible for my feet so I'm willing to traipse around the post-A landscape in knee-high pantyhose. What the hell?

We fall silent as we dig into the trail, keeping our eyes and ears open for the Zs.

Not far in, we have a group of three Zs lock on and have them shambling up the trail after us. We dispatch them quickly, Dallas with the tire iron and me with the hatchet, and get back to hiking.

I'm glad to see Dallas is not pretending every female Z is Talia and taking unnecessary risks to vent her anger. Later, as it gets dark, we use a flashlight so we don't lose the trail.

We have two more encounters with small groups of Zs in the first few miles, but nothing we can't handle, nothing remarkable.

And it's strange. We regularly dispatch the undead, poking knives or tire irons through their eyes, crushing their skulls with a hatchet, and this is just life. Post-A life.

Yeah, we woke up this morning, ran twenty-some miles of river and navigated numerous rapids down the Grand Canyon, took out ten zombies on a go-as-fast-as-you can hike with a five-thousand-foot elevation gain in a desperate attempt to save the woman I love from a psychotic, petty, wannabe warlord. Just another post-A day. What'd you do today?

Lipan Point is a parking lot, a few trash cans, and that is it.

The moon is down and the Milky Way hangs sparkling above us when we get to the top.

"You love the pantyhose," Dallas says as we take a moment and catch our breaths. "Admit it, Beckman."

"That, I do." My feet hurt, a lot, but I'm pretty sure it's the old blisters, not new blisters. "After you, Lonestar, I think those pantyhose might be my new best friend."

It's dark, with only indirect illumination from the flashlight, so I can't really make out much of her expression, but I hear her sniff. "Really?"

"Yeah, really. I love the pantyhose and I don't care who knows it."

"No, no. You said after *me* they're your new best friend. You know... that... that part."

We've got our packs on, and it's awkward, but I pull her into a hug. "Yes, Lonestar. You're my new best friend."

She sniffs more and I know she's crying, but even with my blunted male emotional intelligence, I'm quite sure that this is a good kind of cry.

"It's just that... you know... after Talia relegated me to night patrol, I..."

She's really crying now, and I just hold her, amazed at the wide range of emotions she can express. I am beginning to believe that she really wants to be a good person and all that happened as we escaped the North Rim was induced by pressure from Talia and a life of isolation with Phantom Company.

"You're my new best friend, too, Woody," she says after pulling out of the hug.

And then I feel the tears in my own eyes. Before June it was just me, for a long time. Now I have two amazing people in my life.

Yeah, the pre-A Woody is long gone, as well as the pre-June Woody. This is a different world, a different life, and finally one that is about more than survival.

"Umm... thanks, Dallas, but we better go. You know... the truck is over at Desert View and we've got a couple of miles to go."

She sniffs. "Oh sure. Yeah. Remind me again, what's our next stop."

We're walking right in the center of the road, walking out of the lot and heading east towards Desert View.

"The Best Buy in Flagstaff, Arizona. We need some drones and then we have to find some dynamite... somewhere. Keep your fingers crossed that we find what we need and we don't run into any of Flagstaff's psychotic, petty, wannabe warlords."

Dallas sniffs again, she must still be crying, and to tell the truth, I am a bit too.

"We got this, Beckman," she says. "You and me, we got this. We're going to get June back."

PART SEVEN

WOODY AND JUNE VERSUS THE DARING RESCUE

HE'LL DO ANYTHING TO GET HER BACK

CHAPTER SIXTY-FIVE

I WANT to confess to Dallas... all of my sins, even things that June doesn't know about, and there's a lot June doesn't know about. We've avoided talking much about our pre-apocalypse lives.

Dallas and I are walking at a good clip down Route 64 along the edge of the Grand Canyon, heading east from Lipan Point over to Desert View Overlook where the truck is parked (at least I hope it's still there). Dallas and I are friends. I trust her now, despite our rocky start, but our silent march under the starry glow of the Milky Way has given me too much time to think.

June taken by the psychotic, petty, wannabe warlord Talia, who just happens to be her ex. The challenges Dallas and I have to overcome before even getting our shot at getting her back, and the poor odds of it working out. Even if we do succeed, then what? The three of us trying to find a place far away from the zombies to live in peace, grow some food... That's not going to be easy.

I pat the pocket of my faded army surplus jacket. It's tied to my pack, so I have to twist my arm around. The seed packets are still there, the future is being able to grow food far away from the living and the undead. I adjust my Diamondbacks baseball cap and trot for a few steps, the backpack rattling on my back. Dallas has gotten ahead of me a bit.

It's a cool spring night at seven thousand feet, but cool feels good. There's a slight breeze, the air faintly scented by the juniper trees along the road. Our steps on the blacktop seem loud, ominous.

Dallas has a flashlight out and she's straight backed, a determined silhouette, her footfalls metronomic in their regularity.

I clear my throat, my mouth dry, but I can't get any words out. I want to tell her, like I told June, about when I was six and I accidentally shot my four-year-old brother Joshua in the arm. I want to tell her about the mess in Phoenix and what I did—or rather didn't do—and what it caused... well, what it cost, which is some good people their lives. It's the event that caused me to leave Phoenix and the psychotic, petty, wannabe warlord I had been following there.

And yes, I left because he was petty and psychotic, but more because every time I saw his lean face and grey eyes, I remembered what I didn't do.

I want to confess.

I clear my throat again, trying to find the words to even start the conversation.

"Somethin' on your mind, Beckman?" Dallas asks, her pace not varying, her head pointed forward.

I nod, although she can't see it. I'm not a religious guy, and if I had been, I don't think my faith would have survived the zombie apocalypse. But some of these things feel like sins, like blots on my soul. Infected wounds that need to be cleaned out.

"The past..." I mumble. "Just thinking about the past."

"The past is shit," she says.

Our hustle has erased the elation we felt and the camaraderie of escaping the Grand Canyon and Phantom Company alive.

And the past *is* shit, full of Zs, psychotic, petty, wannabe warlords, and cowards. The latter being my category.

And if you're reading this—if anyone gets to read this—you might think that insane considering what I've done since meeting June. And I get that, but I don't feel it. What I do now doesn't erase what I didn't do in Phoenix.

"You know..." Dallas says a few minutes later, "that angsty funk pouring out of you right now is not going to help us get June back. Quite the opposite, you know."

She stops and faces me, the flashlight on the dirty pavement, but there's enough light for me to see her face. It's intense, but there is a whisper of compassion there.

"I've... I..." I shake my head and take a deep breath. "Some bad shit went down in Phoenix and my inaction cost some good people their lives."

The words come out in a rush, but I don't feel any better, that wasn't a confession, not really.

Dallas bites her thumbnail and slowly nods. She doesn't tell me the bad things she's done. She doesn't tell me that because of the Zs all sins are forgiven. She's got a few years on me, but given how wild she can be, I didn't really expect such a measured response from her.

She rubs her face, the fatigue suddenly showing. She slowly turns in a circle shining the flashlight around the perimeter. At first, I think she's looking for Zs, but she's not. "You and me," she says when she's facing me again. "It's just us out here. No Zs. None of our petty, peculiar warlords. Right?"

I nod, not sure where she's going and crack the smallest of smiles. I've said "psychotic, petty, wannabe warlord" over and over but she never seems to remember it.

"We're humans. We're alive. Right?" she continues.

I nod again.

"I've seen that look on your face before, Beckman. Talia, when she was trying to woo me, seemed to think that opening up to me would create some kind of a bond. She told me all about Albuquerque."

Her face darkens and she looks down. "She's got Albuquerque. You've got Phoenix. I've got that shit I pulled on you and June and much worse. We all have to find a way to live in the present and *live* with our past. No damn magic formula there."

She sighs, turns, and starts walking down the road.

"But..." I say as I catch up to her and fall in line beside her. "But, what does that mean?"

She snorts. "It means you're human, Beckman. And it also means I don't want to hear all your shit. Save that for your girlfriend once we rescue her, because I'm not your priest and I'm not your girlfriend, and we haven't been friends long enough for that."

I'm silent, chewing it over.

"Got it?" she asks, her voice just a bit too high.

"Yes. Got it." And I do get it. Hearing it would be a burden and we have enough burdens right now. It might be the proverbial straw for Dallas. If I told her, it would be all about me, not about her.

But I want to confess, because I'm afraid that if I don't do it now I won't have another chance.

I take a deep breath and shake it off.

First we get June back.

Then we find a place to survive.

And then we can try to heal.

CHAPTER SIXTY-SIX

THE TRUCK IS in the Desert View parking lot. I am so happy to see it that I almost cry. A brand-new—at the time of the apocalypse—crew-cab, jet-black Toyota pickup truck. Just the kind of truck I always wanted, but could never afford.

The keys are under the floor mat. It starts right up. There's gas in the tank and extra in jerry cans in the bed. We shuck our packs, hop in, and get going.

I pull out of the lot and get us back on 64 heading east towards Cameron. The cab is a bit stuffy and we roll the windows down, letting the wind blow through.

Years from now, if humanity recovers from the zombie apocalypse and something comes of this scribbling I've been doing and the efforts of June, Dallas, and myself, I wonder how I'll be viewed.

I've got a big mouth, but not like Dallas. I'm not the best fighter, that would be June. I'm brash and daring, but decidedly mild compared to the mercurial Dallas. And I'm not the smartest. June, once you get to know her, has a very sharp mind.

Even in emotional intelligence, I'm a distant third. They both seem to be able to read me like an open book.

So what am I compared to these two strong women?

Lucky comes to mind. Never bored, that's certainly true. Driven to be worthy of their companionship, without a doubt. Not good enough... yeah, there it is. This is what I fear. I've got my baggage and flaws which seem so big next to theirs. But, then again, I'm the one stuck in my head, so I can hope they don't see my flaws as clearly as I do.

I do think, though, that the one thing I bring to the table is my strange way of thinking. Taking little pieces of things (either literally or figuratively) and pulling them into something useful.

And BS. I'm pretty good at the BS.

"Time to tell me the plan?" Dallas asks, her voice loud, rising above the wind whipping through the cab.

It's dark, the headlights only catching glimpses of the desert, rocks and scraggly bushes whipping by. I've been down this road, there were no wrecks before, so we're going fast. We need to get as far as we can before the sun comes up.

We've lost some elevation and eased into the desert. The night is nice, in the low fifties.

I clear my throat. "The plan requires electronics, at least one drone, explosives, and an epic amount of BS. And caffeine, lots of caffeine."

She nods. "So Best Buy is for the drone and electronics. What about the explosives?"

I shake my head. "No clue, really. I'm thinking after we have everything else, we'll head east on I-40. They always seemed to be working on bridges out that way. I quickly searched one site when June was captured before, but it could be worth a second look. I've got a few other ideas."

I've been thinking about explosives quite a bit since June and my encounter with the Mount Elden psychotic, petty, wannabe warlord. It's valuable stuff in this new world and I think there are probably quite a few places to find it if you know where to look. Besides road construction, mining is a major use of explosives.

Dallas and I have been lucky so far, and I'm afraid that luck is going to run out before we get to June.

"And your psycho warlord friend?" she asks.

I shrug. "Keep your fingers crossed."

"Always, Beckman. Always."

CHAPTER SIXTY-SEVEN

ELDEN LOOKOUT TOWER sits on the southeastern portion of Mount Elden, right above the east side of Flagstaff with a great view of the big box stores behind the mall, including Best Buy, Home Depot, as well as I-40 heading east.

The psychotic, petty, wannabe warlord—we didn't get his name, I thought of him as "Mr. Short and Stocky" and June thought of him as "Asshole"—has a camp up there and mans the tower. I am quite sure that I'm on the "shoot on sight" list, so Flagstaff is not a friendly place, but the only place in the area with the kinds of stores we need.

On the way into town, while it's still dark, I change my mind and route around side roads with headlights off and get onto I-40 east and drive out to the ancient, crumbling Twin Arrows Trading Post.

The beat-up Ford Focus June and I used in our escape from Mr. Short and Stocky is still there, including my faux suicide vest. We get out, approach slowly, and circle the building before I go to the car.

We are hidden from Elden, so I turn on a flashlight, pull out the vest, and watch Dallas's eyes widen. The vest has what looks like thirty sticks of dynamite strapped to it with nails and screws glued to the sticks. There's wires and a dangling dead man's switch.

"What the..." she gasps.

I smile and yell, "Catch!" and toss her the vest.

She curses and dances out of the way, thinking I just threw a bunch of dynamite at her.

"It's fake," I say, laughing.

"Shit, Beckman! Shit!" She marches over and punches me in the shoulder, the one that I bashed into a rock in the Colorado. I go down to my knees in agony.

"Christ! That's the shoulder I hurt."

"Serves you right!"

I make a mental note on the right ways and the wrong ways to tease Dallas. Tossing what looks like a realistic suicide vest at her is definitely the wrong way.

The trunk of the Focus has all the excess supplies I used to create the vest, the dead man's switch, and the fake bag of dynamite I gave to Mr. Short and Stocky. We transfer it all over to the crew cab of the truck.

I brief her on the details of that bluff as we work.

"Talia is looking dumber and dumber," Dallas says. "She should have just put a bullet in your head. And you did all this after knowing June a day?"

"Yeah."

"Before you were in love?"

I shrug. "I got us into that mess. Besides, I think I kinda always was."

I'm moving stuff and Dallas is standing there, dimly illuminated by my flashlight and the cab light of the truck, her hands on her hips.

"What?" I ask, a half-full bag of sand—what the faux dynamite is filled with—in my arms.

She walks up to me, takes my cheeks in her hands, and kisses me straight on the lips. It's not a romantic kiss, she kept her mouth closed and it is only brief.

"What was that for?" I ask.

"Being a decent human being in a world gone mad."

Now I'm staring at her, blinking. Yeah, rescuing June was the right thing to do, but I'm still full of angst about what happened in Phoenix, and the two feelings are at war.

She takes the sand from me, throws it in the truck, and asks, "What's next?"

JUST WEST OF US, I-40 crosses Padre Canyon, a separate bridge for each direction. The west-bound bridge had been recently rebuilt and there's some construction equipment there, a small trailer, and one of those metal shipping containers.

During my bluff with Mr. Short and Stocky, when he demanded that I produce dynamite or he would hurt June, I made a show of driving out here in case they were watching. I did search, but not very well. My bluff was already underway, and I did not want to, under any circumstances, give that psychotic ass any real dynamite. Besides, I didn't have the time.

It's a long shot and we need some shelter anyway, so with the sun just starting to come up, we park the truck behind the trailer and out of view of Mount Elden, and Dallas and I search a second time.

The trailer is useless, but the shipping container is a god-awful mess. It's like when the world went mad, they just threw everything in here. Hand tools, orange cones, construction signs, some jerry cans with gasoline—those go in the truck—, surveying equipment, and some things I just can't identify.

As the sun comes up and the container heats up, we slowly sift through the crap, moving much of it out of the container. We're lucky in that the open end is shielded from Elden by the trailer and we can work quickly.

A few hours later, we get to the back and we find a metal box the size of a small foot locker. I bust the lock and in it, sealed in plastic bags, are stick after stick of dynamite. Plus, a smaller box with several types of blasting caps, wire, and fuse.

Dallas's whoop echoes in the enclosed space and she slaps me on the back. She runs out of the container, points herself north, and screams, "We're coming to blow you up, Talia. You hear that, you sociopathic bitch!"

I pull out one bag and carefully bring it into the light, holding it like a newborn baby, careful not to jostle it. When I get a good look at it, I swear.

"What!?" Dallas asks.

I point inside the sealed plastic at a few crystals that have formed near one end of the dynamite.

Dallas shrugs.

"That's nitroglycerin. The dynamite is old, it's sweating, it's very volatile at this point."

"Volatile?"

I nod. "This little baby gets dropped and then..."

"Boom?" she asks.

I nod. "Boom!"

She's wide-eyed and blinking at me. "June's worth it," she says. Her voice is weak and it comes out as half question.

I smile. "She is." I'm scared, but I have no doubt that June Medina is worth it.

CHAPTER SIXTY-EIGHT

I SPEND the next hour in the shipping container having banished Dallas to the trailer to get some rest. She said she was too nervous, so I showed her how to make the fake dynamite. We are going to need more of it.

I'm not worried about Zs out here that much, although Twin Arrows Casino is not far away and there are likely a bunch there, but it's well beyond zombie radar range. I'm not too worried about Mr. Short and Stocky and his gang either—there's no reason for them to come out this way.

What I am worried about is an explosion.

I tried to get Dallas to go across the highway to the ancient trading post, but her answer was her middle finger. Having spent a few days with her, it's quite clear that it's her favorite finger and she enjoys using it whenever she can.

The trailer is a compromise. I've got one door to the storage container shut and while the blast, if it happens, will direct some energy towards the trailer, I'm hoping it will be mostly contained.

Well... I'm hoping I don't blow myself up. Really, I am.

One stick at a time, I pull the dynamite out. I'm using a flashlight—it's fairly dark back there—and examine them. I am relieved to find that not all of the sticks have sweat an equal amount. Some have almost no nitroglycerin crystals. A few have none.

My heart is beating hard the whole time, sweat dripping into my eyes, my hands slick from the sweat.

But I go slow. I keep rubbing my hands on a towel. I go through one stick at a time, getting the best ones.

I put the good ones back in the box, pack rags around them, and carefully carry it to the truck, put it on the seat of the crew cab, and buckle it in.

"What's next?" Dallas asks. She looks strung out, I'm sure she didn't even try to close her eyes. I know I wouldn't have been able to rest.

"We create a little more faux dynamite and then we sleep. We can't do anything else until dark."

She nods.

"And after that, we rig the rest of the dynamite to blow if someone comes sniffing around."

Her eyes go wide, but there is no Dallas-like whoop. I guess explosives are a bit over her limit. I am relieved to find that the wild Lonestar has a limit.

CHAPTER SIXTY-NINE

AFTER DARK, as we pull away, the shipping container has a couple of sentences scratched on the metal: "Dangerous explosives inside! This will go off if you open the door." Below that, scrawled by Dallas, it says, "Seriously! Walk away now or die, dummy!" And then she drew the image of a hand with the middle finger raised.

The rigging is simple, really. The remaining dynamite is in a cardboard box up high on a shelf with a string tied to the second door of the shipping container. Opening it will pull the box down and the odds of the nitro igniting are high.

No one will see it unless they go through this site, but with the dynamite just getting more dangerous with time, I wanted to both warn and try to keep it out of the hands of dummies.

And, yeah, I'm the one cruising down I-40 with my headlights off as dusk slides into darkness with a container full of dynamite. But hey, I'm trying to save the woman of my post-apocalyptic dreams, so maybe I'm more of a fool in love than a dummy.

I glance over at Dallas and she gives me a weak smile. Even with her around, I think laughter is going to be hard to come by today.

We go "shopping" at Best Buy, OfficeMax, and Home Depot and find what we need. Again, we're lucky. I even snag a few journals and some good pens so I can start writing for real. It's on our way out of town that our luck runs out.

We're just heading out on 89 going north, back towards Cameron and the Grand Canyon. There's a quicker way to get to the Grand Canyon Village on the South Rim, but I don't dare try to drive all the way through Flagstaff. There's another gang at the university.

We've just passed Townsend-Winona Road and all the wrecks and blockages are behind us. I'm picking up speed when a pickup truck lurches into the road and blocks both lanes, men in the bed pointing rifles at us.

I throw the truck into reverse and another truck blocks our way back with more men and more rifles.

There are four lanes here and soon all of them are blocked by trucks, lights shining on us, guns pointed at us. The psychotic, petty, wannabe warlord found us. It has to be him.

Dallas curses with gusto and then adds, "What do we do now?"

I could head off the road, go around them, but there is no getting away from that many trucks and that many guns.

"Stall them," I hiss, "but don't leave the truck. And find out what Mr. Short and Stocky's real name is."

I pull the suicide vest out from the crew cab and put it

on. I then crawl over the seat, into the back, and dig into the dynamite case.

"Hey, officers!" Dallas calls in a cheerful voice. She opens the door and stands in behind it. "Were we going too fast? We kinda thought that with the apocalypse and all that no one cared anymore."

I'm moving as fast as I can with the dynamite, but I really can't go that fast.

"Where is he?" a male voice shouts from the trucks in front of us. I can't see him, but I recognize his voice. Mr. Short and Stocky. "Diamondback and I need to have a discussion."

Dallas sticks her head into the cab and says, "'Diamond-back,' ha! He thinks of you as Diamondback. That, my friend, is your new nickname... for however long we live."

"Just stall," I hiss, my hands shaking from the 5-hour energy drinks we both slammed before hitting the road.

"Yeah, Diamondback will be right with you," Dallas calls. "But in the meantime, maybe you can settle a little debate for us. Seeing as you guys were never properly intro-duced, Diamondback refers to you as 'Mr. Short and Stocky.' Me, personally, I find that a bit ironic given that Diamondback himself is fairly short and fairly stocky."

I have a stick of dynamite out of its plastic wrapper and am inserting a safety fuse into the thin metal blasting cap, my hands shaking, my breath coming fast, the mountain night suddenly hot. I crimp the end of the blasting cap with my multi-tool so the fuse won't come out.

"I mean," Dallas continues, "short and stocky works for me, provided the man is kind, has a heart, you know?"

"What are you talking about?" Mr. Short and Stocky yells. I figure we're still alive because he wants to kill me personally, and up close.

"Oh. Sorry," she replies. "Please forgive me. Not that many people to have conversations with these days. Let me get to the point. Your name. Diamondback thinks of you as Mr. Short and Stocky, but another friend of mine just thinks of you as Asshole. I'm wondering what your real name is, so when we have a conversation about you, we can use the correct moniker."

I cringe and push the completed blasting cap and fuse into the dynamite. Dallas is doing her thing, crossing every line possible. I expect the bullets to fly at any moment.

I hear a chuckle. "Asshole. I like that. Was that what the skinny girl called me?"

"Yes, sir, Mr. Asshole."

"You are not so skinny of a girl," he says. "I like that, maybe I won't kill you. So, get your friend out here. Now!"

"But your name," Dallas says, her voice taking on a girlish whine. "Please."

He sighs. "Brown. Call me Mr. Brown."

Dallas ducks her head back in the cab. "God, that's a boring name. You ready yet?"

I nod and step out of the truck, suicide vest on, one hand held high with the dead man's switch, the other holding the stick of dynamite.

Mr. Brown laughs, it's loud, kind of this overdone guffaw, and very appropriate for a psychotic, petty, wannabe warlord, but it doesn't last long. "I won't fall for that two times, boy."

I nod. "If you don't mind, I thought we might have a quick demonstration before you kill me."

He shrugs. "Sure. Your friend has put me in a good mood and I am feeling generous."

"How did you find us?" I ask.

He points out in the darkness back towards Flagstaff.

"We have someone on top of the tower of the pet food factory now."

I nod. It makes sense, it's the highest thing besides the mountain in the area. He's extended his territory while I was gone.

"I have a deal for you," I say, wiggling the stick of dynamite. "After our last meeting, I've made it my mission to find real dynamite. I've been all over the area. I know where it all is now."

"Bullshit." He spits the word out and I get the feeling he wants to spit on me... for starters. My bluff must have shamed him, and that's really the last thing you want to do to a psychotic, petty, wannabe warlord.

My hands are high as I walk forward a few steps until I'm halfway between our truck and his. The night is cool and all gloomy darkness except for the harsh pool of light created by the headlights.

I carefully set down the stick and slowly step back.

"It's real," I say. "That's about a ten-second fuse. Light it, but I suggest you throw it far."

Brown nods at one of his beefy boys who recovers the dynamite and returns.

"Real, you say?" he calls.

"Yes. Real. No bullshit."

"And your deal?"

"We just raided a store not far from here. I couldn't take it all. You let us go, I'll tell you where to find the dynamite."

He's silent as he fingers the stick of dynamite and I can almost see the wheels moving in his head. He holds the stick to his face and sniffs, his brow furrowing below his brown-grey buzzed hair.

"I must tell you," I say, "that I found C4 as well as dynamite and my employer has it all except for this. She knows where we are, she knows when to expect us. She knows about you. If I don't make it back with this she'll come looking, and believe me, you won't like that."

He's holding the dynamite and starts pacing back and forth in front of the trucks.

"Lies. All lies," he says.

"Light it," I say, slowly stepping back to the truck. "See if I'm lying."

"What have you got to lose, Mr. Asshole?" Dallas shouts. And then quieter to me, but loud enough for them to hear. "I don't think he's got the balls or the sense. Isn't it better to get some dynamite than to start a war?"

I suppress a smile. There are no women among Mr. Brown's group, and having a woman suggest he's lacking balls is perfect. I don't know him well, but in many ways, I think he's worse than Talia.

Someone pulls out a lighter and I duck behind the open door to the truck and yell, "Throw it as far as you can."

The fuse hisses to life and Brown throws it into the trees on the side of the road. He's got a good arm, but the stick hits a tree and falls to the ground. I dive into the truck and Dallas does the same.

There is a bright flash of light and the truck is buffeted right before the sound of the explosion smashes into my ears. A few moments later dirt and pine needles come raining down.

There are curses and whoops and hollers, the loudest, of course, from Dallas who's slapping me on the back. "Oh my God, Woody. Holy Shit! I want to shove one of those bad boys up Talia's ass and light up. Whoop!"

Silence descends as the shock and adrenaline wear off and Brown and his gang start thinking about the implications of dynamite and what it means and what they can do with it.

"Now get out there and sell it, Diamondback," Dallas hisses and shoves me towards to door.

I walk out, the dead man's switch held high. "Do we have a deal?" I shout. The air has an acrid, smoky smell to it and there is some mumbling from the trucks both in front of and behind us.

"You expect me to trust you?" Brown asks.

"Kill me or trust me," I say. "Take a chance on acquiring dynamite or start a war you will lose." I shrug as casually as I can but am shaking inside from the caffeine and adrenaline.

Mr. Brown stares at me for the longest time before nodding his head.

CHAPTER SEVENTY

"I MEAN, the fools are going to get there and probably blow themselves up," Dallas says, the energy in her voice just making me feel exhausted.

I told Brown where to get the dynamite, out at Padre Canyon, even explained that I was so rushed the first time I was there, I couldn't really search properly.

She's driving and I'm in the back rigging more sticks of dynamite and working on the suicide vest. We're past the turnoff to Sunset Crater, 89A making its quick decent down into the desert, the pine trees shrinking to be replaced by juniper trees and then the grasses of the high desert.

"We can hope," I say, quietly.

My mind is spinning. Brown is mean, and fairly smart, but Talia is smarter and with more at stake.

"I mean, what a brilliant combination of the truth and BS. Diamondback strikes again!"

"You know, I don't think I like that nickname."

"Too damn bad, Diamondback. You rattle and the petty, mean... wait, what is your phrase?"

"Psychotic, petty, wannabe warlords."

"Yeah, you rattle and the psychotic, petty, wannabe warlords go-a-runnin'!"

We hit a bump and I almost drop the stick of dynamite I'm holding. Probably nothing would have happened, but my heart does a tap dance in my chest.

"Slow down there, Lonestar. I'm handling dynamite back here. Besides, I've got a lot to do before we meet Talia."

"Sure. Sure. Man, I feel alive. Do you feel alive, Diamondback?"

"Yeah. I feel super alive," I say dryly. "Now, please slow down so we *stay* alive."

WE MAKE it to Desert View without incident and head west twenty-five miles, paralleling the rim of the Grand Canyon to Grand Canyon Village. This is where all the tourists came, and this is where that zombie herd must have originated before it took to wandering along the rim in search of living flesh and delicious brains.

My theory—and you knew I had one, didn't you?—is that the herd started at the Grand Canyon Village and cleaned the area out, either eating or chasing away all the living humans, not to mention the animals.

And then they got hungry, but there were a lot of them, so their fungal super brain (remember their fresh meat radar was much better in a group) had the bright idea of trying different territory, so they probably wandered west all the way out to Hermit's Rest and then back east all the way to Desert View.

From time to time as they wandered back and forth, they'd come across new groups of the living who figured the

Grand Canyon might be a good place to hole up, or trap animals that hadn't long since vacated the area.

They found enough food this way so that their wanderings became something of a regular patrol.

Okay, end of theory, back to the rescue.

We don't stop, we drive right to Bright Angel Lodge, park in front, and get on Bright Angel Trail and start the ten-mile hike down to Phantom Ranch.

It's been four days since we left June with Talia and I'm worried. Worried how Talia has treated her, hoping she is still alive. I'm worried about this plan that June and I sketched out in our three days in the forest on the North Rim. Will it work? Is there even a shot?

In one respect, I am grateful for the encounter with Brown and company. It was kind of like a dress rehearsal and gave me a few more ideas.

Our packs are loaded down and very heavy. We've got the altered suicide vest, water, food, and electronics. Plus, I'm carrying the bag of fake and real dynamite. I have every portable solar charger we could find hanging off my pack to charge the batteries we need. We might actually have to delay a day, so we have enough sunshine to charge them.

"So, what do you think our odds are?" Dallas asks as we start down the switchbacks, lighting our way with a flashlight. It's a few hours until dawn.

"Of what?" I ask. "Saving June or finishing Talia?"

"Let's start with Talia."

"Oh, those odds are good. As long we get her onto the bridge, she's likely going down one way or another."

"And saving June?" she asks quietly. "And all of us hiking back out?"

I shake my head. "Not so good."

We're quiet for a long time and then I add, "But you,

Lonestar, your odds of survival are quite good. You're our sniper so you won't be in the thick of it."

She's unusually silent and angst is almost radiating off her.

"Naw," she says. "If my new best friend doesn't make it, well... let's just say I could get a little crazy."

I open my mouth to argue with her, but who am I to tell anyone how to live in this post-A world. Hell, I'm hiking, caring a bag full of explosives and a suicide vest that isn't quite fake anymore. Who am I to tell Dallas how to live much less die?

"You want to talk that part through?" I finally ask. "I mean if you're going to go 'a little crazy,' you might as well be smart about it."

She sniffs and rubs at her face but doesn't speak right away. "Yeah, that... that'd be great."

So we spend the next few miles talking about how if June and I don't make it, Dallas will ensure that Talia and a few of the crueler members of Phantom Company don't make it either. We even allocate a few sticks of dynamite to the "Lonestar Goes Berserk" plan.

Morbid? Yes. But if the apocalypse did anything, it opened our eyes to the gift of life and the inevitability of death. Best live the former as well as you can before that latter comes calling.

CHAPTER SEVENTY-ONE

PLANS like these are hard to make. They don't descend fully formed from the heavens. Getting boots on the ground can change everything, and having someone more familiar with the surroundings can help.

Dallas and I talk it through on the hike down. We talk sporadically and quietly, keeping our ears open for Zs. We take breaks frequently because of our heavy loads.

So, my first idea was to get Talia and company on the Kaibab Suspension Bridge, but that won't work. Dallas reminds me that the sides are metal railings about five feet high. The same is true for the Bright Angel Bridge, making them both a bad place for the exchange. I need Dallas to have a clear shot.

"If Talia actually goes for trading June for dynamite, June is gonna..." Dallas let out a long, low whistle. "Well, let's just say that hell hath no fury like a military trained woman traded for explosives."

I chuckle, grateful for anything resembling laughter. I can't imagine June being happy to be traded for explosives, but I'm sure she'll be glad to be out of there. But that isn't all the trade is about. We will rain holy hell down on them if Talia doesn't give us June, so there is that.

We switch the trade location to right across the Bright Angel Bridge. We need them in the open and I want Talia to bring lots of her people. Their numbers don't increase our danger and I have a hunch it will help. Well, a hope at least, that June has made some headway down there.

The sun comes up as we descend, and as much as I hate to do it, we stop before the final descent into the inner gorge —where we would be visible to Phantom Company—and hike off the trail a good ways and find shelter.

We spend the day alternating between sleep and prep— there are still some electronics to rig, batteries to charge, and a note to write to Talia.

While Dallas sleeps, I pull my "Woody and June versus the Apocalypse" notes out and scribble down more details. I've got one of the journals we picked up at OfficeMax and I just start to write more notes and then start writing it as a story. I feel this pressure, the need to... well, it's kind of confessing my sins, I guess, but I know I'm a long way from writing about Phoenix, so I start in Flagstaff at the dog food plant, because shouldn't a love story start when the couple meets?

And I am hoping that this is a love story, one with a happy ending.

Really, I need this love story to have a happy ending, despite the apocalypse, despite the prevalence of zombies and psychotic, petty, wannabe warlords. I feel it in my stomach, which is a tight knot, and I'm hungry and nauseous at the same time.

But writing helps, so I give in to the pressure to write, and I write, as fast as I can.

I don't stop to think about that pressure then, but with just a little hindsight, it's clear that I don't believe that we will succeed, that we will survive this rescue attempt, and I need to capture something of Woody and June that will outlive us.

The words just pour out of me and I write as quickly as I can. I focus on remembering our words as clearly as possible, the sights and smells of our journey, how things felt—all the things that will quickly fade from memory.

When Dallas stirs, I stow the journal back in my pack, not ready to talk about what I'm doing, and certainly not ready for a biting comment from her.

I go back to rigging the dead man's switch, making it real this time.

"How'd you learn to do all that?" Dallas asks sleepily as she pushes herself up into a sitting position, yawns and stretches.

"It's not complicated," I say, holding up the jury-rigged assembly. It's the hacked off handle of a leaf blower, red electrical tape over the spring-loaded switch with wires dangling from it. There's a couple of LEDs embedded in the bottom of a handle that glow red when it's powered. "It's a switch, altered to be off when pressed and on when released, some LEDs just for show, some wires, a battery, and an electronic detonator."

"Blasting cap?" she asks

I nod. "The detonator. Some of the blasting caps use a fuse, some can be triggered electronically."

"So... how'd you learn all this crap?"

I nod vaguely to the south. "All post-A. I was in that group in northern Phoenix led by one of those charismatic psychopaths."

"Wait," she says, holding her hand up. "I'll get it this

time." She sits up straight, her face serious. "Petty, pustulant, pouty, psychotic, pedantic person..."

I just sit there shaking my head. "No."

"Hmmm... Let me try again. Psychotic, always-gotta-be-right, power-hungry, post-apocalyptic asshole?"

I crack a smile. "I like that one."

"So... he was one of those?"

"Oh yeah, makes Talia look like a kindergarten teacher. He had an old dude working for him he called 'Q,' à la James Bond, and the guy took a shine to me and taught me all this stuff. Taught me about electronics and explosives and lots of crazy things."

Dallas is quiet for a while, drinks some water, and we share a very stale power bar. "What happened to Q?"

I shake my head. "You don't want to hear my confession, remember?"

Dallas nods. We've all seen the bad side of the apocalypse, and in some ways, we are living it now. But it's different this time, right? I've got purpose and friends, people who aren't psychopaths or petty, and have no desire to be warlords. I can let go of the past, right?

"He's gone," I add, feeling the weight of it bearing down on me again.

"So you're Q now," she says, scooting over the dirt and sitting next to me. "Show me."

Her face is hard to read, maybe she wants to know, maybe she's just trying to distract me—in either case, I can use the distraction. I show her each piece of the dead man's switch, all the changes I made, put in the battery, and feel the electricity when the switch is released. We then get some longer wire, hook up a blasting cap, and make sure it works.

It does. Once I add real dynamite to the suicide vest, I can officially blow myself up.

Now I've got something that in one fell swoop violates both of my rules for each day. First, it will kill me, so survival is out; and second, having real dynamite and a real dead man's switch is going to make it extraordinarily hard to laugh.

And my newly minted third rule of spending time with June... well, that's what this is all about.

CHAPTER SEVENTY-TWO

WE SNEAK down the rest of the way during dusk, when it's light enough for us to see the trail without flashlights, and dark enough so that it will be hard for the Phantom Company sentries to see us.

Dallas assures me that odds are low. She was a sentry, and besides guarding the bridges, they were supposed to watch the trails on the other side, but in reality, they all get bored and don't do nearly enough of that.

Bright Angel Trail ends at the suspension bridge and River Trail connects to Kaibab Trail and that suspension bridge. Much of River Trail is exposed and in clear view of the sentries.

We can't bushwhack around, the terrain is just too rugged, the cliff of the inner gorge too steep, so we have to use the trail.

Once in sight of the river, we stop until it's nearly pitch dark and move slowly and carefully on the trail past the Bright Angel bridge.

My heart is pounding and I can barely breath. The

noise of the rushing river will overwhelm any noise we might make, but they could spot us.

We go slow and steady, in case anyone is looking over this way, so they don't catch any movement in the darkness. We get past the bridge and go up River Trail, which is mostly carved into the side of the cliff and the 1.5-billion-year-old Vishnu Schist.

I think of my old friend Q, his grey hair and wrinkled face, his Boston accent. If this was his territory, he'd have rigged solar-powered motion sensors and what Dallas and I are doing would be impossible. Alarms would be going off by now.

Just because there's been an apocalypse, doesn't mean you have to completely abandon knowledge and technology... not to mention civility and compassion.

Once we get up River Trail a ways, we find a perfect spot for Dallas right off the trail. Perfect in the sense that you can see both bridges and all of the Bright Angel Creek delta that Phantom Company is farming and housing their burros on.

What's not perfect is it's right off the trail and quite exposed. But we don't really have a choice. Dallas tells me this trail gets patrolled every few days, but isn't actually used. If a patrol comes out, we'll see them, but our campaign to get June back starts at first light, so hopefully there won't be any patrols.

We settle in behind a large boulder and try to rest, but I find it impossible. There are too many things that can go wrong. Too many ways to die. And way too few ways for this to work.

CHAPTER SEVENTY-THREE

BEFORE DAWN, I pack up my gear. I need to be closer to the bridge.

"You got this, Diamondback," Dallas says, tugging at my ball cap.

I nod, too nervous to even speak. Success means June, failure means death. I don't see how the stakes can get higher.

"And if you don't..." I see her shrug in starlit darkness. "Well, Talia will have to deal with Lonestar armed with a hunting rifle and not a goddamn thing to lose."

I swallow hard. "I'll do my best so that doesn't have to happen."

We're silent and I hear Dallas sniff. "Get June back, okay? I was awful to you two and want to have a chance to make it up to her."

"Yeah. I'll get her back." I try to sound confident, but am anything but.

She pulls me into a hug and holds me tight and I hug her back. She sniffs more and so do I.

"You are not to shoot unless this goes south, right?" I say.

"Yes, Woody. No shooting."

"And 'goes south' means June and I are already dead. Nothing short of that. Nothing. Do you hear me?"

She lets go of me. "I got it, Woody, I do. If you and June live, Talia lives."

I stare at her, not that I can really see her face with the sky to the east just starting to lighten. I need this mission to be more important than her vengeance. Can I trust her?

I take her hand and squeeze it, my hand shaking.

"I won't let you down," she whispers and then kisses me on the cheek.

I let go and make my slow way down the exposed trail, past the bridge, and take cover behind a mesquite tree right off the trail. It's terrible cover, as these things go, but I won't need it long.

In the dark, I get a drone out, a high-end quadcopter with HD camera and about twenty minutes of run time. I attach a live piece of dynamite, with blasting cap and fuse, and attach the white flag and note we wrote. I power up the tablet and attach it to the drone controller, which is basically two little joysticks, two antennas, and a few buttons.

My hands are shaking, and I have to slow myself down. I whisper to myself, just like I did when Dallas and I walked away from June, "This is not over, this is not over, this is *not* over."

Please don't let this be over.

By some miracle, I've found a reason to live in this world and I so want to live now. Not just survive, but *live*.

As soon as there's enough light for the drone's camera to work, I get my binoculars out and look for June's sign. We had planned this when we were being hunted by Phantom

Company. I search frantically in the dim light trying to find it.

If I don't find it, June and I agreed that I would abort any rescue attempt because it would mean she wasn't alive.

Five minutes of searching, and I don't see it and I decide to join Lonestar in her berserker plan, shed my humanity, and embrace the apocalypse.

But, no, there it is. In the rocks on the hill above the burro stables are five sticks sticking up in the gravelly dirt next to three rocks forming a small cairn. June survived five days. This is day six since we parted.

She's okay.

I wipe the sweat from my brow and launch the drone, sending it up river several hundred yards, across the Colorado, and downstream as fast as it will go.

I stop it just past the bridge, the camera trained on the sentries, two thirty-something men. I recognize them from our time with Phantom Company, but don't know their names.

Their jaws fall open, which makes me smile, the sign must be working, because they don't shoot the drone. The top of the sign says, "Live Dynamite Attached. Do Not Shoot Unless You Want to DIE!"

Right below it says, "Will trade dynamite for June. Get Talia now! Cross either bridge and you die, both are rigged to explode."

In smaller text are more instructions on the exchange and on testing the dynamite. I land the drone and one of the sentries goes running.

This is it. Showtime.

CHAPTER SEVENTY-FOUR

AN HOUR LATER, right after I puke what little I have in
my stomach, I put on the suicide vest, put my green army
surplus jacket on over it, attach the dead man's switch with
the button firmly pressed down, and zip up the jacket.

I am now a bomb.

My heart pounds hard and I feel dizzy, standing there
for a moment until I can get myself under control. I take a
deep breath, pick up the bag of dynamite, and make my way
onto the trail and walk onto the Bright Angel Suspension
Bridge.

The drone's batteries died before Talia got back, but
they have tested the dynamite attached to the drone and
followed the instructions.

At the bridge, I put down the bag and use my binoculars, one-handed of course, and see the group approaching.
Talia in the lead, with Harris, Sal, and Mary. I only see a
glimpse of June's black hair, she's shorter than the rest of
them and in the middle of the group.

I look towards where I know Dallas is and do my best to

smile. I don't feel like a diamondback rattlesnake. I feel like a boy who has gotten way in over his head and wishes the adults would swoop in and straighten it all out.

With the jacket and the nerves, I am sweating profusely despite the cool morning.

This bridge has a series of gates set up, just like the Kaibab Bridge, that are easy for the living to open and walk through. I leave them all open.

I get a glimpse of June as I get towards the other side of the bridge. Her face doesn't look right. I stop and use my binoculars. She has a cracked lip and her left cheek is swollen. I grip the dead man's switch so hard that my sweaty fingers are in danger of slipping off.

Then I see Talia and smile. The tall woman has one eye nearly swollen shut. Whatever happened, it appears both of them took a few good blows. I hope I live long enough to hear the story.

The gate on the far side is tall with razor wire on the top and locked. There is one terrified-looking guard there who opens the gate for me.

"Back with them," I say, nodding towards the group standing just a few yards back from the gate.

He nods and seems happy to be getting away from me.

"Hello, Talia," I say as I approach, getting a better look at her bruised face. I can just imagine Dallas smiling ear-to-ear seeing this through her rifle scope. "Have a bad spill or something?"

Her lips purse, and she raises one thin eyebrow, but she doesn't say anything.

"You okay, June?" I ask.

"Just fine," she says, her tone tight.

"Let's see it," Talia says.

I walk forward a few steps, drop the bag of dynamite,

and back up. There is a blinking LED taped to it with some wires running into the bag, very similar to the pack I gave Mr. Short and Stocky up on Mount Elden.

Talia nods to Sal, who walks slowly up to the bag.

"Unzip it," I say. "Feel free to look, but don't touch any of the wires."

Sal whistles and then says, "Shit! There are a bunch a nails in here with the dynamite."

"Insurance," I say.

"What the hell are you talking about?" Talia asks.

I slowly unzip my jacket with my free hand and reveal the suicide vest, which is covered in sticks of dynamite with nails glued to them. I push my left hand out of the sleeve of my jacket and show them the dead man's switch. "The detonator blows both. If the blast doesn't do the job, the nails will."

Jaws drop and there are gasps. I smile, feeling less nervous now that the confrontation is finally here.

"So there's the dynamite," I say. "June and I will be going now."

Talia doesn't move, her one good eye boring into me. I'm not expecting this to be easy, but I'm not prepared for what she does next.

She steps forward boldly, kicks the bag of dynamite aside and walks right up to me. She's several inches taller than me and I have to look up to meet her eyes.

"Bullshit!" she says. "You wouldn't kill your precious June, you doe-eyed weakling."

She pulls a knife out so quick I can't react and pokes several of the sticks on my suicide vest. They start leaking sand, and before I can say a thing, the knife is back on her belt and her gun is pressed to my forehead, pushing the brim of my hat up. "Any last words, Woody Woodpecker? Because, ttthattt's all, folks."

I blink, my mind still catching up with her boldness. "You're wrong. Some of the dynamite is fake, I'll give you that, but some is real." My heart is pounding and I am sweating all over, drops sliding into my eyes and stinging.

"Bullshit!"

"You haven't pulled the trigger, so you can't be sure, so let me prove it."

The gun leaves my forehead and she backs up a step.

"I am prepared to die today, so is June. We had plenty of time to talk about this out in the forest."

Talia twists around and glances at June's crossed arms, pursed lips, and hard eyes.

With my free hand, I point at a cluster of sticks over my sternum. "Look closely. See those small crystals. These sticks are old, they're sweating. That is nitroglycerin. The bag has fake sticks, but four real ones too, and lots of screws and nails."

Talia's jaw is moving, her cheeks flushing red, I can see the fury in her eyes.

"The first time I did this, it was a bluff, but not this time. I found dynamite, you already proved it. Do you somehow think I only found one stick?"

Talia is breathing heavily and her whole face is red now, she steps back up to me and presses the gun to my forehead. "I don't believe you. Maybe some of the dynamite is real, you wouldn't kill yourself, you wouldn't kill *her*."

"Just because you've never had anyone you'd be willing to die for, doesn't mean I don't."

My mind flashes to Dallas, I can see her, her finger tensing on the trigger, sweat beading her brow, her heart beating fast, wanting to kill Talia, but trying to hold back. I just hope our bond is strong enough, because if Talia dies, June and I are dead... for sure.

And somehow that empowers me, and I feel this growing boldness. I'm going to die, either Dallas will lose it or Talia will shoot. What is there to lose?

"Go ahead, Talia," I say, my voice getting stronger. "Shoot. Kill us all. End this now. Do it!"

Seconds tick by and I can't see her well with the gun to my forehead, but she is getting even redder. "Okay," she says calmly, slowly pulling back the hammer.

Time slows down all cliched, B-movie style, and I can hear each heartbeat reverberating through my brain, each breath flowing past my nose, down into my lungs. The essence of life, heart and breath, becoming so loud right before they are about to be extinguished.

The psychotic part of Talia was the one thing we couldn't predict. What path the pressure of our attack would push her down, whether she would choose death rather than defeat.

And in her mind, there is a chance I'm bluffing with the dead man's switch, that the wires don't actually do anything. She's partially right, the bag is a bluff, I didn't have the right equipment to do a wireless trigger, but the vest is not.

She shoots, we all die.

I hear shouts and see a flash of movement. June breaks free of the others, surges forward, and dives towards Talia.

It's not going to work, she's going to fall short.

The beating of my heart grows louder in my head and my breath seems to slow.

Talia slowly squeezes the trigger.

I love you, June Medina.

You better, Woody Beckman!

June's dive turns into a roll just as the hammer starts to fall. I feel a surprising moment of peace there between the heartbeats, between the breaths, when I'm still alive but everything is still. I love June and she knows it. I found love in this completely insane world. While I do want more time, isn't that really what it's all about?

As the hammer is about to hit the back of the bullet, June's feet slam into the back of Talia's knees and the gun flies up right as the bullet fires, knocking my hat off, parting my hair, scraping my skull, but not blowing my brains out.

And then time falls back on me with more force than the Colorado when I was thrown into that rapid. I fall to my knees holding the dead man switch tight, clamping my second hand over the first, my ears ringing from the gunshot.

Blood is oozing from the wound, trickling down my forehead, the bullet's trail burning, but I ignore it.

Talia scrambles to her feet cursing, there are shouts from Sal and Harris and Mary, but I can't hear them.

June is there, her face just inches from me and I inhale deeply of her sweet and sweaty scent, her blue eyes locking with mine.

"I love you, Woody Beckman," she says.

My heart skips a beat. She's saying that because she thinks we're all about to die.

"You better, June Medina."

CHAPTER SEVENTY-FIVE

THERE'S SHOUTING AND CURSING, a huge argument is going on around us, but I try to suck up as much of the ocean blue eyes of June as I can. I try to breathe her in, memorize her face, feel her breath.

"She shot you," June says, her tone even.

I nod, I can feel the slow trickle of blood on my forehead and a fiery burn where the bullet grazed me. "Just a flesh wound," I say.

"The vest is real, right?" she asks.

I nod. "And Dallas has Talia in her scope right now."

"Okay. I have a *plan*." She ends with a wicked smile, but before I can say anything she slowly stands up and brushes off her jeans.

The argument is fierce and seems to come down to whether Talia almost got them all killed. It's Talia and Sal against Harris and Mary.

"We're just going to leave now," June says quietly, "and let you all sort this out. Seems like a family affair to me."

Somehow, her voice filters through the noise and they all stop and then four guns are pointed at us.

"I don't think so," Talia says.

June ignores her. "Harris, Mary, Sal, listen to me. We talked about this. How much effort and how much risk did Talia expend to get me back? How many of you could I have killed when you captured me? I don't want to be here, Talia knows this. She did this just to have what she wants, to prove that she is right.

"Every deal she's made with us was either an outright lie, or stacked so survival was nearly impossible."

"Shut up, June," Talia says, walking to June and aiming the gun at her head. "I will only warn you once."

"Woody's vest is real. Under Talia's leadership, we will all die. If I hadn't stopped her we would already be dead."

Talia's face is beet red again and I know that June has gone too far. She has crossed the line with Talia and is now the enemy.

Talia cocks her gun, but Harris slides behind her and presses his gun to her back. "Now, now," he says, his jaw bunching. "I want to hear what the young lady has to say."

"Ask yourself," June continues, "are Woody and I worth this war? We didn't want to stay, if we had just been given the option to leave, none of this would have happened." She locks eyes with Harris. "Make no mistake, we either walk away, or people die."

I slowly get to my feet, feeling as weak as a rag doll, and pull a handkerchief from my pocket and wipe the blood out of my face. "There are four real pieces of dynamite in that bag, with blasting caps and a few feet of safety fuse," I say. "My offer was an honest one. But the sticks are old and must be handled with care. We're lucky they didn't blow when she kicked the bag. Yet another brilliant decision on the part of your leader."

Now Sal's gun is pointed at Talia and Mary's too.

"You've got a good thing going here, Tal," June says, gesturing up the canyon towards Phantom Ranch. "But I think it's time for a council, not a petty dictator."

June walks up to me takes my free hand and we walk towards the bridge. I let go of June long enough to pick up my Arizona Diamondback's hat. It has a bullet hole where the bill joins with the hat. I smile and put it back on by bloody head.

"As soon as you are at a safe distance," Talia yells, her voice high-pitched and hysterical, "I'm going to get a rifle and kill you both!"

June turns. "Harris, Sal, Mary, do we have a deal? The dynamite for our safe release, no pursuit?"

"Yes," Harris says.

"I don't care what they say!" Talia snarls. "I'll leave. I'll hunt you down myself. I'll see you both dead."

"I should mention," June adds, "that Dallas has you in her sites right now. She's itching for some payback. Shall I have Woody give her the signal?"

"And I mean," I add, "it took everything I had to convince her not to kill you on sight." I look around the open Bright Angel Creek delta. "And you guys might want to think more about security. You aren't nearly as safe here as you think."

Talia opens her mouth to shout more threats, but Harris hits her on the head with the butt of his gun and she goes down in a heap.

"Can you restrain her for a couple of days? Give us time to regroup and get out of the area?" June asks.

Sal chuckles. "That would be a distinct pleasure."

Just because I can't stand it anymore, I disable the dead man's switch by slowly disconnecting the wires. I'm suddenly panting harder now that the danger of immediate death is past. We can either trust them or we can't, so now or later doesn't make a big difference. I give a thumbs-up signal in Dallas's direction to let her know we're good.

I take June's hand and squeeze it, her eyes bright, her smile wide, and we walk across the bridge towards our future... together.

CHAPTER SEVENTY-SIX

TO SAY our reunion with Dallas is enthusiastic is like saying the sun is hot. It doesn't cover it, not nearly.

"Oh my God!" Dallas cries, tears running down her cheeks as she sprints towards us, her pack bouncing, her hair flying, the rifle in one hand.

She hits me like a linebacker and envelopes me in a hug, her wet cheek against my face.

"She shot you!" she says in between her half laughing, half crying. "I thought I'd have to... Well, I almost... I... I didn't... You..."

I hug her back tight and feel my own tears of relief, very aware that June is standing there watching, and likely much of Phantom Company; we are just across the bridge.

"Live dynamite," I whisper to her. "So, ahh... maybe don't hit me so hard next time."

She laughs, like I just told her a joke and then she disengages and Dallas and June are hugging and I breathe a sigh of relief. June hasn't experienced the last week with Dallas that I have, and I am glad to see them getting along.

They are both crying and I hear "thank yous" from both and then they are whispering. I let them be, dab at my head wound, it's almost done bleeding, so not bad at all, and go get my gear from under the mesquite tree.

I tie my jacket and suicide vest to the pack and get it on my back and look back at the Bright Angel Creek delta with Phantom Ranch beyond. It's nearly a perfect spot to be post-A. Maybe they'll get Talia under control, maybe they'll figure it out, but it's not the place for us.

As I'm looking, I see Harris standing in plain sight looking at us, his hands shoved in his pockets. Dallas told me that he was good with a rifle and was the one we'd have to watch out for. But he's not holding a rifle, he's just standing there, the noisy river between us.

June and Dallas are still talking but have started up the trail and I wave at Harris, and to my surprise he waves back with this half wave, half salute kind of thing.

He's going to honor the deal. I breathe a sigh of relief and catch up with the others.

When I get there, Dallas is saying to June, "...but I'm not sure what to think about it because after me, pantyhose are his next best friend."

My face flushes red.

"Pantyhose?" June asks, her eyes bright.

"Oh yeah," Dallas says with a mischievous smile. "He's a convert. Go ahead, Woody, show June your pantyhose."

They all stop, and with a sigh, I pull up one pant leg and they both laugh, and I just smile. Survival looks good for the day and there's the laughter. I'm okay with it being at my expense.

June gets a serious look on her face and examines my head. She makes me kneel down, takes off my hat, and wets my handkerchief and dabs at the wound. It hurts, but I've suffered worse, a lot worse.

"Not too deep," June says, her fingers gently moving my hair, "but you might need to change your part."

I thank her and we start back up the trail.

"Okay," Dallas says. "We need supplies, we need a destination, but first up, you two need a room."

My cheeks flush red again and I glance at June, but she's looking down as we walk up the dusty trail.

"I mean," Dallas continues, "if anyone, ever, in the history of mankind needed a room, it's you two. First June holds a gun to her head to save Woody, and then Woody nearly blows everyone up and gets shot in the head saving June and only survives because of June's jujitsu magic."

She stops and takes both of our hands, her brown eyes playful. "Don't be shy, kiddies, nod your heads and repeat after me. 'We need a room.'"

We both repeat after her quietly and she joins our hands together and slowly jogs up the trail. "Then let's find a room!" she shouts.

June and I stand there looking at each other; God, I do love those blue eyes of hers.

"Thank you," she says quietly.

I smile and nod. "Thank you." In one way, I'm saying thank you for saving my life again, but more than that I'm saying thank you for giving my lonely life meaning.

Maybe she can feel it too. It's a moment again. I could lean down and kiss her, all the emotions of the rescue still with us, the Grand Canyon surrounding us, the Colorado below. I'm about to lean down when...

"Come on!" Dallas shouts. "The sooner we get to the top, the sooner we can find that room you two so *clearly* need."

June shakes her head and smiles. "It's okay. We've got time, Woody. We've got time."

When we catch up, Dallas says to June, "So, did Diamondback here tell you about the secret scribblings he's been doing while pining away for you?" Dallas has a wicked smile playing on her lips and my cheeks flush red, yet again.

"Who's Diamondback?" June asks.

"Oh," Dallas says with a knowing nod. "That's the nickname Mr. Short and Stocky aka Asshole, real name Brown, gave our hero here." She grabs my hat and puts it on her head. "On account of his ever-present baseball cap."

I feel naked without it, my overlong bangs falling into my eyes. I don't say a thing, I'm hoping the "scribblings" comment is ignored.

We fall into silence, hauling up the trail, the Colorado still near, and the bridge still in sight.

"Wait," June says. "What scribblings?"

"That was private," I say, snatching my hat back from Dallas and putting it on.

"Don't think so," Dallas says, clearly enjoying herself. "We are all in it."

"In what?" June's eyes are serious now.

"I've just... you know..." I stammer. "Been taking some notes on everything that's happened since we met. Writing a little bit."

June grabs my hand and stops me. She's blinking and her face flows through emotions quickly, from surprise, to puzzlement, to a shy smile. "Really?"

"Yeah. I... I didn't know if I'd ever get you back, and..." I can't think of anything else to say and just stand there getting lost in June's eyes.

"And tell her what you're calling it," Dallas whispers, suddenly close to us.

"Woody and June versus the Apocalypse," I say quietly.

June smiles widely and nods. "Are you going to write it?"

I shrug. "If we get the time, if I don't run out paper. Why not?"

She smiles, squeezes my hand, and we start walking back up the trail.

"But the title..." Dallas says. "You know... it's kind of lacking something."

"What?" I ask.

She stops in the trail, her hands on her hips shaking her head and then pointing at herself. "Woody and June and *Dallas* versus the Apocalypse."

I open my mouth to speak, but June speaks first. "No... No, I think it should be 'June and Dallas and Woody versus the Apocalypse.'"

"Yes!" Dallas yells, pumping her fist and heading back up the trail. "Majority rules, Woody, that's the title."

I stand there for a moment getting a glimpse of my future with these two women. It won't be easy, but it won't be boring, that's for sure.

"You know," I say as I catch up, "I can't put your name in the title, Dallas."

"Why not?" she asks.

"Really, you are the most interesting character. You appear to be a villain at first, but then you turn out to be crucial to our success. If I put your name in the title, that tension will be lost to the reader."

Everyone is silent for a moment and Dallas laughs, a full-bodied, echo-off-the-canyon-walls loud laugh. "You got the gift of bullshit, Woody, I'll give you that."

"That's not bullshit," I say. It's not. The story will be better if Dallas is a mystery.

"It's one of the things we love about you," June says with a smile.

I stand there as the two of them continue up the trail. "It's not bullshit!" I yell, but I am smiling. Yup, this is going to be interesting.

CHAPTER SEVENTY-SEVEN

IT WAS dark when Dallas and I rolled into the South Rim and we were focused, so we didn't see much of anything. When the three of us make it out of the canyon, it's late afternoon and despite the pantyhose, my feet are killing me.

As we carefully explore the area, weapons out, we see what happened here.

The historic and sprawling El Tovar Hotel, constructed out of pine logs and Kaibab limestone, burned down. The rustic Bright Angel Lodge and cabins, another one of Mary Coulter's creations, has significant damage, doors bashed down, broken windows, and the bodies... there are a lot of them. Emaciated tourist zombies with bashed in heads, well chewed on corpses too far gone for the fungus to take over, signs of the living versus the undead everywhere.

"It was the horde," I say quietly as we stand on the rim near the remains of the El Tovar. The fireplaces, blackened limestone walls, and a few charred timbers remain, but the rest is a pile of ash. The breeze brings a whiff of the fire long gone.

June nods.

"We didn't come up here after we discovered the herd," Dallas says, her voice uncharacteristically quiet.

"The horde, it roamed the South Rim," I say, "and eventually got each group that set up here." I look at June. "We got lucky."

June takes my hand, nods, and squeezes my hand.

Our initial sweep is clear, and we start to scrounge and find it remarkably easy. These groups that came up here were well equipped, with vehicles and gas and food. In no time, we pick through and load the truck and crew cab with as much as it can carry, the bed loaded high and a cargo net thrown over it.

I even find a bat. It's aluminum, not wood, but I'll take it. I carry it over my shoulder after I find it, feeling a lot more like myself.

Afterwards we find that room. The decidedly not historic Thunderbird Lodge is in good shape. It was built in the late sixties out of brick with lots of windows and looks odd sandwiched between the wooden El Tovar and Bright Angel lodges.

Dallas sets up a room on the second floor and is very secretive about it and won't tell us anything until it's ready.

My breath catches when I walk in. It's got a spectacular view of the canyon and the sun is about to set, the darkening shadows making the Grand Canyon even more beautiful with colors ranging from dark grey to dark red, layer after layer of stone laid out before us.

She escorts us to a round table right by the windows and I pull the chair out for June and then sit across from her. The table has plates and forks and a cold can of chili, crackers, and dried fruit. What you would call a feast in the post-A world.

"One more thing," Dallas says, pulling something from behind the pillows of the king bed and hiding it behind her back. She has a huge smile on her face. I realize that this is the real Dallas. Those smile lines are earned, she is a woman that likes to be irreverent and loves to laugh, but can be remarkably caring. She pulls a bottle of champagne from behind her back and says, "Ta da!"

She produces two crystal goblets, pops the cork and pours.

"Warm, I know," she says, "but as the saying goes 'any champagne in an apocalypse.'"

She leaves the bottle and walks to the bed and pauses, her brow furrowed. Her expression turns to a smile and she pulls out another bottle of champagne, puts the new one on the table, and takes the open bottle. "I gotta have some fun," she says with a shrug and walks out of the room and closes the door.

Suddenly it's just June and me. And it's... sweet and shy and way too awkward.

We've been waiting to have our moment, and now that we have the space, the moment doesn't appear to be here. We caught up on the hike out, so what is there really to talk about?

"You look beautiful," I say. It's the only thing I can think of. We had enough water for us all to wash up a bit, but she always looks beautiful.

"Thank you," she says shyly, her hand straying to the bruise on her face. She takes the chili and portions it out. "You look very nice, too."

I smile and thank her. I combed my hair, trimmed my beard with some scissors we found, have a clean T-shirt on, and actually took my Diamondback's cap off.

I got a good look at my forehead when I cleaned up.

The bullet grazed a path about an inch and a half long. I cleaned it as best I could, even found some hydrogen peroxide, but it's a scabby mess and I'm going to have an interesting scar. I feel a bit self-conscious about it, but this doesn't feel like the right time to be wearing my hat.

"To being alive and being together," I say holding my glass up, finding myself staring at the bubbles, suddenly feeling shy, wondering, yet again, if this thing between us is real.

"To being alive and being together," she says with a sniff.

I look up and she's crying and I'm pretty sure it's a good cry, but I still feel that desperate need to do something about it.

We hold the glasses there for far too long, just staring at each other and then I feel the tears sliding down my cheeks too. It's been three weeks and we've been through a lot. I feel not one bit of shame about those tears.

She clinks her glass against mine and we sip the warm champagne, which isn't that great, but the alcohol is a wonderful treat. Dallas is on watch—albeit with her own champagne—so we can actually relax.

And then the ice breaks and we're chatting. I'm telling her details about rafting down the Grand Canyon with Dallas and she's telling me about her slow campaign with Harris and Sal and Mary, and the knock-down, drag-out fight she had with Talia in front of the whole company.

"What started it?" I ask.

She shrugs. "I refused an order. It was a stupid order."

"Who won?"

She snorts. "Did you see her face?"

"To Talia getting her face punched," I say, holding my glass up. She clinks hers to mine, the sound like music.

Soon the food is gone and we're most of the way through the second bottle of champagne and I'm worried it's about to get awkward again.

"So what's next?" June asks.

"I have a plan..." I say with a big smile.

She smiles and shakes her head. "Well, let's have it, partner."

"I... I don't know," I say, touching my lips. "My lips are tired of talking right now. They need something... something soft, something sweet..."

My heart is pounding so hard I think she must be able to hear it.

"Soft? Sweet?" she asks, putting down her glass and getting up and walking over to me. She puts her finger on my lips. "Like this?"

I shake my head, but not enough to dislodge her finger. "Sweet, yes, but not soft enough."

"Hmmm," she says, looking around the room. "I might think you meant my lips, but mine are still pretty chapped." She picks up a napkin. "This?"

"Soft, but not at all sweet. And, by the way, chapped lips can be *very* soft."

"Really?" she asks, bending towards me, her sweet scent mingling with the smell of the soap she used. "I don't know."

"Yeah," I say, my breath coming faster. "My lips are chapped, too, and there is nothing better for chapped lips than another set of chapped lips."

"Well...."

And then she puts her hand on the back of my head and presses her lips to mine and...

And the world disappears. There is no apocalypse, pre or post. There are no psychotic, petty, wannabe warlords, or desperate fights for survival. There is only June and me and our lips and then our tongues and then our bodies.

We have our moment, finally, and many wonderful moments after in the room our best friend Dallas prepared for us.

ꓘꞀꞀ ꓔꞁ ꞀꞀꞀ

SUNRISE over the Grand Canyon is a gentle affair, with sunlight streaming in from the east, filtering through and filling the depths of the canyon with warm light. It's magic light, soft and gentle, making the reds darker and the taupes more yellow, the easterly faces of the pyramids and temples warming, the westerly sides remaining steeped in dark mystery.

June and I stand there holding hands in our room in the Thunderbird Lodge watching the silent play of light. We are packed and ready to go, but the sunrise moment is not one to be missed.

I sigh, my eyes flicking to the empty rim trail. Not one being, living or dead, out there, the black pavement littered with leaves and dust and sticks, weeds forcing their way through cracks, the detritus of time no longer swept away by park staff and the endless trodding of human feet. No more tourists here at one of the world's natural wonders.

"You okay?" June whispers, her hand squeezing mine.

I don't answer, my eyes going to a motion coming from the direction of the burned down El Tovar. My heart quickens and my maudlin moment is replaced by fear... of the living and the dead. But it's just a couple of mule deer meandering through the grass, munching their breakfast, their large ears flicking a bit as they listen for danger, their ribs showing under their brown/grey fur.

This is their canyon now.

"Yeah," I say, quietly, reverently. "It's so beautiful, it's just that..."

"Yeah," she echoes. I know she feels it too.

The scene itself seems to speak volumes about this new post-apocalyptic world. Nature is coming back and taking over as humanity recedes, holding on desperately for survival.

A few weeks ago, I was alone and desperate, but now my world, with June and Dallas in it, doesn't seem so much like an apocalypse anymore. Maybe, just maybe, things are turning around for us.

CHAPTER SEVENTY-EIGHT

THE TRUCK IS PACKED tight as we head along the South Rim towards Desert View Overlook. The sun is shining and there are no Zs, and no psychotic, petty, wannabe warlords, just the three of us with more supplies than we've ever had.

The desert is lit by the sun's early morning orange-yellow glow making the world look almost friendly. I glance at June and can't help but smile, she catches my eye, smiles back, and then looks away.

"Oh, God!" Dallas says from the backseat. "Maybe that room wasn't such a good idea.

"I mean," she continues, "is this what it's going to be like from now on? You two all doey-eyed and mushy, me all alone and grumpy."

I open up my mouth to speak.

"No!" Dallas shouts. "No details, not a word. I'm going to die an unloved spinster, the last thing I need to hear is any details from you, young man."

I just smile as I drive, catching glimpses of the canyon to our left.

"And by no details," Dallas whispers to June loud enough that I'm clearly meant to hear it, "I mean, tell me everything once we have some girl time. And I mean *everything.*"

I glance at June, her cheeks are flushed, but there's a mischievous look in her face.

"I don't know," June says to Dallas. "I can't stand the thought of you a lonely, old, dried-up spinster. What can we do about that?"

There's a moment of silence and I swear the two of them are communicating telepathically or something, you can almost feel the unsaid words bouncing around the cab of the truck.

Dallas takes a deep breath and says, "Well, the only decent man left in the world is right here. You know, maybe..."

June finishes the sentence, "...maybe we can share him."

My eyes wide, I glance at June, who looks very mischievous now. Dallas's head is close to mine and I can hear her breathing. I look ahead and have to swerve hard because I almost ran us off the road. Both of them laugh.

"I mean, if humanity is to continue," Dallas says, "you have to face facts, Woody. You're going to have to get both of us pregnant and become the father of the new human race."

My hands are sweating on the steering wheel and my heart is pounding in my head. The images of "sharing" colliding with the images of crying babies and dirty diapers exploding in my head... and not in a good way.

"But...," June continues, "why not share all the way

around? I mean, Dallas, you're the whole package, and I wouldn't mind..."

"Neither would I, honey," Dallas says. "Or, you know, all of us at once."

My brain is about to explode. I put Dallas firmly in the "sister" column during our quest to get June back. And now they're talking about sharing, and babies, and...

I slam on the brakes and bring us to a stop, the canyon visible to the left. "Are you guys being serious here, because... I... you know..." My cheeks are hot and I can't find the words.

They both laugh, it's a good laugh, free of restraint, truly joyful, and I know that laugh is coming at my expense, but I can live with that. Their faces are both bruised, Dallas's going to yellow at the edges and June's to purple. They need a good laugh, so I really *can* live with it.

"We might be..." Dallas begins.

"...but, honestly, I don't know that you're ready for it, even if we are," June ends.

"Yeah," Dallas adds. "I don't think he could handle the both of us."

Well, that is certainly true. I don't even know if I can handle June. Both of them still have smiles on their faces and I have no idea if they are serious, and no idea if I want them to be serious.

I nod slowly, looking into the blue eyes of June and then the brown eyes of Dallas. "You guys are just messing with me." I don't say it because I believe it, but because I need to focus. We've had a good laugh, now we need to survive.

"Sure... we're just messing with you," June says, that mischievous look still on her face, her tone leaving the question open.

"I think of you like a brother," Dallas says with a wide

smile. "My little, snot-nosed brother, I might add, but a brother. Besides, as I told you before, Beckman, I'm nobody's second choice."

I take a deep breath and sigh, trying to shake free all the images floating around my head. "Okay, onward." I put the truck back into gear.

"So what's the plan?" Dallas asks.

"Yeah," June adds. "We... ah... didn't have time to talk about it last night."

"Details," Dallas stage whispers to June. "Later."

I shake my head, stop the truck, get the map out of my pocket, and get out. "I'll show you."

We found a good collection of maps when we were scrounging, and this one of Arizona is one of them. After looking around the desert landscape—trying to get my brain back into survival-first mode—I lay the map out on the warm hood of the truck.

"We're here." I point to Route 64 about halfway between the Grand Canyon Village and Desert View Over-look. "What we need is year-round running water, some-where where we can grow food, somewhere remote."

"Where we can fish," Dallas adds.

"And horses would be good," June says. "I used to ride when I was a girl."

I smile, glad to see them focused. I run to the truck, grab my jacket, and pull the seed packets out. There are about eight of them in a plastic bag. Carrots, tomatoes, lettuce, a few varieties of beans. "Food," I say. "We need a place to grow food." I point at Sedona. "Oak Creek runs year-round, but too many people, which means too many Zs, and the ever-present psychotic, petty, wannabe warlords." I point southeast of Flagstaff. "Lake Mary is near Flagstaff, which is not a good place for us, and it's too cold."

They nod. Given our requirements, there are not a lot of places in Arizona that meet them and I'm worried about heading out of state, who knows what we might run into. At least I know Arizona.

"Anyone ever heard of the White Mountains or the Black River?" I point to eastern Arizona.

They both shake their heads.

"Mountains, lakes, rivers, and huge amounts of wilderness. We should be able to get lost there. There can't be that many Zs or that many psychotic, petty, wannabe warlords."

After I'm done, there's silence and the wind picks up, the sound of cawing ravens floating in on the breeze.

"That's a long ways to go," Dallas says quietly.

June points to the map, "And it looks like Flagstaff is the easiest way to get there."

"And we can't go through Flagstaff," I say. "Brown may have blown himself up, but he may not have."

Any city could have encampments, and unlike when I met June, we now have a lot of valuable stuff, a lot to lose.

Dallas slowly nods. "I can fish, get me there and we'll eat." We have fishing gear that we found on the South Rim.

"And if we can switch to horses on the way," June says, "we can stay away from people and keep moving."

"But how do we get there?" Dallas asks.

"Slowly. Carefully," I say, placing my hand on the map near the White Mountains.

"As a team," Dallas adds.

"Partners," June says, putting her hand on top of mine and Dallas does the same.

I look at them both and feel... Well, these things aren't simple, are they? I am quite sure that when we aren't in survival mode, I will be teased mercilessly, and while that will be uncomfortable, it will also be nice in a way. While I am in love with June, relationships are complicated in the best of times and these are not that. And then there is all the healing we need to do. Our bodies and our souls.

So I feel excited to be on a new adventure. I feel grateful to have such competent companions. And I feel scared and nervous for what me might face.

But I'm not alone. Underneath it all, I feel hope for a better future.

"Partners," I say, and then Dallas says the same and then all at once, together, we all say "Partners!"

We hug, I fold up the map, and June and Dallas get in the truck.

I stand there for a moment, looking down the road. I take off my Diamondbacks hat and finger the bullet hole and shake my head and feel... well, there is no getting around it, despite the challenges and the apocalypse, I feel happy.

I smile, put my hat back on and get in the truck. I put it in gear and head us towards our future.

AFTERWORD

I love Arizona.

This must not come as a surprise after reading this book. I was transplanted from an eastern suburb to the mountains of Arizona at the tender age of seven. I loved it. I had a mountain right in my back yard (well, a few houses between my house and the mountain) and spent a lot of time wandering through the forest and scrambling up the slopes.

At ten, I was transplanted to the high desert of Arizona onto a small ranch in the rolling foothills of another mountain. I had animals to care for and a lot of responsibility, but soon I had a horse and so very much freedom.

The terrain of this state is awe-inspiring, from mountains that rise above tree level down to the harshest deserts. There's not much water here, but wow, the Colorado River carved the Grand Canyon out of the upthrust of the Colorado Plateau laying bare the geology of this amazing planet.

You can see here and breathe. Living in the kinds of

places I've lived in Arizona, it's not hard to get away from all the people and be in nature. Being out there in the forest and the desert, I have found, is a balm for our too busy, technology-laden lives. The forest doesn't care how far behind you are at work or what indignities you've suffered lately. The desert doesn't mind if you are happy or sad, it is what it is without all the judgements that we bring along.

So, this book is, in part, an ode to Arizona. Not the state I was born in, but my home state.

Mixed in is a love story of a regular guy who encounters a woman who he thinks is way out of his league when he had given up hope on love (and really, any satisfying human relationships). I've always felt that way compared to my most amazing wife, Aleia. I'm the regular guy, she's... well, she's the kind of person that goes in "where angels fear to tread" and helps people through very difficult times (see, way out of my league).

This book is also the most fun I've had writing.

When this story tumbled out in May of 2017, I was preparing to do what I called a Short Story Writing Marathon with my writing mentor Dean Wesley Smith. May was my "training" month. I'm a runner and thought it might be a good idea to get my output up before trying to write 30 short stories as fast as possible (I gave myself 60 days, but ended up doing it in 34). The first episode of Woody and June popped out and I wrote three more episodes during the Marathon. They are far too long of stories when you're trying to write a story a day, but I was having so much fun I couldn't stop myself and was happy despite the exhaustion and the extremely long days (I had to keep working my day job during all of this).

After those, Aleia kept asking for more Woody and

June. She will never watch or read a zombie anything, but she *loves* Woody and June, so I kept writing them.

In August of 2017 we were on vacation and when I had time alone, the most fun thing I could think of was to keep writing this story. (I'm not really sure what this says about me, but I really wanted to find out how it ended.)

Since then I've revisited some of the locations in the story (I just had to, you know!) to make sure I got them right, especially as it became clear that this was something of a travelogue along with everything else.

So here you have it. I hope you had fun reading this. If you want more Woody and June (and Dallas too) and their adventures, please let me know. There a bunch of ways to do that:

1. Got to WoodyAndJune.com and join the *Woody and June Fan Club*. You'll get the inside scoop on all things Woody and June (we've got some fun ideas) and encourage me to keep going.

2. Spread the word in any way you feel comfortable. The first episode is free at WoodyAndJune.com, so there's no risk in trying it out. If you like writing reviews, please do that. They can be super simple, and it really does help.

3. I'm on twitter at @RobertJMcCarter, reach out and feel free to use the hashtag #WoodyAndJune

4. I've got a page on facebook, come join in the conversation: www.facebook.com/RobertJMcCarterAuthor

5. You can contact me through my website at
   robertjmccarter.com/contact

Okay, enough babbling on. I need to get the pups and
head out into the forest and enjoy some Arizona sunshine!

Robert J. McCarter, August 2019

ACKNOWLEDGMENTS

This book was, obviously, inspired by *The Walking Dead*. I've watched the show (sometimes with my eyes not quite open) and played the Telltale Games videogame, as well as watching *Fear the Walking Dead* and *iZombie*.

But less obviously, this work was inspired by fun, adventurous shows like *Chuck* (from whence the "versus" in the titles comes) and *The Last Man on Earth*, plus movies like *Romancing the Stone* and *Raiders of the Lost Ark*.

These stories have zombies and those horror elements that come with the Zs, but that really takes a backseat to the fun, just like those TV shows and movies I listed above. I tried to keep things realistic (if you can buy into zombies) and fun at the same time. *The Walking Dead* is often about how far humans will go to protect themselves and the ones they love in the direst of circumstances, and there's some of that here, but it is much, much lighter. On purpose.

The most credit, though, goes to my wife Aleia, who kept asking for more and more, so I kept writing more and more (more about that in the Afterword).

Thanks to my team of beta readers for finding my goofs and making this story better: Susana Acosta-Cavert, John Bifano, Roni Hornstein, Chris Kalinich, Peter Klein, and Gary McClellan.

Big thanks to Elizabeth Fitzekam for helping with this very complicated launch and, as always, thanks to Diana Cox for proofreading this and making me look good.

And thank you for reading. I hope you enjoyed this adventure!

MORE ADVENTURE?

There is so much more Woody and June (and Dallas too) coming. If you loved these stories (and if you got to the end here, I sure hope you did), please join the Woody and June Fan Club at WoodyAndJune.com, and for bonus points, tell everyone you know! The more support these books get, the faster I'll get to writing the next volume. And if you join the fan club it guarantees you won't miss a thing and you'll get exclusive behind-the-scene details and cool free stuff.

Until then, remember that your life is an adventure and no matter what current "apocalypse" is befalling you, love hard, be kind, and take it all in stride.

While you wait, you might be interested in my super-hero / love story series: *Neutrinoman & Lightningirl: A Love Story*. In this series I take a similar spin on the super-hero genre as I did here with zombies. Real characters in extraordinary situations that are full of adventure, fun, and romance. Season 1 is out, with Season 2 coming soon. All the details are below.

SUPERHEROES... FALLING IN LOVE... SAVING THE
WORLD.

Follow Nik Nichols (aka Neutrinoman) and Licia Lopez
(aka Lightningirl) on this wild adventure past "happily ever
after" into the heart of love while they try to protect the
Earth from aliens bent on our destruction.

Join my newsletter and get the *Meteor Attack!* ebook for
free!

Meteor Attack!: *Falling in love and saving the world...*

Toxic Asset: *Friend or Enemy?*

Protocol X: *An Alien Encounter*

Season 1: *Episodes 1-3 for a great price!*

Find out more about the series at Neutrinoman.com

ABOUT THE AUTHOR

Robert J. McCarter is the author of six novels, three novellas, and dozens of short stories. He is a finalist for the *Writers of the Future* contest and his stories have appeared in *The Saturday Evening Post, Adomeda Spaceways Inflight Magazine, Everyday Fiction,* and numerous anthologies.

He has written a series of first person ghost novels (starting with Shuffled Off: A Ghost's Memoir) and a super-hero / love story series (Neutrinoman and Lightningirl, A Love Story), as well as two short story collections.

Of his latest novel, *Seeing Forever*, Kirkus Reviews says, "Sci-fi as it should be: engaging, moving, and grand in scope."

Find out more at:
robertjmccarter.com

BOOKS BY ROBERT J. MCCARTER

WOODY AND JUNE VERSUS THE APOCALYPSE

1. Woody and June versus the Wannabe Warlord
2. Woody and June versus the Fungus-Head Zombies
3. Woody and June versus the Grand Canyon
4. Woody and June versus the Ex
5. Woody and June versus the Third Wheel
6. Woody and June versus Phantom Company
7. Woody and June versus the Daring Rescue

Join the Woody and June Fan Club at WoodyAndJune.com

NOVELS IN THE "GHOST'S MEMOIR" WORLD:

- Shuffled Off: A Ghost's Memoir, Book 1
- Drawing the Dead
- To Be a Fool: A Ghost's Memoir, Book 2
- Of Things Not Seen: A Ghost's Memoir, Book 3

OTHER NOVELS:

- Seeing Forever

BOOKS IN THE NEUTRINOMAN AND LIGHTNINGIRL
SERIES:

- Meteor Attack! Neutrinoman and Lightningirl,
  A Love Story. Episode 1
- Toxic Asset: Neutrinoman and Lightningirl, A
  Love Story. Episode 2
- Protocol X: Neutrinoman and Lightningirl, A
  Love Story. Episode 3
- Season 1 (Omnibus edition of Episodes 1 - 3)
- Off Book: Neutrinoman and Lightningirl, A
  Love Story. Episode 4 (*Coming soon*)

WALTER ANCHOR, GHOST DETECTIVE STORIES

- **Case 1: "Detecting Haley"** (part of *Life
  After: Stories of Life, Death, and the Places in
  Between*)
- **Case 2: "The Ghost Brides Gift"**
  (exclusive to newsletter subscribers)
- **Case 3: "A Long Hard Fall"** (coming in
  2019)

*For a complete list of Walter Anchor stories, go to
RobertJMcCarter.com/WalterAnchor*

SHORT STORES AND COLLECTIONS

- Life After: Stories of Life, Death, and the Places
  in Between

For a complete list, go to RobertJMcCarter.com

CPSIA information can be obtained
at www.ICGtesting.com
Printed in the USA
LVHW021219041119
636250LV00002B/426/P